CINDERELLA.COM

RIVER LAURENT

Georgia Le Carre,
You let me stand on your shoulders.
No gratitude will be enough.

ONE
Cass

"**O**pen this damned door now," my landlord yells, banging his meaty fists on my door.

Not even daring to breathe, I press myself tightly against the wall in the only blind spot that cannot be seen through the keyhole of my tiny, one-room apartment.

"I know you're in there, Harper. I saw you go in," he growls.

Please God, please. Make him go away, I pray silently as a bead of sweat slips down the inside of my arm.

"I have another key that I can use to get in," he threatens darkly.

I squeeze my eyelids tightly. Don't fold, Cass. Don't fold. Stay strong. He's totally lying. Just trying to scare you. In the last year, I've seen him walking around with that heavy ring of keys only once.

Suddenly, to my horror, I hear the jangle of keys.

Oh, shit.

My eyes fly open and I stop breathing. He brought the whole damned thing. I freeze with panic when I hear him put a key into the lock. I can't face him and tell him another pile of lies. I just need to buy myself a little bit more time. One of the people from my job interviews could still call. In fact, that guy from Chips-R-Us said he'd call tomorrow. Impulsively, I drop to the floor and roll under the bed just as the door flies open.

With my cheek stuck to the bare floorboard and my heart pounding like crazy, I stare wide-eyed at the doorway. Mr. Tanner is standing with his feet wide apart. From this angle, his legs look like tree trunks. For a few seconds, they remain planted on the floor while he surveys my small room. Then his feet move as if to leave. I clasp my hands together. Thank you, God. Thank you. But just as I exhale a sigh of relief, his scuffed black shoes turn back into the room.

No!

They come to a stop in front of the bed.

Shit. Shit. Shit.

Suddenly, his fat face appears in the gap between the floor and the bed.

Busted.

My cheeks burn, but I plaster a fake bright smile on my face. "Hi, Mr. Tanner."

There is no smile in response. His brown eyes are irritated. "You think this is funny?"

I drop my smile instantly. "No, no. Of course not."

"Get out of there," he orders.

I scramble out and stand nervously in front of him.

He smells of sweat and bacon. "I thought you said you'd have my rent money by today."

I swallow hard. "Yes, I know I said that. But I've had a bit of a problem, Mr. Tanner."

He folds his hands in front of his distended belly and stares at me coldly.

"But please don't worry about it. I swear I'll have the money by this weekend."

5

He frowns. "That's what you said last week and the week before that."

"Yes, and I should have had it." I clear my throat. "I was let down, but this time I promise I'll have the money."

"Look. I like you. You're a good kid, but I ain't runnin' a charity here. If you don't come up with the money by the weekend, and that means Sunday—6:00 p.m. at the latest—you're out. Am I making myself clear?"

I nod. "Absolutely, Mr. Tanner. I hear you loud and clear. I'll have the money. I promise."

"I don't get it. You work all the time. You never go out. What do you do with your money?"

"I told you, Mr. Tanner. When my father was sick, I took a short-term loan from some people to pay for his medical bills. I have to service that loan every week. They've cut my hours at work, but I've gone for some interviews. I should hear back this week." I bite my lip and look at him imploringly.

"Hmmm…that's a shame." He sucks at his teeth. "You could, you know, pay your rent in different ways."

My eyes widen with disbelief. "What?"

He scratches his double chin while his greedy eyes crawl over my chest like slimy fingers and his tongue comes out to wet his lips. "We could come to some…arrangement."

"No," I blurt out in disgust.

I see a flash of surprised anger cross his face and quickly smile to soften the blow. "What I meant to say is, thank you. It's a truly great offer, but it won't be necessary since I *will* have the money for you."

He throws me a sour look. "Fine. I'm leaving now, but you keep your word this time. Don't think I won't haul your sorry ass out on the sidewalk and change the locks."

"Okay. Thank you, Mr. Tanner," I whisper.

He turns around and walks out of my room.

I walk to the door, close it, and sag against it. My knees give way. I slide down and sit slumped on the floor. It's like the weight of the whole world is bearing down upon my shoulders. I stare at the blank wall above my bed, feeling sick to my stomach.

I don't know how I'm going to manage. It is now clear that Mr. Tanner is deadly serious. He is going to kick me out unless I come up with my rent money. I am so lost in worry and stress, I jump when my cell phone rings. I pull it out of my pocket and look at it hopefully. It is my bestie, Jesse.

"Hey," she says, her voice bubbling with excitement. "I've got great news for you."

"Yeah? What is it?" I ask without enthusiasm.

"It's too good to tell over the phone. I'm coming over right now," she says and cuts the connection.

TWO
Cass

Jesse's eyes are shining when I open the door.

"Howdy, partner," she greets jauntily.

"Howdy? What's with the cowboy talk?"

Instead of answering me, she grins, grabs my arm, and pulls me over to the mirror, positioning me in front of it. "What do you see?" she asks excitedly.

I don't even want to see my reflection. I'm rocking the shadows under the eyes, deathly pale skin, and haunted blue eyes look. I turn away from the tragic sight. "Look, Jesse. I'm really not in the mood. What's this about?"

Undeterred by my lackluster tone, she cups her palms on either side of my face and turns it back toward the mirror. "I see money."

Frowning, I ask, "What?"

She leaves me standing at the mirror and goes toward my bed. Hopping on it, she sits cross-legged and pats the space in front of her. With a sigh, I go and sit opposite her.

"You know how everybody is always mistaking you for Tamara Honeywell?"

"Yeah," I agree cautiously. Tamara Honeywell is a hotel heiress, famous for being infamous. I think she cut a record where her voice was compared to cats wailing, and she might also have starred in a Hollywood movie her father produced that flopped big time. She does a bit of modeling and has a clothing line but seems mostly to be photographed at parties and clubs looking wasted, or making out with perfect strangers. I don't have the time to read gossip magazines, but there might also have been talk of a sex tape. So, it's not exactly a compliment to be compared to her, and I can't imagine why Jesse is so fired up.

Jesse leans forward eagerly. "Well, I had an idea, so two months ago, I secretly signed up as you on Cinderella.com."

I stare at her. "What the hell is Cinderella.com?"

She smiles proudly. "It's a body double agency. Normal people who look like celebrities can impersonate them for a night or a day, feel like a star, and get paid for the pleasure. They have all kinds of doubles on their website. The Queen of England, Taylor Swift, Nicole Kidman. Are you getting the gist of what I'm saying?"

"Kind of, but I'm going to need a bit more."

"Basically, I sent them your photo, as well as your height and weight, to be on their books as an impersonator for Tamara Honeywell. Two days ago, they contacted me because they need you to impersonate her for an entire month!"

My head starts swimming. I dare not believe. I stare at her silently.

"Guess how much this gig is worth?" she asks.

For her to be this excited it has to be…quite good. I shake my head.

She grins. "Five-hundred smackeroos a day plus expenses."

My jaw drops. "Five-hundred dollars a day? For a whole month? Are you sure?"

"Abso-fricking-lutely," she says with a laugh. "I've been emailing Mrs. Carter, the owner of the agency, for the last two days, but now she wants to connect on Skype to make sure the photos are not photoshopped and stuff."

I open my mouth to ask her more about the job, but no sound comes out. My chin starts trembling, the backs of my eyes sting, and tears start rolling quickly down my face.

"Hey," she soothes, hugging me. "Don't cry, Cass. Please don't cry. It'll be all right, I promise."

"I'm sorry," I sob. "It's just the relief. You can't imagine what it's been like. I've been so frightened. I didn't know what to do, Jesse. Mr. Tanner is planning to kick me out on Sunday, and I'm behind with my loan payment, which they've just doubled again. I've already paid them everything I borrowed, but the figure never seems to go down. There's always interest and penalties being added for no damned reason. It's starting to feel as if I'll never be able to pay it off. I'm already working two jobs, and though I'm trying really hard to find another, it's been impossible to find something that I can fit around the other two."

Jesse pulls away and gazes at me. "Why didn't you tell me how bad it was?"

I shake my head. "What could you have done?"

"To start, you can stop being such a dork and move in with me. Our couch is very comfortable and you can sleep there."

I wipe my tears with the backs of my hands. "I'm not going to sleep on your couch, Jesse. It wouldn't be fair to Adam."

"Adam won't mind."

I sniff and shake my head. "Jesse, you live in a one-bedroom apartment. Of course, Adam will mind. Who wants to have someone living on their couch?"

"Anyway, we don't need to worry about that anymore, do we? Let's just get you this job and see where we go from there, okay?"

"Tell me more about the job. What will I be doing for a month?"

Jesse grins widely. "You'll be learning to ride a horse on a ranch in Montana."

I look at her in disbelief. "Are you kidding me?"

"Nope."

"I'm going to be impersonating Tamara Honeywell for a month on a ranch in Montana?"

"Yep."

I open my hands, palms up. "Why?"

She shrugs. "Mrs. Carter said she can only give more information once you've signed a Non-Disclosure Agreement."

"Me on a ranch in Montana. Pretending to be Tamara Honeywell. Riding a horse. It's just…surreal."

"I'm thinking breakfast with cowboys," she says, rubbing her hands like some evil witch in a Disney cartoon. "Mmm…sausages."

I start giggling and so does she.

"Speaking of sausages, Bacon Belly told me we could come to some *arrangement* over my rent."

Her warm brown eyes flash with disgust. "Ew. Thanks a bunch for that. Now I need to go flush my brain out with bleach." She wrinkles her nose with disgust. "It's practically pedophilia. What a dirty dickwad. I hope you told him what he could do with his wrinkly old thing."

"I didn't. I was too shocked, actually."

"I'll give him a piece of my mind the next time that—"

For a second, I stop hearing the torrent of abuse spewing out of her mouth and see only her kind, sweet face. I say a silent prayer to God for sending her to me. Now that Dad can barely recognize me, she's all I've got. Jesse and I met in ninth grade. She was lousy at math and I helped her with it. We've been best friends ever since.

"Thank you, Jesse," I say, my voice breaking with all the emotions swirling in my body.

"Stop being weird, Cass. I love to do things for you, but you're always so damned independent you won't accept even the slightest bit of help."

I reach for a tissue from the box by the bedside and blow my nose.

"Anyway," she adds, "I'm so happy this job's come up for you. It's about time you got a break in your shitty life."

I hug her tightly. "I love you."

"Break my ribs, why don't you?"

THREE
Cass

Mrs. Carter, the owner of Cinderella.com, turns out to be super-efficient. Less than four hours after we speak, a courier comes with an NDA agreement; a ten-page affair written in the strictest, most pretentious sounding words I have ever come across. I skip through most of it since it's basically Miss Honeywell's solicitors trying to impress me with just how prepared they are to take me to court and see me behind bars if I don't keep my mouth shut. I've never been a talkative person anyway, so I sign the document on the spot and give it back to the courier.

The next day, Mrs. Carter calls me.

"Can you ride?" she asks as soon as I answer the phone.

"No," I confess, my heart lurching with disappointment. I thought Jesse said I would be learning to ride. I should have known it was too good to be true.

"Excellent," she says crisply. "Are you prepared to learn?"

"Yes."

"Good. Let me tell you about the job. Miss Honeywell seems to have gotten herself into a bit of a scrape. Something to do with driving while under the influence. Anyway, her father negotiated a probationary sentence for her on the understanding that she must live on the ranch of a friend of his. It is not meant to be a holiday but a kind of rehabilitation. The plan is for her to learn how to ride, take care of the horses, and generally help around. At the end of her stay, her father will come to the ranch to see what progress she has made with her riding skills.

"Miss Honeywell has decided she does not care to be on a ranch in the middle of nowhere for a month, so she has hired us to find a body double to take her place. And that's where you come in. Are you available to drop everything starting tomorrow and take her place?"

I didn't even have to think about it. "Yes."

"There is a catch. If the ranch hand who is in charge of teaching her reports back to her father that he is unhappy with her general attitude or her willingness to learn or do as she is told, she will have to stay for another month. If that happens, you will not be paid a single cent."

I take a deep breath. "Wow!"

"Is that a deal breaker for you?"

"No," I say immediately.

"Can you confirm that you are prepared to work very hard on the ranch for a month?"

"Yes." I say the word at the speed of a bullet. Of course, I can work hard. I can work very hard.

"And you are prepared to alter your appearance slightly and wear the clothes provided to you?"

"No problem."

"Good. It looks like we have a deal."

"I may be having a blonde moment here, but if I learn to ride, how will Miss Honeywell ride for her father?"

"Er...yes. I was getting to that. Miss Honeywell has a solution to that problem. Her plan is that you should pretend to fall and feign injury on the day before her father

14

comes. While you are in a separate living accommodation, she will exchange places with you."

"She wants me to fall off a *horse*?" I ask incredulously.

"Well…" Mrs. Carter begins.

"I could break my neck," I splutter.

Mrs. Carter clears her throat uncomfortably. "Miss Honeywell suggested that you arrange to fall into bushes or a body of water. I suppose you could ride out on your own and pretend you have fallen off and sustained an injury."

How shockingly selfish and sick rich people are. But I need the money. I take a deep breath. "And then what?"

"Then, Miss Honeywell will simply pretend that, as the result of the fall, she is too afraid to get back on a horse."

"And her father will buy *that*?"

"Miss Honeywell is certain that he will believe that story. There is no reason for him not to because all the ranch hands would have seen you ride."

We are both silent for a few seconds while I digest this new requirement.

"By the way, I didn't mention it before, but there is an extra reward. If you stick the month out to the end, Miss Honeywell is prepared to pay not five hundred dollars, but one-thousand dollars per day."

A thrill runs through me. My God! At that rate, I'll be able to pay off my entire loan. "A thousand dollars a day?" I echo.

"Yes, but you will only get that sum if you stay to the very end and execute the fall in a manner that is believable to those around you."

15

I clutch my phone tightly. It sounds almost too good to be true. I don't care if I break a bone anymore. "And that's guaranteed?"

"You'll have it in writing. Miss Honeywell is my client. She is not your employer. I am. As soon as you agree to the terms of this assignment, the entire sum will be put into escrow for you. If you make it to the end of your assignment, my agency will release the payment into your account."

"Thirty days at a thousand dollars a day is thirty thousand dollars! That's what I'll get?"

"That's correct. You'll have to pay taxes on that, obviously." She pauses for an instant. "Will you do it?"

"Yes. Yes, I'll do it," I respond instantly. My head is swirling with excitement.

"Fantastic. Miss Honeywell will be pleased to hear that. Can you leave for LA tomorrow?"

"Er…I don't have any money," I admit quickly.

Her voice softens; loses that professional edge. "I'll send you some pocket money with your ticket. We'll put it under expenses. She can well afford it." For the first time, I hear a sarcastic, disapproving tone creep into her voice.

I sigh with relief. "Can I also have a small advance? I need to pay my rent."

"Certainly," she says immediately.

"Thank you, Mrs. Carter."

"Don't mention it."

"What do I need to bring?"

"Nothing. Just yourself. Someone will pick you up at the airport and take you to Miss Honeywell's home and her PA, Ms. Nora Moore, will take over."

******

That afternoon, I go to the diner where I work. The manager, who knows my dad and understands my financial situation, agrees to hold my job for a month. Nonetheless, I have no choice but to give up my second job stocking shelves at Target.

Afterward, I go to visit Dad at the hospice. He is sleeping soundly, so I don't wake him. When he is awake, he's in pain, so sleep is a good thing. I sit silently by his bedside until it's time for me to leave. As I'm leaving, a woman from the office runs up to sternly remind me that another bill is already overdue.

"I'm sorry. I've had some problems, but I'll settle it at the end of next week," I promise.

When Chips-R-us calls to say I've got the job, I respectfully turn it down. That evening, before I leave to have dinner at Jesse's, I pay my landlord. He snatches the money from my hand grumpily and stalks off. Behind his back, I flip him the bird.

At Jesse's apartment, for the first time in a long time, I feel no stress. I relax and taste the food I am eating. Pasta with meat sauce. Jesse is a truly terrible cook. The meatballs are green and she doesn't know how they got to be that color, but I can't stop smiling. When the evening comes to an end, Jesse kisses me on the cheeks and wishes me luck.

The next morning, I hop on a flight to LA.

FOUR
Cass

I get out of the cool, scented limo air into the fiery heat of LA's sun. Standing on the wide driveway, I look up at Miss Honeywell's ginormous white mansion. Wow! What a place. It's more like a palace than a house. I've never been inside such a majestic building.

The driver closes the door and indicates that I should walk up the steps to the house. I ring the doorbell, suck in a breath of scorching air, and straighten my spine. One of the tall double doors opens and cool air-conditioned air pours out. The round, middle-aged, Mexican-looking woman standing at the entrance widens her eyes in surprise at the sight of me.

"Santa Maria, you're prettier than her," she cries gaily.

Slightly embarrassed, I smile politely. "Hello, I'm here for my meeting with Ms. Nora Moore."

She moves back to allow me access into the house. Above us, there is a massive chandelier hanging from the tall ceiling, and beneath my shoes, the granite floor gleams like a mirror. A few yards in front of me is a sweeping, white marble staircase. Amazing. All this to accommodate just one person.

"Come in, *chica*. Ms. Moore is not here yet, and Miss Honeywell has company, but she asked me to take you up to her when you arrive."

I take a small step forward. "Company?"

"A man," she stage-whispers. "And I should warn you that she's been drinking."

"It's ten o'clock in the morning," I blurt out.

"Miss Honeywell likes bubbles for breakfast, but today she's had a bit more than usual, so be careful," she confides.

A chill runs up my spine. "Is she…drunk?"

"A little bit." She smiles apologetically.

"Do you think she'll remember that I'm supposed to be here?"

She rolls her eyes heavenward. "God only knows. But don't worry. Ms. Moore will remember and she'll be here soon."

"Well, shouldn't I just sit somewhere and wait for Ms. Moore to arrive then?" It seems like the most logical solution to me.

She ushers me further into the house. "No, no, my orders are to take you up as soon as you arrive."

I hang back. "But don't you think it will be better if we just wait for Mrs. Moore?"

"Do you want me to lose my head?" she cries dramatically.

My mouth drops open. "What?"

She laughs uproariously. "I was joking, *chica*. This is a madhouse you have come to and without a sense of humor, you won't survive it."

I stare at her.

Her face suddenly becomes serious. "What's your name again?"

"Cass Harper."

"It's not as bad as it looks. If you agree with everything she says and treat her like a princess, there should be no problem." She shrugs. "After all, you only have to deal with her for a month."

"Okay," I agree with a nod.

She puts her foot on the first step of the marvelous white staircase. "Don't take her insults to heart. She belittles people to seem superior to everyone, but you're a very beautiful young lady. Don't let her bring you down."

"All right," I mumble, reluctantly following her up the stairs.

"You need anything at all, you come and see Maria, okay?"

I nod again, glad to have found a friend in that vast, cold house. "Thank you."

She grins widely. "Don't worry, you'll be fine."

"How do you do it?" I ask. I can't imagine that her job is simple, especially working for such an egotistical rich girl.

"*Chica*, I have two boys at home. They need a roof over their heads and food in their bellies. Miss Honeywell's father pays better than anyone else. Once you learn to be lower than her, it gets easier," she explains gently.

She leads me down a large landing toward a gilded door. I'm not sure if I'm nervous to meet Tamara Honeywell because she's drunk, or because of what I know about her, but either way, I'm not looking forward to meeting her. A door is slightly ajar at the end of the hallway and there are strange grunting noises coming from inside the room. Maria stops outside it.

"Good luck, dear," she says, patting me on my back.

I push the door fully open, walk into a pink and gold room, and come to a complete standstill.

What the...

FIVE
Cass

I stare at the scene in front of me with shocked, disbelieving eyes. A buck-naked woman, presumably Tamara Honeywell, is bouncing on the erect shaft of a beefy man double her size while his hands squeeze her extremely endowed breasts.

"Oh, I'm sorry," I exclaim, immediately turning away.

"Don't go," the man's voice orders.

I freeze in my tracks.

"Watch us," he says, his voice deep and persuasive.

My jaw drops. I couldn't possibly have heard that right. That would be too weird. And gross. Sick bastard.

"Is she watching yet?" a woman's voice pants.

"Not yet, baby," the man says.

Oh, my God! Tamara Honeywell wants me to watch her having sex! What the hell have I gotten myself into? I feel as if I have fallen down a rabbit hole. Think of the money, Cass. Think of the money. If I leave now I'm in a worse position than I was two days ago. Not only have I said no to Chips-R-Us, I've even given up my Target job. So what if she wants to be a mini porn star, or have people ogle her while she's doing the dirty. As long as I don't have to join in, what does it matter? I'm not going to turn tail and run just because she has no shame. I take a deep breath and whirl around slowly.

"She's watching," he tells her.

"Do you think she's jealous of me?" she grunts.

"Yeah, baby."

"Her panties must be soaking wet watching us fucking."

"Yeah, baby."

"Do you think she wishes you were fucking her up the ass while she sucks me off?"

"Yeah, baby."

Yuck! More nasty and vile things come from her mouth as she bobs up and down on the man, but I tune out and stop hearing them. I let my mind wander off to that day three weeks ago, when in a rare moment of lucidity, my father opened his eyes and recognized me. I stroked his thin hand and he whispered that he loved me. I leaned in and listened to his hoarse murmurs. He thought Mom was still alive, and I pretended she was. He was happy that day.

A shrill scream pierces the bittersweet memory and I return with a jolt to the sight of Tamara Honeywell pulling herself off the man. His dick is thick and red and flops onto his belly like a wet fish. While she wraps herself in a silk gown, he leans over and takes a cigarette out of a silver box on the bedside table. He flicks open a lighter, lights it, and holds it out to her. She knots a tie in front of her gown and plucks the cigarette from him. Putting it to her lips, she takes a deep pull.

"Get out," she tells him rudely, exhaling smoke from her mouth.

Without a word, he jackknifes off the bed and walks naked to the door. As he passes me, our glances touch briefly and he winks at me. I look away quickly. The door closes behind him with a soft click.

"So, who the fuck are you?" she slurs.

She's drunk and I'm not good with drunk people. "I'm, uh, Cass. Cass Harper."

"That doesn't tell me anything. The question was why the fuck are you in my house?"

Jesus! Where the hell is Mrs. Moore? "I'm your body double. I'm supposed to go to Montana in your place," I say slowly.

"Montana?" She scowls.

"One month on the ranch," I remind.

She grimaces. "Oh, fuck, that."

She starts walking in my direction, swaying drunkenly, and I feel like I'm staring at one of those appearance-warping mirrors. She is the version of me without errors. The Barbie version. Her hair is platinum blonde, her lips are two times plumper, her nose is perfect, her boobs are bigger, her waist is about a mile smaller, and her skin is a lovely Californian golden brown.

Standing in front of me with her head tilted to one side, she lets her glazed eyes rove my face then down my body. I'm wearing my best button-down white blouse and black skirt, but by the look in her eyes, I don't come up to scratch.

"You're too fat," she spits spitefully. "And you look nothing like me." She takes a long drag from her cigarette, her critical eyes locked on mine. "I can't have people looking at *you* and thinking that you're me." She shakes her head decisively. "No. The agency must send someone else."

The hairs on the back of my neck stand. I can't have come all the way here for her to send me back with nothing. "I'll look more like you once they get the hair and the make-up going," I say desperately.

She walks around me. "Great hair and make-up are not going to cover that enormous ass of yours." She comes back to stand in front of me and peers into my face. She is so close I can smell the alcohol on her breath. "Is your nose deformed or something?"

I'm usually quite good at defending myself, but I *need* this job, so I resist the instinctive urge to say something equally nasty. "It's just a nose."

She looks scandalized. "Have you looked in a mirror? Fuck, if I had a nose like that, I'd fucking throw myself under a bus." Her lips curve upwards maliciously. It is clear that she is thoroughly enjoying herself.

It's a good thing I've never been self-conscious about my nose, or given it a second thought, because this woman is so wealthy, so beautiful, and so confident that she can totally rob someone of their self-esteem and make them question their own self-worth. I remember Maria asking me to appease her.

"You're right. I'll consider getting a nose job," I say monotonously. If I agree with everything she says…

"Are you like a robot or something?" she screeches suddenly, her eyes flashing.

Whoa, she just flipped into fury mode without any warning whatsoever.

"Why are you agreeing with everything I say?"

I realize that I've tackled the situation the wrong way. Maria said make her feel superior. She cares about being better than me. To her, I'm a bit of gum at the bottom of her shoe and she wants me to act like that. "Because you're right. I am very unhappy with my appearance."

"You should be disgusted by your appearance."

25

I put on a sad expression. "I know I have many flaws."

"How dare you patronize me? You're intolerable," she shouts, shoving me backward.

I usually have good balance but I was not expecting the push, so I fall straight into the door and crash to the floor. My elbow and hip hurt. Her spitefulness toward a total stranger who has never done her any harm is shocking, and I clench my fists in anger but quickly release the tension. I must try my hardest to ignore it and concentrate on not saying anything else to piss her off. I can't lose this opportunity, and that's exactly what will happen if I get into a fight with Tamara Honeywell. I'm too poor to walk away, and I'm not too proud to beg. This round can go to Miss Honeywell.

I only have to survive until Ms. Moore comes.

"Miss Honeywell, I know that you are far more beautiful than me, but it won't matter because I'm just going to be on a ranch. The only eyes looking at me will be workers and the animals," I say from my position on the floor. I keep my voice low in the hope it will ease the tension swirling around the room.

It works. The fury drains out of her. She slouches, turns, and walks to a table where there is a bottle of champagne in an ice bucket. Idly, she picks up a glass and fills it. Bubbles overflow down her fingers.

Without bringing too much attention to myself, I pull myself to my feet and stand awkwardly. What exactly am I supposed to do? Stay? Go?

"Well," Tamara says, sucking her fingers, "do you know what you'll be doing in my place?"

"I'll be working hard on a ranch."

She whirls around and almost loses her balance. Righting herself clumsily, she raises her glass in a toast. "That's right. You will be," she makes air quotes with her fourth and fifth fingers, 'learning responsibility' as Daddy Dearest puts it. Cleaning up after dumb animals and working alongside a bunch of illiterate, filthy workers."

I rack my brain to say something neutral that will not make her fly off into another rage. "I'm not a stranger to hard work."

"And while you're learning responsibility, I'll be topping up my tan on a friend's private island," she announces gleefully.

"You deserve it," I say quickly.

She frowns. "I know I do. The last few months have been so difficult. With all the stress of my new movie being released next month, I can't believe Daddy would try to do this to me."

She sounds like a caterwauling cat, and I cannot understand how this whining, self-pitying woman came to be so famous. She's horrible. "I know. It must be so hard," I commiserate.

She nods her head solemnly.

Thank God I am spared from spouting more insincere remarks about how difficult her situation is by a soft knock on the door.

"Come in," Tamara shouts, and a beautifully preserved woman walks in. She has iron-gray hair swept away from a stern face, and she is dressed in a sophisticated, two-piece, black and white box suit. Her bright red shoes accent her outfit in an out-of-context, throw-on, totally glamorous way that all the money in the world cannot buy.

SIX
Cass

Tamara twists her head toward the woman. "Why did you pick her? What happened to the girl we usually use? What's her name?" she demands. There is no longer any aggression in her body or tone.

"Unfortunately, Miley was not available," the woman says mildly.

"Why not?" Tamara's voice has become petulant, like a spoiled brat that is being denied something it wants.

"Her sister is getting married on the seventeenth of this month and she's the maid of honor."

She flings her hand out in my direction. "I don't like her. She was rude to me."

I blink at the unfair accusation. What? When was I ever rude to her?

The woman does not even turn to look at me. "You won't have to deal with her. I will."

"Why can't we get someone else?"

"There is no one else. It's either her or you'll have to go to Montana yourself," the woman says patiently.

"But she looks nothing like me," Tamara grumbles, glaring at me.

"Oh, I don't know. I think she'll do very well."

Tamara gasps with outrage that anyone would dare think I look like her. "My nose does not look like that. Her eyes are the color of dirty dish water. And she's at least twice my size."

The woman smiles tightly. "We haven't worked on her yet. Besides, she's going to a place where no one knows you and she'll be stuck inside a stable for most of that time. I don't think it's going to matter too much if her nose doesn't look like yours or if she's carrying a bit more weight than you."

Tamara drains her glass and looks sulky. "If this goes wrong, you're fired."

"Nothing will go wrong. As long as you stay under the radar and don't draw media attention to yourself during that time …"

"I'm not stupid," Tamara scoffs before turning to me and jabbing her finger in my direction. "As for you. You better Skype me twice a week and keep me informed."

I nod.

"And you better make sure your performance is believable. I hope that Carter woman told you that you have to finish your month. If you drop out halfway you don't get paid, but don't make the mistake of thinking if you do a bad job and you have to stay for another month that I'll be coughing up for that extra month too. You won't get a cent if you screw this up for me."

"Understood," I say quickly.

Her eyes glitter. "You'll be wearing real jewels. My jewels. Don't take that as an invitation for you to steal anything, because old Nora here keeps an inventory of every fucking thing I own in her head." She picks up a black pearl necklace lying by the champagne bucket and holds it up. "How many pearls are in this necklace, Nora?" she asks while keeping her hostile eyes fixed on me.

"Thirty-six," Nora says after a brief pause.

Tamara throws the necklace at me and I catch it mid-air.

"Count the pearls," she orders.

My hands are shaking as I count the smooth orbs. I guess it's the fear of thinking I nearly lost the job and outrage of being treated like a common thief. I finish counting and realize there are thirty-seven pearls. I look up. "Thirty-six."

Tamara laughs triumphantly. "See. So, don't get any bright ideas."

"I won't take anything that belongs to you," I say quietly.

Tamara yawns.

"Would you like to have a little nap?" Nora asks.

"Yeah," Tamara slurs as she walks toward the bed. "Will you come and cover me?" she asks sleepily. I watch the older woman cover her as if she is a child then walk toward me.

"Come on," she says softly.

I follow her out and wait while she closes the door and turns toward me with a smile. "Hello, Cass. You've probably already gathered that I'm Nora Moore."

I nod vigorously. "You cannot begin to imagine how glad I am to see you, Ms. Moore."

She suppresses a smile. "I'm sure you are. I'm afraid you got off to a bad start with Miss Honeywell. It's my fault. I'm sorry, I was late, but it couldn't be avoided." She grimaces. "She might not remember when she wakes up, but I suggest you stay out of her way for the rest of your stay here."

"I'll be happy to do that," I say quickly.

"Now. Let's take a good look at you," she says and takes a step closer. She comes within a few inches of my face and looks at me carefully. Her vanilla scent is a nice change after being around Tamara's alcohol-soaked breath.

I stare straight ahead.

"Hmm," she says.

My eyes swivel to meet hers.

She steps back and smiles. "As much as Miss Honeywell hates to admit it, your features are remarkably similar to hers and you've actually got a better figure. All you need to be her is a bit of a makeover with some new clothes, a change of hairstyle, the right makeup, colored contact lenses, a tan, and some HA fillers."

I stare at her. "HA fillers?"

She smiles reassuringly. "It's a perfectly safe temporary lip filler. The beauty of it is it can be completely erased with an eraser enzyme injection if you don't want big lips once your month is over, or you can leave it and let your body naturally metabolize it between four to six months."

"Right," I say, relief bubbling into my veins and making me feel almost dizzy. I've got this job and I'll be able to pay off all my debts.

"Obviously, your accent is very different, but since you're leaving for Montana tomorrow afternoon, nothing can be done about that. Fortunately, it won't matter since you will not be around anyone who knows her. How are your acting skills?"

"Acting skills?"

She tilts her head toward the door we just came out of. "Can you imitate the behavior you just witnessed in there?"

31

I think of Tamara shamelessly jumping up and down on the beefy man's dick and push it firmly out of my head. "You mean can I be rude to total strangers?"

A ghost of a smile appears on her stern face. "At least at the beginning you'll have to act sarcastic and spoiled."

"Sure, I can veto conventional manners for a few days."

She nods. "Then you'll do just fine."

"Thank you, Ms. Moore. You don't know how much I need this job."

Her eyes flicker. "Hmmm…ready to start the makeover?"

"Sure. I'm ready when you are."

"Good. I believe the hairstylist is already here, and Tamara's makeup artist will come tomorrow morning after you've had your tanning session. She'll teach you how to do your makeup the way she does Tamara's for her."

"We don't even need to leave the house to make me look like her?"

Her lips twitch with amusement. "No."

I decide I really like her. There's something special about her and I'm glad I didn't get her into trouble with the pearl necklace.

We make our way through a small corridor and go to the ground floor where we happen to see Maria coming from the opposite direction. It is a very different Maria that we pass though. Instead of the gossipy and warm woman I met, this one walks with her head down and her eyes locked on the ground. Taking her lead, I don't say anything either. I guess she wants to draw attention away from herself, which is probably how she keeps her job in a treacherous place like this.

Down a short corridor to the left of the staircase, Ms. Moore leads me into a pure white room. The lighting is cleverly cast from different angles around the room, so not one part is darker than another. The air smells of perfume and the glass cases lining the walls are filled with expensive looking little pots of cosmetics. In one case, there are hundreds of bottles of nail polish.

The room is also equipped with two sleek hair washing stations and cream barber chairs facing full body mirrors. There are small carts beside each station stuffed to the brim with hair products, brushes, rollers, and straighteners.

"Selene," Ms. Moore calls.

A redhead suddenly pops up from under a side counter. I furrow my brow. Had she been under there the whole time? She looks to be in her thirties.

"Hi, Nora," she greets with a friendly grin. "Oh, my," she says, running her pale eyes down me. "What have we here?"

"This is Cass," Ms. Moore introduces.

"I can see this is going to be a walk in the park for me. She's gorgeous." Selena turns toward me. "You will make a perfect Tamara."

I nod, unsure of how to take the statement. I can't be offended that I look like Tamara Honeywell. She is a beautiful woman, after all. I guess I just don't like being compared to such a rude and disgusting person.

"Right, I'll be off. Will you give me a call when you're finished?" Ms. Moore says briskly.

"Yes. See you later."

We watch Ms. Moore walk out the door before Selene turns to me and grins impishly.

I smile back. "Where do we start?" I ask, unsure of how this process works.

"We start with your hair. Take a seat in one of the chairs and I'll get to work cutting it."

I take slow steps toward the closest chair, hoping to prolong the process. My waist-long hair has always been a trademark feature of mine, and I've never changed its dark blond color either. I'd rather not mess with the color or the length, but if it means paying off the loan sharks and keeping Dad going, then it's a very small price to pay.

"Honey, don't be nervous. It will be a great style for you," she states confidently.

"I hope so," I whisper. My dad always loved my long hair. I try to remember that I'm doing this for him as well.

I lie back in the cold leather chair and Selene comes up behind me. "Do you need any last pictures? Last words to your hair?" she asks with a cheeky grin. I know she is just being nice, but Tamara has made me feel so paranoid, I almost feel like she's mocking me.

"No," I say firmly.

"Good," she says, spraying my head with water from a plastic bottle.

With a muted snip, the first lock falls to the floor.

SEVEN
Cass

For the rest of the day, I am kept busy with the makeover.

The injection filler doesn't really hurt—okay it stings a bit—but it's really nothing. I've had worse. The colored contact lenses are harder to get used to. They feel like grit in my eyes.

"That's it," the nurse—I'm assuming she's a nurse because she wearing a white nurse's uniform—says cheerfully.

The reclining chair is raised to an upright position and I look into the mirror she holds out to me. Oh, my God! My lips look like ten bees have stung them and they feel weird, but she tells me that as she has used a blunt tip cannula there will be hardly any bruising. My lips will settle in twenty-four hours and will look the way they are supposed to for the next few months.

My next destination is a small cubicle where, turbaned and completely bare, I stand in front of a stranger called Clarise while she spray-tans me. The mist feels cold and smells like malty biscuits. After two all-over layers, my skin is basically the color of mud.

"Are you sure about this?" I ask, feeling quite concerned.

Above her face mask, her eyes crinkle at the corners. "Don't freak out. The color will fade and you will look great by tomorrow."

It takes two more hours for Helen, Tamara's makeup artist, to complete my transformation. My nails and eyebrows are shaped and colored in. When I look in the mirror, a stranger with blue eyes stares back at me.

"Wow," I whisper through numb lips.

Selena comes and stands behind us. "She'll die if she sees you. You're better looking than her."

"Shhh…" Helen says, giving her a funny look.

Selena shrugs nonchalantly. "Why can't I say it? It's the truth. Tamara used to be pretty, but she's just gone too far now. I swear if she has another nose job, her whole nose is going to fall off. Besides all the drugs and drink…"

Helen narrows her eyes in my direction as if to say, not in front of her.

"She doesn't look stupid enough to repeat that to anybody, let alone Tamara," Selena says carelessly and flounces off.

For the next hour, Helen teaches me all about makeup. Some of it is useful and I file the information away to tell Jesse. She tells me that while blondes are generally advised to wear only fiery, orangey reds if they're going to wear red lipstick, the most dramatic and stunning red lipstick for blondes is blue based.

"It will make your teeth look brighter too." She twists open a lipstick. "Like this Cherry Lush by Tom Ford."

She applies it on me and she is right. It makes my lips, already big and swollen, look even more prominent. "Try wearing this with a blue dress," she advises.

She drops the lipstick into a big cosmetics bag on the table in front of me. By the time the lesson is over, the makeup bag is full of all kinds of cosmetics.

After the lesson, I am shown to another room where Tamara's personal dresser, a woman dressed from head to toe in black, is waiting with a tape measure. I cringe inwardly, but she is deft and quick.

"Now that was not so bad, was it?" she asks a couple of minutes later.

"No, it wasn't," I agree.

She puts her tape measure into her bag. "I'll see you tomorrow, then."

"Are we finished?"

"Uh-huh. I'll get a couple of suitcases ready for tomorrow."

"Don't I get to see any of the clothes I will be wearing?"

She smiles apologetically. "Sorry, my instructions were to fill two suitcases of clothing that will suit Tamara's style in your size."

I can't help it. I become a bit anxious about what I'll find inside the bags.

That evening, I join Ms. Moore for dinner. We sit at the kitchen table and eat a delicate chicken dish made with olives and white wine served on a bed of wild rice.

"Not only are you required to look like Tamara, but you need to mimic the way she walks, talks, and moves," Ms. Moore says and switches on the DVD player. When the videos come to an end, she pushes a notepad toward me and gives me a brief rundown of Tamara's childhood, likes, dislikes, hobbies, mannerisms, favorite foods, and drinks. "You can start practicing to be like her from now."

I pout the way I saw her do earlier.

"Good. Toss your hair a lot like this too," she says, tossing hers as if she is in a shampoo ad.

It looks ridiculous but I follow her and she smiles approvingly.

"When you get there, you'll have to make some calls to Tamara and me. You better key our numbers into your phone now."

I realize that I must be extremely blunt with her. "I don't want to sound disrespectful, Ms. Moore, but I have twenty-three dollars and a pack of mints in my pocket. That twenty-three dollars is all the money I have left after paying my landlord. Since my cell phone is a pay-as-you-go, I will not be able to call anyone long distance."

Ms. Moore's eyes narrow. "If you want to act like Tamara, you must do better than that. Neither your attitude nor your words were disrespectful."

I place the palms of my hands against my temples. "I'm sorry. I promise you that I can and I will impersonate Tamara's behavior to the best of my ability as soon as I get to Montana, but for now, the last thing I want to do is be ungrateful to you. You have taken me under your wing and given me a huge break. You cannot imagine how big a break, so please don't get upset with me for not being rude to you. I just needed to make you understand my situation. Mainly, that I don't have any money at all."

She sighs, her eyes suddenly filling with compassion. "I was in your position a few years back."

I find that hard to believe. To me, she is the epitome of effortless glamor and sophistication.

She stands up and goes to the kitchen counter where her black patent leather purse is. She reaches into it, pulls out a wallet, and extracts a few bills.

When she extends the bills in my direction, I take them awkwardly and look at them. Five hundred in crisp new bills. I shake my head. "I can't take all this from you."

"Don't worry. It's not coming from me. You can't go to Montana without any money. I'll make sure you have a phone by tomorrow too. Tamara Honeywell would *never* be seen without the latest one."

I fold the bills. "Thank you, Ms. Moore. I can't tell you how much this means to me."

"Like I said, I've been where you are before, maybe even worse. You're a strong girl, Cass. You'll find your way out of your pit." She smiles and stands up. "Time you were in bed. I'll see you bright and early tomorrow morning. Your flight is at eleven and there are still some things to iron out."

"Okay."

"Oh, please don't go wandering around the house. Tamara tends to be active at night."

"I won't," I promise. The last person I want to meet ever again is her.

"Tamara and you will leave from the same airport, only she will be getting on her friend's private jet and you'll be flying first class to Montana."

My eyes widen. First class. My, my what will Jesse say?

"Goodnight," she says and starts walking away from me.

"Ms. Moore," I call when she is almost at the door. She turns to me with an emotionless expression on her face. She may seem to be all business, but the woman has a hidden heart of gold. "Just so you know in case it happens again, there are thirty-seven pearls in her necklace."

"I knew that," she says with a faint smile.

"So why did you say thirty-six."

She gives a small shrug. "It was a test to see what you would do."

"Did I pass the test?"

"You passed one and failed another."

"Passed what and failed what?'

"You're trustworthy, but you're too naïve to survive around Tamara."

She was a lot braver than me. "You took a chance. I could have gotten you in trouble and she could have fired you."

She smiles confidently. "Tamara knows better than to fire me. Her loss will be her competitors' gain, and she has many of those. Sleep well, Cass."

She opens the door and walks out.

Alone in the kitchen, I go to flip my hair over my shoulder and realize that it's no longer the same. The tips brush against my shoulder blades and I try to ignore the fact that I'm no longer myself. My mouth, my hair, the color of skin...

For thirty thousand dollars, I sold my individuality.

EIGHT
Lars

hat?"

"Ryan broke his leg," my brother, Matt, repeats patiently.

"How the hell did he do that?" I yell into the phone.

"He got tossed off Thunder."

"That dumbass! What was he doing with him?"

"Trying to ride him," my brother says dryly.

"Why in heaven's name? I told the damn fool to keep away from that beast."

"You know how he is. He was trying to please you."

I take a deep breath to calm myself. This is the last fucking thing I need. "Right. We have to find a backup trainer. The spoiled brat has to be picked up," I look at my watch, "in an hour. Who do we have?"

"Nobody," my brother says cheerfully. "Thunder put Jimbo out of commission last week with a few cracked ribs, remember?"

"So, who's going to pick her up and train her?" I almost growl.

"You."

"Like hell I am. I'm not taking one damned minute out of my day to train a talentless, uninteresting, fake ass, ditzy drama queen."

"Don't hold back. Tell everybody how you really feel about a girl you've never met. She could turn out to be nice, you know." My brother sounds amused, which pisses me off even more.

"Nice? God vomited and there was Tamara Honeywell is how one film critic described her, and I'm inclined to agree."

"One man's vomit and all that…"

"Why do I have to do it? Why can't you?" I demand.

"Me? Why should I? Bucking Bronco is your ranch."

I swear under my breath. "If I get stuck with Honeywell, I swear she'll be working her pampered ass off until she breaks every fucking artificial nail on her fingers."

He laughs.

"I don't know why you don't take her? I hear she's a gem at riding dick," I say persuasively.

He chuckles. "Thanks for the kind offer, but I've got my hands full with Erika. You're on your own with this one, bro."

"Fine." I don't like it, but I don't have an option in the matter, so I'll cowboy up and take it on the chin. "I'll pick her up. Maybe I'll put her on Thunder."

"Be nice," he says. "Even vomit is precious to its father."

"Whatever."

"What should we do with the racehorse, Lars?" Matt asks.

I sigh and rub the back of my neck in frustration. Thunder is one of the fastest stallions this side of Montana. I know he has potential stored up in him, but I just can't understand why he won't work with any of our men. They've never had a hard time with any other horse.

"I just hope he has not become of one of those wildly independent horses that can never be tamed."

"We spent good money on him, so I'm not giving up yet," I insist.

"If he keeps hurting our trainers, we'll have to get rid of him. Money doesn't matter in a situation like this."

"Understood," I say. My brother holds no power here, but he makes a valid point. It will be tragic to get rid of Thunder, but until he takes to a trainer, we're wasting time and funds on him.

I hang up the phone and stand up from my office chair. There's a farmhand who tends to the broncos, so I don't often interact with them, but I'll have to do something about Thunder soon. However, there are more pressing priorities that need to come first.

I walk through my house and go outside. Bucking Bronco is a cattle ranch about 44,400 acres and expanding. With eleven full-time employees, the spread supports a sizable herd of Angus cross, mostly black hided, fall calving cows. We also farm one thousand acres of baleable forage crops and nearly two hundred acres of permanent pastures.

"Hey, Lars. Did you hear about Ryan?" Chance, one of the ranch hands shouts.

I nod and stride in the direction of the cattle barns.

"Yeah, Thunder made him chew gravel too." Catching up with me, he keeps pace by jogging backward a couple of paces in front of me. "So, is it true that Miss Tamara is coming right here to this very spread for a couple three days?" he asks.

I spare him a glance. Chance is a good kid but naïve. His eyes are fucking on fire with excitement. "Chance, she's not staying for a couple three days. She's staying for a *whole* damned month. And stop looking so pleased about it. It's not a good thing."

"Whoopee. She's hot," he hollers, and taking his hat off, throws it into the air.

I sigh and hop into my truck. "Hot or not, she'll still be a pain in my ass."

It takes me forty-five minutes on dusty roads to make it to our meeting place and I am expecting her to pull up any minute. Most men would be thrilled to meet Tamara Honeywell, but brainless, pointless celebrities like her just make my skin crawl. I don't even want to be in the same room with them. I swear, if she's not careful, she's going to end up bent over my knee getting what her daddy should have given her.

Fifteen minutes later, she arrives right on time in a blacked-out limo. I fill my lungs with air, step out of my truck, and lean against the hot metal. The back door of the car doesn't open immediately. Instead, the driver exits the car and nods at me before going around to open the door for her. I scowl at the act. It is completely unnecessary for the driver to leave the vehicle. Tamara is perfectly capable of getting out herself.

Once the door opens, one sparkle infested, sky-scraper high shoe makes its way out of the car. Attached is a disconcertingly smooth, long, golden leg. Another shoe slips out. Followed by another endless leg. Something starts happening to my temperature. Both shoes hit the ground, rustling up small clouds of dust.

Languorously, God's own vomit unfolds itself from the limo and...whoa! It goddamn kills me to admit it, but hell, blood rushes south and I pop wood right there for

Tamara Honeywell. I was a pimply-faced kid the last time just the sight of a female had that effect on me. Somewhere at the edges of my vision, I notice the driver of the vehicle moving toward the back of the car, but I can't really focus on anything except the shining vision in front of me. I've had my share of women, more than my share, but this one, I can't take my eyes off.

Sunglasses cover her eyes, but her hair is glowing like white gold—a color not one woman around these parts would dare —and her skin is apple fresh. She is wearing a short white dress that clings to her every curve, and fuck me, she has a lot of those. Like some sex zombie, my eyes latch on to and get unwittingly stuck on her full, round tits. I must look like one of those cooking show chefs who pretend to smile while they are stuffing bread up a bird's ass.

"Up here, buddy," she scolds. Her voice, contrary to what Rolling Stones magazine once claimed sounds something like a mix between a screeching cat and a Baccarat champagne glass being smashed in a fit of temper, is sweet and despite the angry undertone, is all kinds of sexy.

"Lars," I introduce myself, extending a hand to her.

She doesn't take it. "Yeah, well you know who I am. So, are you going to get my bags?"

That brings me down to earth with a bang. Reality check. That's right, I detest what this woman stands for. Despite the banging body, she's a lousy excuse for a human being. I turn my head toward the bags left behind the limo, which the driver has unloaded while I was examining her with my mouth hanging open. I bring my gaze back to her face. I wish she'd take those fucking shades off. It'll help if I can see her eyes and look into the empty voids behind them.

"You came here to work. Start by carrying your own damned bags," I tell her.

I notice a small smile on her lips before she tosses her hair like some goddamn horse and tilts her head. The minx pushes her sunglasses down her little nose and peers up at me with laughing blue eyes. Oh, man, I'm so fucked. How could these eyes belong to a vapid creature pairing all the sad dick hopping with alcohol and drugs?

"I figured a handsome cowboy like you wouldn't mind carrying a few bags for little old me," she says with a teasing lilt.

Fuck. Part of me wants to do it. Manipulative little bitch. I'm gonna need all my wits about me. "Lil' old you had better get strong fast because you'll be lifting things much heavier than those bags."

She pushes her sunglasses so they lie on top of her head. "I have a secret to tell you," she whispers with pouting lips. Tamara takes another step closer and stands on her tiptoes to speak into my ear. Her lips only come as far as the middle of my neck because of our height difference. Her breath fans over me and goosebumps run down my arms. Jesus, she smells like a slice of heaven.

"I'm not really a bitch," she whispers. "I'm very sweet if you do what I want."

Even the dust motes stop swirling. And for one crazy second, I experience the primitive urge to grab her sweet smelling soft body and kiss the hell out of that sexy, pouty, slutty mouth. My hands open into claws, ready to squeeze her flesh. Then sanity asserts itself. What the fuck am I thinking? This is Tamara Honeywell. STD-guaranteed-

Tamara-Honeywell. Suddenly, I see the thick layer of greasepaint she has troweled on her face. The blazing heat must have affected me while waiting for her in the midday sun.

I take a giant step backward.

The suddenness of my action makes her teeter in her high heels, and she almost loses her balance. It would have done her good to land on her pampered ass, but she manages to right herself. Shame.

"You think you're so hot ice cream would melt on your fingers, don't ya?" I ask, laughing.

"Says the man who stared at my breasts like they are a saucer of milk and he's a cat dying for a drink."

I suppress a smile. "I know I was looking at your chest, but I got news for you, honey. I'm a man. That's what we do. We look at breasts. Especially big ones. And yours are…big. However, let's get something straight. I'm not attracted to you. You might be smoking on the outside to…some people, but beneath that, you're a manipulative, selfish, lazy, careless, ditzy bitch."

Her eyes widen.

"You nearly killed someone because you were so zoned out on drugs and alcohol, and as far as I'm concerned, the right place for you is behind bars or in one of those fancy rehab centers. If I catch you making those kinds of skanky offers to me or my men again, I'll send you back to your father so fast you'll be nursing an ass full of rope burn."

I feel as if I have gone too far, but I swear, she doesn't look disappointed or put out in the least. In fact, she looks a mixture of relieved and extremely pleased with herself.

"Okay," she agrees coolly.

That is not the response I expected. This is turning out to be nothing like I thought it would be. I clear my throat. "Good. I'll wait in the truck. Put all your shit in the back," I order gruffly.

I walk to the front door of my truck and jump in. Surreptitiously, I watch her break into a sweat from my rearview mirror as she struggles to walk toward her bags in her tall heels. She has a fine ass on her.

She'll have to make at least three trips to load them all into the truck—especially since she's likely never carried a bag in her life; then it will be interesting to see her haul everything into the truck. She starts with the largest suitcase, dragging it behind her, the wheels catching the gravel and causing the bag to shake and tip dangerously. Once she reaches the truck, instead of lifting it, she grabs the bottom of the suitcase and flips it into the truck bed without much effort.

My jaw drops open.

As she moves away, I notice her shoulders shaking and for a second, I think I've reduced her to tears, but then she turns sideways and I realize she is laughing!

In a couple of minutes, her bags are expertly stacked. Quickly, she ties the straps of the bags to one another to prevent them from falling. Is this girl full of surprises or what?

She must have inherited the old cunning fox's brains.

She hops into the passenger's seat, takes the heels off her feet, and sits up straight. I stare at her curiously, but don't say anything.

"Are we leaving, or are we just going to sit here, cowboy?"

NINE
Cass

$\mathbf{F}$irst impressions can be everything and I hate that I blew mine with the hunk who came to meet me at the dirt strip. If it had been a movie, that moment I got out of the car and our eyes met should've had the Blues Brothers track, Rawhide, playing in the background. I can almost hear it playing in my head.

Rolling, rolling.

I've never seen anything as mind-numbingly and fabulously macho in Chicago. A real, honest-to-goodness cowboy. His skin is deeply tanned, his hair sun-streaked and curling around his shirt collar, and his features cut as if from pure granite.

He is casually leaning against a beat-up truck with the thumb of his right hand hooked into one of the belt loops of his faded jeans. It makes the big muscles of that arm strain against the sleeve of his plaid shirt. And the low riding jeans that hug his lean hips and fall onto cowboy boots...someone, anyone, just kill me now.

As I watch, one tip of his hard mouth curls into a sarcastic, lazy grin, and my mouth goes bone dry. It should be a crime to smile like that. He tips his solid black Stetson back. Nice. When he pulls away from the dusty pickup and starts walking toward me, my heart hammers like crazy.

No, it doesn't happen in slow motion, but it sure feels like it does.

Act one, Scene one.

Spoilt bitch meets to-die-for cowboy.

Tearing my eyes away from his approaching form, I pretend to nonchalantly dust my clothes with my sweaty palms and take the first step. I can feel my hands fidgeting and twitching as he walks toward me. I get OCD when I'm nervous and I'm shaking with nerves.

Even under the shade of his hat, his icy gray eyes, framed by paintbrush eyelashes, are piercing. When they drop to my chest and stay, I feel as if I'm gonna melt into a puddle. I know then I need to cool down and hit the right note of blasé or I'm gonna to ruin everything for myself.

There's only one way I know to do that. I channel Tamara Honeywell. And to be honest, I'm a much better actress than I thought. I take a gamble and offer myself to him in the most unsubtle way possible. That's usually good to scare all but the most desperate man. And this one is definitely not desperate. Jessie always says men like a chase. Put it on a platter and shove it under their noses and they'll run a mile. He falls for it like a rat falls for cheese. He doesn't run a mile, but his lips thin and he takes a long step back.

I can tell by the expression in his eyes that he has declared war, which is fine by me. I'm not here to get laid or have my heart twisted and torn. I'm here for a month because I have bills to pay, and then I'm gone. Forever. With chivalry dead and buried in the dirt, I start dragging my suitcase toward the truck. I'm used to hard work, but I'm wearing high heels. It's boiling hot and I nearly break my ankles. All the while I can see him watching me in the rearview mirror.

Asshat!

Once I've thrown everything into the bed of his truck, I join him in the front. I don't care about sweat or dirt, but Tamara would, so I make a big deal about it. When I sit on the dust covered seat and my skirt rides up my thighs, so high it's nearly obscene, he gives me an odd look before quickly looking away. The backs of my legs stick to the leather and I want to wiggle under his glare, but I know not to do so. Tamara would be confident about getting attention.

"Are we leaving, or are we just going to sit here, cowboy?" I ask, putting extra sass into my tone.

"I'll pull away whenever I damn well please," he responds, but he starts the engine with a scowl. Even when he is angry he looks as delectable as three scoops of ice cream and a big ole cherry on top.

"Are you smiling or just breaking wind?" I ask cheekily.

"Yeah, very classy," he says sarcastically.

Hmmm…what would Tamara do? Be obnoxious. I stick my lower lip out in a belligerent pout the way I saw her do to Ms. Moore and snarl, "Don't talk to me like that."

He fixes the brim of his hat. "Maybe if you'd stop acting like a spoiled child I'd stop talking to you like that," he retorts, his big brown hands clenching the steering wheel.

I contort my face and pick up my discarded heel— which probably costs more than my old apartment—and hit him on the shoulder with it. I'd love to say that I'm acting, but his manners are starting to piss me off.

"Quit acting like a selfish bitch." He snatches the shoe from my hand, cranks his window glass down, and without any hesitation, hurls it out. "Oh, whoops. There goes your precious designer shoe," he says, smiling smugly.

I gasp. I don't care about the shoe as much as the money it costs. I hope Tamara doesn't expect to get it back. All the same, he is insufferable. "You act like I give a shit about a stupid pair of shoes. There's plenty more where that came from," I scoff as I crank my glass down and toss my other shoe out into the endless stretch of prairie extending out on either side of us.

He stares at me in shock for a moment before turning back to the road and roaring with laughter. It breaks the tension and I bite my lip to keep from laughing along with him. I have to stay in character.

When I look in his direction, I notice his straight black hair blowing around his face from the breeze of the open windows. He has two dimples, but the one on his right cheek is more noticeable than on the left. He is a truly gorgeous specimen. One I would love to have for myself. Christ, where did that come from? I hope I don't have to spend too much time with him or there could be trouble.

"You're not going to be my trainer, are you?"

"Unfortunately, yes. The man who should have been training you broke his leg," he explains morosely.

"Are you good enough to teach someone?" I ask. I know the terms of the deal—I have to be able to ride well enough to fall off of a horse at the end of the month and not hurt myself too much. I might as well get the pieces into their rightful places on the chessboard.

"That's up to you. Will you listen and do exactly as I say?"

Cass would listen to everything he says while being respectful toward him, but I'm not Cass. I'm Tamara Honeywell, Queen Bitch. "Probably not."

"Well then, you'll probably fall off the damned bronco," he says with a frown.

He swerves suddenly for no reason at all and I grab the holy-shit bar over the window and glare at him. "Are you sure you're qualified to drive?"

His laugh has an edge to it. "I was avoiding a gopher."

"What is a gopher?"

"Technically, it's a ground squirrel."

I turn my head back quickly but all I see are clouds of dust.

The rest of the ride is silent. I don't want to push the man's buttons too hard, even though I know Tamara would. She went out of her way to push mine and if I had not needed this job so badly, we would have come to blows. We drive through a tall wooden arch with Bucking Bronco Ranch written on a hanging wooden board and pull up at a large white house with a deep wraparound porch. I automatically reach to open the car door, then halt in my tracks and sit inside the car instead. Tamara would wait to have the door opened for her.

Lars opens his door, steps out, and slams his door shut. "What are you doing in there?" he asks, staring at me through the open window.

"I'm waiting to have my door opened," I say, sitting a little straighter.

He shakes his head in wonder. "You'll be waiting a long while if that's the case."

I sit back in my seat stubbornly. I hope he doesn't concede to opening my door. I hope that he teaches me to be independent soon so I can drop this snobby act. "And I don't have shoes," I add. "I need to be carried in."

His eyebrows disappear into his hat and the expression of astonishment on his face almost makes me burst into laughter. As I watch, the shock of my request is wiped away and replaced with a scowl. "Here's another option. How would you like me to throw you into the house?"

I lift my chin arrogantly. "Well, at least get me some shoes then."

"We're on a ranch. It won't kill you to walk barefoot on a bit of dirt."

I love being barefoot—feeling the soil between my toes and the rocks beneath my feet—but I pretend to make a revolted face. "That's disgusting. I am *not* getting my feet dirty."

"Okay, I've had enough already. Let me make this crystal clear. If you don't stop acting like a spoiled brat, I will make one call—one—and this will be over. I don't care if you get hauled off to prison. It's the best place for you as far as I'm concerned. While you are here, I expect nothing less than blind obedience. Do I make myself clear?"

Good man. Tamara's father had a brilliant idea to send her here. This man and this place are exactly what she needs. Shame he has such a cunning daughter that she schemed her way out of his plan. I make a face. "Fine, I'll listen, but I'm not doing all the gross things you people do.

I'm just going to learn to ride a horse and go back to my life in LA as soon as possible."

"I don't give a shit what you get up to when you get back to wherever you came from, but while you're here, you'll do whatever I tell you to do," he says sternly.

"How about not," I snicker.

He stares at me with another priceless expression of disbelief.

Ignoring him, I open the door. Jumping to the ground, I wiggle my toes in the lovely hot soil. I almost moan with pleasure. I absolutely adore the feel of it. Up above, an eagle is circling in the hot blue air. In the distance, I can see animals that look like deer grazing.

"Are those deer?" I ask, squinting at them.

"No, antelope. We have about a hundred of them."

I turn toward him. "Really?"

He nods. "The spread is heavily populated with wild pigs too."

I have always loved animals and wanted to have a lot of them around me, but living in Chicago obviously deterred me from owning any. At that moment, I want nothing more than to go see all the farm animals, but Tamara Honeywell only loves animals when they come in the form of a handbag, a coat, or on her plate. "We passed a ton of little cottages on our way here. Are they all separate farms?"

"Most of what we passed belongs to this ranch. There are dozens of small homes lining the spread since many of the employees live and work on the land. It's much easier than driving through the old country roads daily."

"What kind of ranch is this?"

"We're producers of grass-fed, grass-finished, pasture-raised beef, and we're one of the finest stock farms in the state. Our prize cattle are sold for premium prices, but we also have dairy, sheep, hog, poultry, orchards, and we're starting an Arabian horse operation soon." His voice is filled with quiet pride.

TEN
Cass

I could have listened to him talk about the ranch all day long but that kind of talk would have bored Tamara silly, so I cut him off by walking away from him.

"Show me where I'm staying," I command as I reach the back of the truck.

Without any shoes, I find it far easier to pull myself up and stand inside it. I grab the tightly bundled bags and throw them onto the ground, jumping down after them before they can fall over. Again, he just stares at me with a bemused expression. God, how can a man be so effortlessly gorgeous?

"Well?" I prompt rudely.

A tick starts in his cheek and I have the impression that he is struggling to control himself. I follow as he marches forward, his back straight and rigid with tension.

"Am I staying in the house?" I ask. I really don't want to live in the same house with him for a whole month. He is too attractive for my liking, and I hate the idea that I'll have to keep on antagonizing him just to keep him insufferable and arrogant. It's either that or I blow this job by doing something stupid like falling into bed with him, or worse, getting emotionally entangled.

He inclines his head toward the white house in front of us. "Yeah, you'll be staying in the guest annex. It's downstairs and connected to the rest of the house by the kitchen." He turns his face toward me.

That suits me just fine, but I can imagine how offended Tamara Honeywell would be to be living next to the kitchen. "Next to the kitchen?" I grumble. "What am I, a fricking servant?"

His mouth lifts in disgust. "It makes it easier for you to wake up every morning and tend to your horse."

"What exactly am I supposed to be doing with the horse?" I roll my eyes as if I'm bored to death and not brimming over with excitement at the thought of caring for my very own horse. A horse that will be mine for the next thirty days!

His voice hardens. "You will clean your horse's stall, feed and grain all the horses, and once a week, you will clean out the barns."

Lars opens the door and signals for me to walk inside ahead of him. He says nothing as he strides through the big house. We go through a large airy kitchen and down a short corridor. He opens a door and stands back.

I almost break into a smile, but force myself to remain passive. "This is it?" I complain in a whiny voice.

"You won't be inside for anything but sleeping, so I'm sure you'll manage," he says tightly from behind me.

I take a step into the room. The floor is cool under my bare feet and I drop the suitcases. Knowing he can't see my expression, I let go of my facial muscles and start beaming with happiness. God, I could live in this annex forever and ever. It's simply the most beautiful room I've ever been in. I look around me in amazement. It is decorated in exactly the way I would love my home to be done up one day when I am married and have my own little family.

The windows are large and sunlight pours onto the duck-egg blue walls and makes rectangles of light on the gleaming wood floors. There are French doors that open out to a patio that overlooks gorgeous country. I can already see myself sitting out there watching the sunset with a tall glass of something cool.

My eyes move to the bed. It is large, intricately carved, and painted white. The sheets are all crisp and smooth like in a hotel. The furniture is all white. There is a pretty dressing table with a little dusty-pink velvet-covered stool pushed up against one wall and built-in cupboards on another. Someone has put a blue vase of wild flowers on the nightstand.

I hear him come into the room, and as I turn to look at him, he grabs my suitcases from the floor and hauls them onto the bed.

"Are you bipolar?"

"What?" he growls.

"Why can't you make up your mind? Either help me with my bags or don't. I can't understand why you'd refuse to help me when I needed assistance, and take my bags when I really don't need your help anymore."

He runs his hand behind his neck and frowns. "I don't know why I did either. You're easily the most ungrateful, cranky woman I've ever had the misfortune to meet."

He looks so adorable my stomach flutters. I can't think of a single thing to say.

"There's a bathroom through there." He sighs, indicating a door on his right. "When you finish unpacking, go to the horse barn. It's down the hill on the left. Choose a horse that takes well to you. Isadora and Pumpkin are both gentle. So is Misty. Devil's Ride is mine," he says, walking away.

"Thank you," I say to the closed door.

I don't bother to unpack. I'm far too excited about the horses to concentrate on anything else. Only one suitcase is mine anyway. The two big ones are filled with the things Tamara will need when she come to take over on the last day. Shoes, bags, jewelry, dresses, rollers, hair straighteners, and all kinds of things you'd never think one woman would need for *one* night away from home.

I quickly open my bag and sift through the clothes, trying to find something to wear on a farm. There is one risqué dress, a very short sundress, a pair of white shorts that I wouldn't be caught dead in, some T-shirts, and finally, a couple of pairs of jeans. I get into one of them and pull on a black T-shirt. Then I run out barefoot.

The house is absolutely deserted as I run through it. A pair of men's muck boots sit beside the door and I question whether to take them or to go to the barn barefoot. Unfortunately, while I do enjoy the feel of soil between my toes, I won't feel the same way about horse crap. I run back to my bedroom, get some toilet paper and fill the boots with it, and slip into them. A bit uncomfortable and heavy, but they'll do.

Wearing them, I stomp out the door. The driveway is a small hill, so I walk down it and turn left as instructed. I get a weird, almost awed look from a boy in the cow barn, but I ignore him. I am Tamara Honeywell, after all.

It takes only a few minutes to reach the horse barns and I'm practically bouncing with excitement. It's hard to stay in character when I care so much about this part of the job. As soon as I step foot in the barn, I crinkle my nose. When I thought of barns, I typically imagined a well-groomed building, but I never really thought about the smell. Then a horse in one of the stalls in the rows on either side of me neighs, and I smile widely. Oh, yes. That is exactly how imagined it. I walk into it with a heart full of joy. I seem to be the only one in the barn, which means I can be myself.

Some of the pins are empty, but the majority are full of large, healthy horses. Inside the single barn, there are fourteen stalls—seven on either side. Only a few of them are labeled with names—I see Pumpkin, Isadora, and even Devil's Ride. The animals watch me nervously, all standing in the back of their stalls. Only one, a gorgeous, sleek black stallion with a star on his forehead, comes forth and sticks his head out. I smile and reach forward to rub his snout while he exhales loudly.

"What's your name then?" I ask, leaning my face on his warm neck. His black mane is not slicked back like the others, as if he hasn't been groomed in some time. He huffs beneath my gentle fingers.

"Tamara, you took my boots," Lars shouts through the barn, and the horse's head shoots up.

"Shh…He's mad because I stole his boots but it'll be all right," I say soothingly.

"Tamara," I hear Lars call hesitantly behind me.

The horse nudges my shoulder playfully and I turn around with a laugh. Lars is standing behind me with wide eyes and a gaping mouth. My laugh dries up in my throat. "What?"

He closes his mouth. "Can you please come here?" he says quietly.

"Why?"

I see him take a deep breath. "Do you remember what I said about obeying me?"

"Yes."

"Now is a good time to do that."

"Fine, but just so you know, I want this horse," I say firmly.

"Of course, you do," he mumbles, "but maybe you should select something other than a wild Arabian that spooks easily and doesn't usually even let people touch him."

I laugh and reach back to pet the stallion's long face once more. "He's doing fine with me."

"He won't let you ride him," he explains and shifts uneasily as if he is hoping I'll move away from the horse.

"Yes, he will," I retort confidently, and climbing over the door, jump into his stall.

Lars doesn't move a muscle as I snuggle up closer to the animal. "He looks like a beast, but he's just a big softie."

"He's never let anyone this close to him," Lars says in amazement.

I lean against the fence with the horse standing beside me. "Okay, well now he does. What's his name?"

"His name is Thunder."

ELEVEN
Cass

"**N**o fucking way," Lars roars when he finally gets me to jump out of Thunder's stall. With an iron grip around my upper arm, he roughly tries to steer me out of the barn.

"Let go of me," I yell, shocked by his sudden transformation from calm to furious.

He releases me so fast I nearly fall backward.

I try to argue with him, but he isn't having any of it. The horse, he insists, is untamed. It has already bucked off two highly seasoned men. One broke his leg and the other a couple of ribs.

"If you insist on breaking your neck then go do it on someone else's watch. I'm not having it on my conscience," he shouts.

"Please. He won't throw me off. He…likes me," I implore.

For a second he stares at me as if I've just turned green, or I've uttered the most insane thing he's ever heard. Instantly, I realize that I have already slipped out of character. Tamara would never be begging like this.

"Why do you want him?" he asks, his forehead furrowed.

I can't tell him because Thunder is the most beautiful horse I've ever laid eyes on, or that it is love at first sight, because Tamara would never say such a thing. "Because, I know I can ride him," I whisper.

He takes his hat off and runs his hand through his hair. "No way. I'll have to tell your father about this and he can decide what to do."

My blood runs cold and my hands rise in fear. Bringing her dad's attention to me would be a very bad idea. "No, no, please," I plead. "Don't tell him."

His eyes narrow into slits.

I swallow hard and think up a lie that would work best. "I just want to do one thing that will make him proud of me."

Something flashes in his eyes. A softening. Thank God.

"I'll be very careful. I promise to listen carefully to everything you tell me."

In the end, we agree (although my fingers are crossed behind my back) that I will learn to ride on Isadora and only attempt to get on Thunder once he can be trusted not to throw his rider.

****

That evening after a lovely shower, I have an early dinner of cold chicken sandwiches on my patio. The sky is velvet black and studded with millions of stars that shine like diamonds. I mean there are stars in Chicago obviously, but holy hell, the stars in Montana are something else. They glitter like diamonds. I have never seen such a sight in the city, and for a very long time I sit in the cold night air, wrapped up in a blanket, staring at the night sky.

Everybody seems to go to bed early, and by ten o'clock, silence descends. I remain in the darkness alone, more at peace than I have been in my whole life.

My real life feels like it is thousands of miles away. In a different world.

Eventually, I go in and close the French doors. Lars told me to be at the barn by 7:30 a.m., so I set my alarm clock for 6:45 and slip between the fresh, sweet-smelling sheets.

****

The first thing I do when I wake up is to check the sheets for brown stains from the spray tan. Relieved that the sheets are clean, I pad over to the bathroom.

It takes me nearly twenty minutes to get my make-up right, but I am in the kitchen by seven sharp. There is a delicious smell wafting around and a tiny, white-haired woman is bustling around making breakfast. She must be at least seventy, but she seems to be very sprightly and energetic.

"Morning child," she greets cheerfully as soon as she sees me.

"Morning, Ma'am," I say. I don't know how Tamara treats the elderly, but I was raised to be polite to them above all else, and I'm doing just that. No way I'm going to be rude to this little sweetheart. Ever.

She grins. "Take a pew, honey."

I sit gingerly on one of the wooden chairs arranged around the long wooden table.

"Lars wants you to fill your belly before going out to the barn to start your chores, so I've made you eggs, bacon, beans, and toast," she says, pushing a plate of warm food in front of me.

"Are you the cook here?" I ask as I start buttering the toast.

"That'll be me," she says as she walks over to the stove and stirs whatever is cooking in a small pot.

She spoons some into a bowl and puts it in front of me. "Go on and get it all down you."

The porridge is still steaming hot so I reach for the fork and knife and start eating my eggs. "This is delicious."

"I wouldn't be late if I were you. Lars is very punctual. If he says seven-thirty then he means not a minute later."

I look at her warily. "What time is it?"

She glances at a clock on the wall. "It's already seven-fifteen, child."

I follow her gaze and momentarily panic. I'm fifteen minutes later than I thought. Something must be wrong with my alarm clock. "Shit," I mutter under my breath, and then scarf the food down my throat. Even though I rush like mad, it's 7:20 by the time I finish.

"I was told to give you these before you leave," she says, handing me a pair of small muck boots.

"Thank you so much..." I begin, realizing I don't know her name.

She folds her hands over her chest and beams. "Emma Jean Jansen, but you can call me Emma Jean."

I grin back gratefully. "Thank you, Emma Jean."

I step into the boots—they are a perfect fit—and rush out of the house. The morning air is lovely and cool as I run down the hill at full speed and race to the barn. I don't have a watch and I left my new phone on my bedside table, so I pray that I am on time.

"I'm here," I shout as soon as I get through the entrance.

Lars is standing in between the stalls with a shovel in his hands. He turns his wrist, looks at his watch, and glares at me as I stand there panting hard. "You're a minute late," he chastises sternly.

"You've got to be freaking kidding me. I'm late by a minute. I woke up at six forty-five. I wolfed my breakfast down as fast as I could and I ran all the way here. Give me a break." At that moment, I'm not even attempting to act like Tamara. The arrogance of this man irritates me beyond words.

"For the record, I am not 'freaking kidding you'. I am trying to make this month manageable for you. Maybe you should have woken up a little earlier. I was up at five and I'm now doing your job for you. If you are late one more time, I won't help and you'll just damned well have to work right through your break."

My fists ball up. I'm generally a very placid person, but this man inspires violent thoughts in me. He makes me want to smash my fist into his smug face. "I'm here under duress to learn how to ride, not to be one of your servants. Actually, you are my servant. You're paid to teach me."

He laughs suddenly and I'm tempted to throw horse shit at him. Why would he be laughing at me when I've just called him my servant?

"Someone woke up on the wrong side of the bed this morning," he chuckles.

"Don't you dare patronize me," I cry, infuriated.

"Then get your little ass over here and start shoveling," he says. "You have to be here, I don't."

"Nice try, but you work here. You don't have a choice, I do," I shoot back.

"Last time I looked, it's you who doesn't have a choice."

"Whatever," I say in the most irritating way I can, and walking toward him, try to snatch the shovel from his hand.

"Get your own shovel," he says, pulling it back from me.

I, of course, do not let go. "No, you get your own shovel," I shout at him. Acting like Tamara seems to be turning me into her, but I can't help it. Lars is an ass and he needs to be put in his place.

"Tamara, let go of the fucking shovel," he says quietly, but his voice is suddenly so cold and menacing I flinch backward, lose my grip on the shovel, and start falling back.

"Shit," I cry as I desperately try to find my footing. I expect to crash on the floor, or into the gate behind me, but what happens is worse. Lars' arm tangles around my waist and my entire body gets pulled tight to his chest.

Breathless from our argument, I attempt to push away and fill my lungs with air, but he doesn't let go and that doesn't help my breathing whatsoever. Our faces are inches apart. His scent: clean soap, leather, and just pure man, fills my nostrils. My panicked eyes lock with his and my flimsy façade fades along with my inner strength.

I feel like goo in his arms.

I hear the clank of the shovel falling to the ground, but I can't look away from his hooded, icy-gray eyes. He's a brute. A rude, egotistical, sarcastic piece of shit, but in his arms, he morphs into a mass of strong, hard muscles, and I become a woman who wants the feel of his lips on my body. My heart races like crazy; a fire starts in my belly, and instead of pushing, my hands start pulling. I feel as if I am drunk as our faces move closer together.

A voice inside my head screams, *What the heck are you doing?*

I am not Cass Harper.

I am Tamara Honeywell and Tamara would not be enveloped in the arms of a mere farmhand. But I can't do a thing to stop myself. Like a leaf in a gust of wind, I have no power of my own.

Suddenly, Thunder emits a loud neigh. That does the trick. It jolts me out of my dream state and I jump out of Lars' arms. He stares at me with an unreadable expression as I stand there breathing hard and trying to rebuild my composure. Summoning all my strength, I square my shoulders and tilt my head to the left like I watched Tamara do in the videos whenever she was caught in uncomfortable situations.

Then, I run my tongue over my lip and let it shape itself into a sly grin and say the words I don't want to say, but I must. "So, you want me, cowboy? Sorry, I'm out of your league." Even as the harsh words calculated to ruin any connection I might ever have with Lars drops out of my mouth, my heart shrinks.

It knows I've made a grave mistake.

TWELVE
Cass

Shoveling horse dung for nearly four hours is not a great start to my stay. It isn't merely shoveling the crap into a pile; I have to shovel it into a wheelbarrow until the barrow is full. Then, I have to drag the heavy wheelbarrow down the lane and across the road into a compost pile and dump it. And compost piles smell worse than shit.

My lessons are not supposed to start until after lunch, but I'm already dead on my feet. After my rude and condescending remark, Lars stalked off and left me to finish on my own. I understand his anger. I was unforgivably ill-mannered. If I were him, I wouldn't be happy with me either.

Even if I was not pretending to be Tamara, I recognize that he brings out the worst in me.

Judging by how high the sun is in the sky, it must be nearly noon. My stomach is grumbling, my arms and legs are like jelly, and my poor hands are red and sore. I need to fall into a bed and sleep for a week. I sprinkle a thick layer of hay in each of the empty horse stalls then rush up to the house, hoping to avoid Lars. If he sees me, he'll almost certainly make me do some other disgusting job.

I open the front door and step into the house. My boots squeak loudly on the polished floor. Screwing up my face and trying not to make a noise, I take off my boots and leave them by the door. Then, I close the door as quietly as I can and walk through the deserted living room. If he knows I'm here, I may not be able to eat my lunch in peace. I peek around the corner of the corridor into the kitchen. There is no one there either, but I see that a sandwich wrapped in tinfoil is lying on the counter. There is also a note right beside it.

I pick up the note and read the large scrawling letters.

Eat and be back at the horse stables by 12.00pm.
Don't be late. -L

I glance at the clock and note that it's 11:35. Just the thought of being back in the stables so soon makes me groan. If I had gotten up a bit earlier, I would have had more time to eat and relax. As it is, I'll barely have half an hour. I hold the sandwich up and look at it. Ham and salad. Emma Jean must have made it a while ago judging by the fact that the meat is already at room temperature.

I walk to my bedroom in my socks and sit on my bed, but I am so tired my body naturally falls backward. With a sigh, I unwrap the sandwich and, rolling over, take a bite. It has cheese and ranch sauce on it and is very good, but I'm too exhausted to really appreciate it. Chewing dispiritedly, I grab my new iPhone and scroll through my contacts. Other than Tamara's and Ms. Moore's, I've added only my father's caregiver and Jesse's numbers.

Pulling myself up, I lean against the headboard of my bed. It's going to be so damned hard to leave this bed. I hit the FaceTime icon and stare at myself on the screen. I don't look anything like myself. I'm wearing a sweat-drenched V-neck shirt that cost far more than what I normally earn in a week. My hair is slicked back into a tight ponytail, but the color is not mine. My face is at least five shades darker than it usually is, which isn't a bad thing, I suppose. Still, that was real and this is fake.

But even worse, my eyes are not my own anymore. After just two days of being someone other than myself, my eyes are lifeless and without sparkle, not to mention they are now blue. With a big sigh, I hit Jesse's number.

"Cass Harper," Jesse shouts into the phone. "Why did I not get a call from you yesterday?"

"This is Tamara Honeywell, actually," I correct, rolling my eyes.

"That's no excuse," she says smartly.

"I'm busy living the life of a Montana ranch hand."

"Girl, you look like dog poo and it's only one o'clock. What have you been doing all morning?"

I look at the clock on my phone, which says noon. "It's actually noon here," I respond tiredly. "And I probably look like crap because I've been shoveling it all morning." I know I should be getting back out there, but I can't. I'm no stranger to hard work, but four hours of continuous hard work is a different story.

"You've been shoveling what?" she asks with a laugh.

"You heard," I say dryly.

"Well, are there any cute cowboys over there?"

Lars' face pops into my head and I know Jesse will be able to see a change in my expression. I feel a blush sneaking onto my face.

"There *is* one," she squeals excitedly.

"Yeah, there is," I admit with a sigh, "but he hates me."

"Why?" she blurts out.

"I'm Tamara, remember? Queen bitch?"

"It can't be that bad." She laughs. "Why don't you make an exception and be nice to him?"

"What's the point, Jesse? It's not like I can start a relationship with him. I'll be gone in a month. It doesn't matter. Let him hate me all he wants," I reply.

"Well, can't you just tell him the truth and tell him to pretend too."

"Whoa…Jesse. Not so fast with the 1001 bright ideas of the easiest ways to get your best friend behind bars. His employer is Tamara's father! Don't forget I signed that NDA, and her lawyers really sounded like they meant business. One wrong move and I could end up in prison. Anyway, the last thing on my mind is a relationship. The loan sharks will be looking for another chunk of money this Friday and I don't know how I'll keep them going for another twenty-nine days."

Jesse looks sympathetic. "I can pitch in about half of what you owe," she offers, but I know that she can't do that without giving up something herself. She doesn't have much to give away when it comes to money.

"No. I'll work it out with them somehow. I'll tell them I'll be able to pay it all off when I get home."

"Other than bad vibes from a hot cowboy, what's it like?"

"I hate acting like a snobby rich girl, or shoveling horse crap for four hours because I've made Lars so mad with me, but I really enjoy the country air. It's so much cleaner. I like the peaceful atmosphere. God, you should have seen what the sky looked like last night. And I love being around the horses."

She nods and smiles. "Yeah, you've always liked animals. Chicago isn't the place for you."

"I know it's not. I wish staying here was an option," I say wistfully.

Outside my door, I hear the floorboards creak and I shoot up, sitting straighter in bed. "I've got to go, Jesse. Much love," I say, looking at the door.

She gets the hint, smiles, and kisses her camera. "Love you more. Bye, Tamara," she says with a wink.

I laugh and end the call.

It doesn't surprise me when Lars barges through my door with a scowl. "I thought I said to be back at the horse barns by noon."

His body fills nearly the entire doorway. I lie back on the bed and pull a tomato slice out of my sandwich. "Don't you ever knock?"

"What the hell do you think you're doing?" he glowers, his face as dark as a thundercloud and his eyes burning like twin gray fires.

I slip the tomato into my mouth unhurriedly. "I'm eating my lunch and taking a break."

"Have you been in bed yapping on your phone for the last four hours?" he asks in an incredulous tone.

I laugh harshly. "Yeah, that's what I did. You caught me," I spit sarcastically.

"You're impossible," he snarls and looks at me as if I am some sort of flesh eating parasite.

I guess if I were him, I wouldn't believe me either. "Have you even been in the horse barn since this morning?"

His eyes narrow suspiciously. "No. I've been working in the cattle barns."

"Doing what?" I challenge aggressively.

"Not that it is any of your damned business, but we're short-staffed so I milked six dairy heifers and cleaned out their stalls. What have you done?"

"You called it," I say airily. "I was on my phone for a few hours. I stopped when it needed to be charged." I wave my hand vaguely in the direction of my phone. "Oh, and while we're at it, let's get something straight. You're *not* the boss of me."

"I don't think you get it, poor little rich girl. Let me put it in simple English for you. I *am* the boss of you. In fact, I have express permission from your daddy to discipline you in any way I see fit. That includes putting you over my fucking knee if necessary," he roars furiously.

My back goes rigid with shock. Over his knee? Nobody talks to me like that. Not even my own father has ever laid a hand on me. Enraged, I lean forward. "I've been out there since seven- thirty this morning working my butt off. For your information, I didn't get back to the house until eleven thirty-five. I've been here for less than half an hour"

"That's twenty minutes too long," he says coldly.

I start boiling with frustration and anger. "I'm not a robot that can work all day without a break."

"More's the shame."

I throw my hands up in a huff. "You know what? I give up. Work me until I drop dead. Then we'll see how grateful my father is to you. What do you want me to do now?"

"I want you to finish cleaning out the barn so I can put the horses back inside. They shouldn't out be in the midday sun."

"What do we do after I finish?"

"The plan was to start your lessons today, but since you can't get your basic chores done, you can't work with the horses."

Now we're getting somewhere. "Okay then. If I finish, I get to ride a horse today?" I ask craftily.

"You won't finish quick enough. It's a long job."

"But if I do?"

"Then I'll teach you some basics."

I smile and sit up on the bed. If it's possible to be more sore from lying down, I am. "Let's go."

I allow him to lead as we walk back down the hill toward the horse barn. His strides are long and I have to trot to keep up.

"So, why did it take you so long to clean out six stalls?" I ask, for the sake of making conversation.

"Not that you'd understand work if it bit you in the ass, but cleaning stalls properly and milking cows takes time. It isn't as easy as yapping on the phone for a few hours."

"You're right. I wouldn't know," I reply. My voice is so calm he glances back at me suspiciously, but I keep my face expressionless. He thinks I was lying when I claimed I worked for four solid hours.

Once the horse barn comes into sight, I start smirking, all soreness forgotten. We come to the entrance and he stops so suddenly I almost run into his back.

"What-" he exclaims.

I step nimbly around him and get right in his face. He's almost a foot taller than me, but I make my presence seem larger than it truly is by squaring my shoulder and straightening my spine. I tilt my head sideways. It used to be Tamara's habit, but it's now becoming mine as well. I should be careful. I definitely don't want to pick up any more bad habits from her.

"Looks like it's my turn to make something clear, huh?" I say triumphantly.

He just stares at me, and I have to admit, the man really has astonishingly beautiful eyes. They glisten like wet jewels. I take a deep breath and continue. "For some reason, you've had me stereotyped from the first moment you laid eyes on me. Rich, spoiled bitch. Maybe you shouldn't listen so much to gossip. There may be more to me than meets the eye."

His neck flushes dark red and something shifts in those amazing eyes. It has the bizarre effect of making my stomach flutter.

I plow on. "Here's a novel idea. Why not treat me like a human being? It might make both our jobs a lot easier."

His eyebrows shoot up and he opens his mouth to say something, but I stop him by putting my palm out.

"I'll do the same in return. I'll try to be nice…if you stop acting like you're so much better than me."

He folds his arms over his chest. "I don't act like I'm better than you. It's you who acts like you're better than me."

"I *am* better than you," I say sweetly.

He blinks and I laugh at his stunned expression. "Just kidding. I'll try to be nice if you agree to do the same. Deal?"

He nods his agreement but his face is still dark and wary.

I hold out my hand and he grabs it and shakes it.

A strange thrill runs up my arm. I jerk my arm back, suddenly aware of how close he is to me. He keeps on staring at me as if he is seeing me for the first time and I realize that it is unlikely for someone like Tamara to suddenly become a pleasant person. Batting my eyelashes innocently, I say something to get his motor running. "So, tell me again about how difficult it is to clean six stalls in four hours. Because it looks like I cleaned thirteen in the same amount of time."

THIRTEEN
Cass

One by one, we bring all the horses back into the barn until they are all in their stalls except Thunder, who refuses to allow Lars to put a halter on him. He runs around the pasture and comes close enough only to tease him.

"Do you need help with him?" I ask.

"There's nothing you can do," he says in a long-suffering tone.

I make my way to him and grab the halter from his hand. He gives me a dirty look but continues shaking the bucket of grain. Thunder charges in our direction. Lars jumps in front of me and the horse immediately halts in his tracks about twenty yards away and shakes his head.

"For God's sake, you're scaring him. Now move," I say, and push at the wall of muscle. It doesn't budge an inch.

He gives me an irritated look and takes a step back.

"Thank you," I say with excessive politeness before turning toward the horse. "Here, Thunder," I call softly.

Keeping a close eye on Lars, he starts wandering in our direction, snorting with each step.

"Why does the damned horse listen to you? You're not even a trainer," Lars mutters. Thunder stands before me and shoves his snout under my armpit.

"Good boy," I coo, pleased beyond measure that he seems to prefer me to Lars.

Lars takes a step toward him and the stallion immediately lifts his head and paws the ground with his right hoof.

"Seriously, Lars. Just stay back," I say, barely able to keep the satisfaction out of my voice.

Glowering, Lars walks backward.

"How do I do this?" I ask.

From a few feet away, Lars explains how to place a halter around a horse's head. Fortunately, the lead rope is already attached, so I exclude that step and pull the halter up behind Thunder's ears. To my surprise, it seems as if the stallion has no problem being handled.

"This makes no sense," Lars grumbles. "He used to be a racehorse so he should let anyone handle him."

"Why don't you just leave the halter on him when he's in the pasture?" I suggest. "I'm pretty sure that's what they do in movies."

He shakes his head and rubs the back of his neck. "We've tried every type of halter out there and he always manages to get them off."

I pet Thunder's face and smile at him. "He seems to be doing fine with me. I can't understand why you have such a hard time with him," I deliberately gloat.

"Well, if he's so cooperative with you, why don't you try to lead him?" he asks snidely.

Thunder takes a step back when I take his lead, but I pat his cheek gently and give a small tug on his lead rope. To my delight, he follows obediently.

Lars groans and marches off into the barn while I laugh out loud.

When we make it to his stall, I look at the narrow entrance with confusion. How am I supposed to get him inside without going in first?

"Lead him in and turn so that you're beside the door. Then take off the halter and the lead rope," Lars explains.

I do exactly as he instructs and exit the stall. Thunder neighs happily and I smile up at Lars.

Lars looks down at me, his mouth tilted up on one side. "Do you realize what you've done?"

I shake my head, my body filling with a warm glow of happiness.

"Nobody here has been able to tame him yet. We were going to have to put him down if he wouldn't cooperate. You just saved that horse."

I smile and rub my hands together. "All in a day's work," I say with a broad, happy smile.

There is reluctant admiration in his eyes. "So, are you ready to start your riding lessons?" he asks.

"Yes," I say with a great grin, and for the first time since meeting him, he gives me a genuine smile. It lights up his whole face.

Ohh...totally sexy!

There is a moment of awkward silence then he moves toward one of the stalls.

"We'll start with mounting Misty," he says, guiding a brown mare in my direction. I bounce on my toes with excitement and reach a hand toward the animal, but it is so placid it barely acknowledges my presence.

"How difficult is this part?" I ask, thinking back to all the horse movies I watched as a child.

"It's the easiest thing I'll be teaching you. How's your balance?"

"Balance? Just fine," I lie. Balance is not something that comes easily to me. I had more evidence of my lack of it when I was trying to walk in Tamara's four-inch heels.

"Good. That will make this much easier," he says.

I stand back as Lars ties the horse's lead rope to a post and lays a blanket on the horse's back before tossing a saddle over it. He nudges the horse's front hoof forward and begins connecting the straps. He turns to me and raises an eyebrow.

"What?" I ask.

"You have to take care of your horse for a month. You may want to know how to do this."

I take a few small steps in his direction until I'm so close to him I can feel the heat coming from his body. The horse snorts and I lay my hand on its back instinctively. Lars grabs my wrist with his gloved hand and I stare at how big and powerful it looks compared to mine.

He places the strap in my hand. "Tie the back cinch to the one on the other side," he instructs. He releases my wrist and it feels suddenly strange and empty.

I do as he asks.

"Make sure that it's tight. We don't want the saddle to flip halfway through our lesson."

I tighten it slightly more.

He frowns. "Tighter."

"I don't want to hurt her," I protest.

Lars laughs, takes the strap, and pulls it harder than I would have ever done. "You won't hurt her. She's our training horse. She's used to being saddled. Besides, it is almost impossible to make the straps too snug, somehow it always ends up being too loose after a while."

He finishes tightening the cinches—as he calls them—and I observe carefully, taking mental notes of the process and the way his muscles tighten beneath his shirt with every twitch of his body. When he lifts his arms to put the halter on the horse, his shirt catches on the saddle and the glowing ripped muscles of his abdomen show. I can't help but stare at them in amazement. How does someone look this magnificent and be so totally unaware of their own beauty?

"Tamara?" It takes me a moment to realize that he's speaking to me.

"Yeah," I respond in a dreamy tone. My eyes travel slowly upward. That dip in his throat is just begging to be licked. Then my eyes collide with his and there is a knowing look in his. Shit! My face burns with shame. This is so not like me. Why am I behaving like some sex-starved nympho? I clear my throat and stand a little straighter. "I'm ready to begin," I squeak.

"I'm sure you are," he retorts with a smirk.

"Are we going to start? I'm getting sick of standing in here and smelling the horses," I say rudely. The barn does hold the undeniable stench of animals, but I don't mind. I just need an excuse to stop this awkward moment where I've stupidly revealed my attraction.

Lars' jaw hardens and his eyes become flinty.

I try to pretend that I don't care that he has seen me check him out. I'm not Cass after all—I'm Tamara. And Tamara wouldn't blush at a handsome cowboy. She would be crude and, if she liked him, probably come onto him. God, the way she bounced on the red dick of that blond man.

Untying the horse's lead rope from the door, Lars guides Misty out of the barn. We walk along the road and I sneak a look at his profile. It looks like it has been carved out of stone. He hates me, but it doesn't matter. He can never know who I am so I mustn't stop antagonizing him, or I'll end up crushing hard and making a complete fool of myself.

We approach a small horse ring and my heart suddenly starts pounding. In the barn with all the other bigger horses, Misty seemed smaller, but out here on her own, she suddenly seems so high off the ground. Doubt fills me. Will I be able to do this? What if I fall off the horse and can't get back on? What if I am unable to finish this project? Why did I think I'd be able to do this?

"I don't know about this," I mumble, stopping cold in my tracks.

Lars turns to face me. "It's not hard. Come on. You can do it," he encourages softly.

"I don't know," I whine. Amazing, but after just one day, complaining has become almost second nature. If my father could hear me now he'd be shocked.

"What are you talking about? You were so excited about learning to ride just a moment ago."

I gulp and shake my head. "I'll fall and break my neck. I won't be able to stay on the horse. I lied before. My balance is awful. I'm the clumsiest person I know," I admit.

His lips quirk up with amusement. "Tamara," he croons, and I stare at him with surprise. He's always been so gruff and stern with me I would never have guessed he could be so gentle. "I've taught children in wheelchairs and kids with other physical handicaps to ride horses. For a while, we even used to have a summer program for autistic children. You will do great as long as you listen to me." He looks deep into my eyes and the gentle simplicity in his face makes my breath hitch. Suddenly, I know without a doubt that I can trust this man with my life.

"I believe you," I whisper.

FOURTEEN
Cass

He doesn't take his eyes off mine and something so animalistic and feral flows between us that our surroundings fade out of existence. It is only me and him. We're alone and I have no interest in moving. Lars takes a step forward until we are chest to chest, breathing the same throbbing air.

What the heck am I doing?

I'm here for a purpose and it's not to flirt with the help. I know that I should step away, and my brain wills me to do so, but my body wants something different. It feels almost as if he is the strongest magnet known to man and I'm a tiny sliver of metal.

Suddenly, the expression on Lar's face changes. He breaks eye contact and takes a step back. The world around me zooms back into focus, and I have to hurriedly stumble onto the grass edging the gravel road to avoid an approaching diesel truck. It sounds like it has a busted muffler. How on earth did I not hear it coming from a mile away?

The man driving it gawks at me while simultaneously waving at Lars and calling out a greeting. His accent is too thick for me to catch, but Lars raises his hand in an answering wave.

Feeling confused and shaken, I follow Lars into the ring. He stops the horse and stands still for a moment before turning to face me.

"Ready?" he asks, his face now devoid of all expression.

I nod nervously. Why do I have a feeling this will not turn out the way I'd hoped?

"Always start by facing the horse," he instructs.

I move to obey.

"Then hold both reins in your left hand and gather them with a tuft of mane, tight enough to prevent the horse from wandering off, but not tight enough to make it go backward. Mount it from the left side. Misty won't mind which side you mount her from, but most horses are adamant about the left side. It's a habit for them and anything else is unusual. You may be in charge most of the time, but if you do something a horse doesn't like, they'll take control, and that's when you get hurt."

I clasp my hands nervously. "Don't I need a mounting block or something?"

He shakes his head. "Just trust me."

"Okay."

"Facing the rear of the horse, take the stirrup in your right hand and turn it clockwise toward you. This way, you won't end up with the leather twisted under your leg once you're seated. Once you've done that, place your left foot in it so that the ball of your foot rests on the bottom of the stirrup. Be careful at this stage not to kick or poke the horse with your foot, or it will start walking forward. Got it?"

I nod nervously.

"Put your right hand on the horn, but don't try to pull yourself up with your arm. Just use it to balance yourself.

Rely on the power in your right leg to spring up then swing it over the back of the horse while moving your right hand forward like this," he says, demonstrating the movement of grasping the reins. "Just make sure to raise your leg high enough. You don't want to kick the horse or hit your leg on the saddle."

"Okay."

"At that point, all there is left to do is gently sit in the saddle. Go on. Give it a try," he says. Both his voice and his manner are cool and purely professional.

As confidently as I can, I make my way to Misty's left. Fortunately, she is calm and excellent at remaining still. I place my right foot in the stirrup and find it almost impossible to lift myself clear off the ground.

Lars clears his throat.

"What?" I ask, irritated.

"Left foot."

I switch feet and use the handle sticking out of the saddle—the one Lars called a horn—to pull myself upward with my right hand.

"Do a couple of light springs to gain momentum."

I do as he says and I'm almost upright when Misty decides to rearrange herself. With a frightened shriek, I fall back to the ground, thankfully, on my feet.

"Again," Lars say.

I give him a hard, unfriendly look. Using all the strength in my right leg, I propel myself upward, but of course, before I can drape myself properly over her, she readjusts herself again. This time, though, I'm ready for her. Even though the muscles of my arms are screaming, I grab the horn tightly with both hands. I'm hanging on for dear life, but for the first time in my life, I'm on a horse. I'm actually on a horse.

"I'm up," I cry excitedly, looking over the edge of the tall animal. Oh, my God. I am so high up. And this is the height I have to fall off...I don't even want to think of that.

"Damn, that was a hell of a lot quicker than I thought it would be," Lars admits, nodding his head approvingly. "Now get off."

Misty moves, making me sway dangerously.

"How?" I ask.

Lars stands so his chest is pressed against my leg. I lean down to him, hoping he is going to help me get down, but he has no intention of helping me at all.

"First, make sure the horse has stopped moving. Grip the reins, remove both your feet from the stirrups, then lean forward and use the momentum of your right foot to swing off and land on the ground," he orders.

White-knuckling the reins, I lean forward and swing my leg over the horse. The last thing I expect is for my left foot to get tangled in the stirrup. "Lars," I scream.

His arms wrap around my waist as he effortlessly pulls me backward. Immediately, my mind reels at his touch, and I am suddenly acutely aware of all his hard muscles pressing into my body.

"Don't panic," he says softly.

"I doubt you'd be saying that if you were the one hanging upside down like some demented bat," I huff.

"You're not hanging upside down," he says coolly, but I swear I can see more than a glint of amusement lurking in his eyes.

"Don't you dare laugh at me," I cry.

"Never," he says, and easily shifts all my weight to one arm. His unoccupied hand wraps around my ankle. His clasp is sure and gentle, but it doesn't loosen my foot and I hiss.

"How much longer?" I mumble and wrap my arms around his neck to take some of my weight out of his arm. Only, once I lift myself, I realize that he isn't straining at all. He is juggling my weight and undoing the stirrup almost effortlessly. And all I have done is effectively maneuver myself into the warm, masculine smelling crook of his neck. Um…since when do I like the smell of sweat? Still, the man has a delicious neck. Tanned and thick. And smooth. And…my breathing goes up a notch.

"Damn it, what did you do?" he mutters as he tries to free the stirrup tangled around my foot.

"How the hell…" he mutters, as he continues to work the twist.

"I can stand on one leg. Put me down," I demand from my awkward and humiliating position.

"Hang on. I've almost got it."

Seconds later, the stirrup releases my ankle. As I ease down his body, his hands move to my hips. His touch scorches me and I suck in a quick, shallow breath. The second both my feet touch the ground; his hands launch off my body.

"That's never happened before," he remarks, his nostrils flaring. There is a dull flush on his cheekbones.

"I think I didn't remove both my feet from the stirrups," I confess as I take a distracted step backward and bump into the poor horse. It startles her and she whips her head around. "Sorry, Misty. Sorry," I whisper, stroking her.

"Right. Get back on," Lars instructs.

I know I need to keep trying until I get better at mounting, but I don't want to fall, or get my ankle all twisted up in the stirrup again. "I'm tired. Can we do it tomorrow?"

"Nope," he says crisply. "It'll be harder tomorrow. You've got to get straight back on or your mind will build this failure up into something bigger than what it is."

I rub my arm anxiously. "What if I fall off the other side of the horse? You can't catch me over there, and I could get seriously hurt."

"Tamara," he says in a tone I don't recognize. "You won't fall." He brushes past me and effortlessly mounts the horse, not even taking hold of the reins.

I watch him with new admiration.

"Come on," he urges, extending a hand toward me.

"Uh...don't I need to know how to do this on my own?"

"All in good time," he says with his hand outstretched toward me.

I'm getting thirty-thousand dollars for this. All I have to do is figure out this first step. *You can do this, Cass.* Without overthinking it, I grab hold of Lars' big hand. It curls around mine and he swings me up in front of him. To my surprise, I find my balance without much assistance, and once I'm sitting comfortably—or as comfortably as a person can be on a saddle—Lars scoots into me. My breath catches in my throat.

"While I'm up here, I'm going to teach you a few basics," he says with an odd inflection in his voice.

I twist my head back to look at him and find his disconcerting gray eyes so near it makes me gulp. They are wiped clean of all expression though. I clear my throat.

"You're already a step up from the people who ride side-saddle." He moves forward slightly and his body rubs against mine, causing all kinds of forbidden images to rush into my head. I blush furiously and his eyebrows rise. Now he knows how affected I am.

Flustered and exposed, I lash out. "Let's finish this lesson already. I'm exhausted after cleaning your entire horse barn and getting a fifteen-minute lunch break for my troubles."

"Calm down. You'll get your break when we finish," Lars grates close to my ear.

His anger is easier to deal with. Saying nothing, I hold onto the horse's reins, but I don't need to clench them as tightly as I had earlier. I feel incredibly safe with his powerfully muscled legs wrapped around my outer thighs and his rock-solid chest inches away from my back

"To get the horse to move, lift your legs out and prod the horse's side, but not forcefully. You'll spook it."

I do as he instructs and Misty takes off at a slow canter around the ring. With each step and with Lars' tight grip on my hips, I lose all my nervousness of slipping and falling off.

"Oh, my God, this is awesome," I squeal excitedly as we finish our first circle.

Lars says nothing but his hot breath billows on my neck. After a few minutes, he releases his thigh-grip on my hips, but it still doesn't feel like I'll fall. I adjust myself so that I lean in with each step Misty takes.

"If you want her to halt, pull on the reins," Lars says.

I do as he says and Misty immediately comes to a standstill.

"Now, how would you feel about riding on your own?"

I hate to admit it, but I don't want to ride alone. Sure, I'd love to experience the freedom and independence of riding the horse by myself. But the sensation of his legs wrapped around me and his firm chest radiating heat and power behind me are not something I want to give up just yet. I turn my head in his direction and look into his eyes. They're unlike before. His irises are like molten silver, full of something unnamable, wild, and beautiful. It makes me forget myself.

"Stay close to me for a few more minutes," I whisper.

For a second, his eyes widen and his pupils dilate, then it's like a shutter falls over his face. His jaw hardens and his eyes become frighteningly blank. He scoots backward and hops onto the ground without the help of the stirrup, using only the brute muscles of his legs.

"Use the skills I taught you and you'll be just fine," he says tightly.

I'm on my own. On a huge horse.

Gently, I prod Misty and she begins to move. She takes one step, then another, and another. I'm riding a horse on my own. Being so high above everything should have been scary—and it was at first—but now that I've gotten used to Misty's rhythm, for the first time since selling my soul to the loan sharks, I feel on top of the world.

FIFTEEN
Cass

Feeling fantastic about my first riding lesson, I walk back to the house with Lars. He doesn't enter with me, but goes his separate way up the road. I open the door, and as usual, it is silent and still. Taking off my muck boots, I pad over to the kitchen. Emma Jean has left a pot of beef stew on the stove and cornbread in a skillet. I'm starving and the smell of the food makes my mouth water as I open the pot and ladle it on to a plate. There is a note stuck on the refrigerator. Emma Jean's writing is small and neat.

There's Huckleberry Bear's Paw going to waste in the fridge, Poppet.

I open the refrigerator and to my great surprise, it's a dessert that looks exactly like a bear's paw. While the stew is heating in the microwave, I cut a thick wedge of bread and fill up another plate with a big helping of bear's paw.

I carry everything out to my patio and eat the delicious meal while watching the sky turn pink and orange. It's an indescribably beautiful show. The remote setting and the barrenness of the scenery makes me feel as if I have stepped back in time. As if I am looking at exactly what the early settlers coming across the prairie in their covered wagons must have seen. When my food is all gone,

I do what I've never considered doing in my life. I bring the plate up to my face and lick it clean like some sort of savage.

Mmmm.

I'm too exhausted to sit and watch the stars come out, so I have a hot shower and am asleep as soon as my head hits the pillow. The insistent sound of my phone ringing wakes me. I peer groggily at the screen and come awake with a jolt. Crap! Tamara. I switch on the bedside light, which blinds me for an instant, and tap the green button.

"Where the hell have you been?" Tamara demands furiously, her face contorted and ugly. "I've been calling for like hours."

"I was asleep," I reply.

Her eyebrows meet, making her look crabby and surly. "Asleep?" she repeats. "Why are you asleep during the day? Aren't you supposed to be working?"

"It's two o'clock in the morning here," I explain tiredly.

"Oh, right. Well, it's bright and sunny here. Look," she says, and waves the phone around her so that I can see the blue sea close by and the pristine white sand that she's lying on.

"Great. You're on a beach," I say, injecting as much enthusiasm as I can into my voice.

"So, how's it going?" she asks casually before taking a sip of champagne. It's amazing what a selfish creature she is. She didn't bother to check the time before calling, and even now that she knows it's two a.m., she just won't piss off.

"It's okay, but it's very hard work," I say, trying to keep my eyes open.

"What did you expect?" she shoots back.

I groan inwardly. As if I need this in my life. "I'm not complaining."

"Good. You better not be. You're getting paid to do this."

"I know. I know," I say quickly.

"Have you learned to ride yet?"

"No, I just got here yesterday."

She stares at me sullenly.

"Uh…I did get on a horse today. Maybe by next week, I'll be able to ride."

She scowls. "Next week? Are you sure you're going to be able to ride properly by the end of the month?"

"I think so, but I'll call you next week and let you know how I get on."

"You better learn fast," she warns. "I'm not staying on this godforsaken island for one day longer than necessary. I've got no friends here, there's nothing to do at night, and I'm already bored out of my head." Her voice is whiny and petulant.

"Don't worry. I'll learn how to ride well enough for Lars to give your father a good report."

"Remember, you don't get paid if you don't learn to ride."

I sigh inwardly. "I know."

"So, who's Lars?" she asks perkily, like she is my best friend and we are having a heart to heart.

For some weird reason, my heart contracts. "He's just one of the trainers."

"And?"

"And nothing."

"Oh," she says in a disappointed voice, as if she was expecting to me to gossip with her about Lars.

Someone calls to her so she turns away from the screen and shouts, "What?" I wait while she listens to someone say something indistinguishable, then she faces me again and rolls her eyes. "No rest for the wicked. My hairdresser is here. The sun is wrecking my hair."

"Bye, Tamara," I say quickly.

The line goes dead.

I blow out a puff of air, switch off the light, curl up with my hands under my pillow, and fall straight back to sleep.

****

"Morning, Poppet," Emma Jean greets, looking up from her pots and pans to smile at me.

"Morning," I reply and smile brightly even though every muscle in my body is in agony.

"Take a pew. You've got a big day ahead, and you'll be needing some food that'll stick to your ribs." Pulling a slip of paper from the notepad on the counter, she walks over and puts it in front of me. I peer down at the page and sigh heavily. Lars has written a specific to-do list to ensure that I don't slack off on my chores. The list includes disgusting stuff like picking up trash, cigarette butts, and dog poo from around the property, as well as feeding and watering the horses; and of course, shoveling manure.

"Will I not be learning to ride today then?"

She pours coffee into my mug. "Lars is away, so probably not."

"Oh."

Disheartened, I curl my hands around the mug and take a sip. While Emma Jean fills the kitchen with mouth-watering smells as she makes veggie browns, bacon,

Croquet-Monsieur, and waffles, I ask her about the ranch and its surrounding area. She tells me that the mountain range visible from my patio is the Pryor Mountains and that Bucking Bronco Ranch is located on the east slope of it, right in the heart of the historic Crow Indian Reservation.

I fill my belly with the food that she piles high on my plate and listen to her talk about life on the ranch. It seems to be completely dependent on the seasons. The men drive the cows and horses fifty miles into the ranch in spring, then it's back to winter pastures all the way in Wyoming during the late fall. Spring, I learn, is also when the mother cows bring forth their calves. The branding of new calves happens in June, and weaning is in September.

"What's done about now?" I ask, shoveling another mouthful of waffle drenched in huckleberry jam and maple syrup into my mouth.

"This is the season for the arrival of the new foals."

"Really? Will I get to see a birth?" I ask excitedly.

"I don't see why not."

Once I have eaten, I start on my chores and do not stop until it is time for a quick lunch. The work is never ending and I only finish at sundown. I walk through the deserted house and find chicken, a baked potato, and chocolate cake with a gooey center waiting for me in the kitchen. My mouth is watering as I walk to my room. I have never eaten anything like the food Emma Jean serves up. Possibly because everything here is freshly grown, slaughtered, and collected, instead of being frozen and store bought.

I suck it all down like a starving savage, shower, and hit the sack.

SIXTEEN
Cass

For the next three days, my life revolves around the same pattern of drudgery. A long to-do list that keeps me going until late, and no sign of Lars. The work is hard but it leaves me time to think, and the more time that passes, the more I realize how much I want to see Lars again. Somehow, I manage to avoid other people, which is for the best. I don't want to act like Tamara to anyone else. I hate being horrible and rude to these simple, good-hearted folks.

By day four, I arrive in Emma Jean's kitchen, mentally and physically beat. I'm used to hard work, and I knew working on a ranch wouldn't be easy, but the workload I've been given is beyond difficult.

"What's on the list today?" I ask tiredly.

"There's no list today," she says with a satisfied expression.

I perk up. "What do you mean?"

"He's been overworking you. Twelve hours of physical labor every day with only one break all day ain't right. Even the highest paid employees here only work a few hours a day and have multiple breaks. It's too hot to work the way you've been doin'."

I stare at her. Lars dialing down my hours without a good reason? "Wait—what? How did you get him to agree to that?"

Emma Jean smiles and takes the scrambled eggs off the heat. The pan is full to the brim and I wonder how she manages to cook it all so evenly, or avoid spilling any on the stove top. I'm used to Jesse's burnt scrambled eggs.

"I've been around a long time, Poppet. I've seen people come and go, but I've never met anyone as passionate as you. It's been three days. You look like you can barely keep your eyes open, but you won't give up or admit defeat. If he carries on with this silliness, he'll run you into the ground."

"I am a bit tired," I admit with a smile.

"You're dying on your feet, child. Today you'll have time to digest your breakfast. You're not to go to the barns until gone nine-thirty." I look at her with wide eyes then glance at the clock. It's only seven.

"What will I do until then?"

"Go look at the animals. Go back to bed. Go explore the ranch. Whatever tickles your fancy."

"When will Lars come back?"

"Probably in the next couple of days."

"Does he go away a lot."

"Some," she says cautiously. It's obvious she doesn't want to gossip about him.

I nod unhappily. The next time Tamara calls, she'll be expecting me to tell her that I've mastered riding and at this rate... "I'm only asking because I need to be able to ride a horse by the end of my stay, and if he's not around much to teach me then..." I leave the sentence trailing.

"I'll mention it to him when he calls," she says, switching off the stove.

I stand to grab a plate from the cupboard and Emma Jean gives me a look best described as sit-down-and-don't-you-dare-try-to-do-my-job.

I raise my hands up and drop back into the chair. "So, you just asked him to shorten my hours and he did it?" It still seems too unbelievable.

She begins to fill my plate and my stomach growls.

"You still have to be in the barns at nine-thirty today, but anytime in the future if you ever get in later than nine o'clock at night, you don't have to be back in the barns until noon the next day. Also, you get a small fifteen-minute break every hour and an hour lunch break," she adds with satisfaction.

I gawk at her and shake my head in awe. "Thank you so much."

"Lars is a good lad. He always tries to do the right thing. The two of you might have gotten off on the wrong foot."

Might? "That's an understatement if I ever heard one."

"I know your reputation isn't great, but you're not a bad person. Your eyes show that you've been through hard times, and eyes never lie."

"Thank you so much." To have a stranger who doesn't know me acknowledge and empathize with how hard my life has been, fills my eyes with unexpected tears. I blink them away, but I can't stop the tremble in my lower lip. To hide it, I hurriedly stuff a forkful of eggs and sausage into my mouth.

"Do you miss your life back home?" Emma Jean asks.

I slow down chewing to give myself some time to think. I don't want to lie to her. I like her a lot and find solace with her every morning. In a funny sort of way, she's almost like a mother to me. Even though she doesn't even know my real name, she knows me better than most people do. I pick up my glass of orange juice and down it in one long gulp. No longer able to put the moment off, I shift in my seat and look up into Emma Jean's kind face.

In a flash, I come to a breathtaking solution. I don't need to pretend to be Tamara with her. Why should I? She's never meet the real Tamara. I'll be myself and show her the real me, and all she'll remember is that someone called Tamara Honeywell was nice and kind to her. I smile warmly at her. "Not really."

Her eyes sparkle. "So, you *do* like it here?"

"I should hate it, shouldn't I?" I ask rhetorically, "with all the endless chores, but I don't. It's an awesome place. I've always loved animals and the idea of a farm, but I thought of myself as a city girl because that is how I grew up. I realize now I couldn't have been more wrong. Even with the punishing workload, I still love it." Other than to Jesse and Emma Jean, I wouldn't admit this to anyone else.

She nods triumphantly. "I knew your daddy did the right thing when he sent you here. How could anyone hate it here? It's wide open land and you never run out of things to do. When I was a girl about your age, I was a lot like you—aside from the celebrity aspect, of course. I lived in Dallas, Texas, and I didn't know hard work a day in my life until I married a ranch hand. Over the years, we drifted about all over the States until we finally found this place five years ago. We've been working here ever since."

I smile at her. "You and your husband are lucky."

"We are," she says, smiling softly. "We got each other and we live in beauty."

I pick up my empty plate to take to the sink, but before I can even take a step forward, Emma Jean snatches it from my hands. She heaps more eggs and a sausage on it and slaps it down in front of me. "After all the work you've been doing, Poppet, you need more sustenance."

I'm not going to argue with her. "Where's your husband now?" I ask, slicing into a sausage.

"One of the stallions broke a couple of his ribs, so he's home resting."

"You mean Thunder?"

"That'll be the one."

"How old is your husband?" I ask curiously. She must be at least sixty.

"Jack just celebrated his sixty-eighth birthday last month," she says with a smile. "After this stunt, I won't be letting him go back to training horses. He's getting too old to be jumping on and off horses. It was good of Lars to agree to pay his medical bills."

"Lars paid for your husband's medical bills?"

She looks anxious. "You won't tell anyone I told you, will you?"

I shake my head. "Cross my heart and hope to die."

Maybe I've misjudged Lars after all.

SEVENTEEN
Cass

I have a surprise the next day. Emma Jean says that I'm getting a riding lesson after my chores. Someone called James will teach me. I wonder why Lars can't be around. What is it that makes him too busy to see me for days at a time. He's supposed to be my trainer, after all.

Nevertheless, I rush through my chores excitedly. As I am running to the barn, my phone rings. It's Ms. Moore checking up on me. I quickly assure her that everything is hunky dory.

"Has Tamara been in touch?" she asks.

"Yeah, she called me last night at 2 a.m."

"Hmm," she says disapprovingly.

We talk a bit more before she rings off. I have just enough time to race to the barn for my four o'clock lesson.

"Are you James?" I ask breathlessly.

A man, maybe twenty-eight or twenty-nine years old, with a Miley Cyrus hairstyle, turns around with a broad smile on his face. "And you must be Miss Tamara," he says, walking in my direction with long strides. Like Lars, he too is good-looking, but where Lars is rugged and masculine as hell, this man is more of a pretty boy with sparkling blue eyes and cute lips.

"I am her," I say.

He stops right in front of me, and to my surprise, pulls my hand to his lips and kisses my knuckles.

My eyebrows rise. I did not expect this type of gallantry from a guy in the middle of nowhere.

"You're nothing like..." he begins, and I know exactly what he's thinking. I'm not what he was expecting. My hair is scraped back in an unglamorous ponytail and I've stopped wearing the thick foundation I'm supposed to wear. Mainly because it takes too long to slap on, but also, it seems stupid to layer it on thick when all I seem to do is the most disgusting tasks anyway. So, I'm not glamorous but I'll have to do because I don't have enough energy to be painstakingly put together and fulfill my responsibilities on this ranch.

"... what you expected?" I finish his sentence dryly.

"No," he says, his eyes calculative. It's obvious he's read stuff about Tamara and thinks she's some kind of slut he can have a roll in the hay with. He has no idea what a tyrant she really is. If I had been her, he'd be licking my boots right about now.

"Life is full of surprises," I say lightly.

"It sure is." I see him make a quick recalculation of his strategy. His eyes darken as he takes his time looking me up and down.

I frown at the slow look. "Shall we start?"

'Sure thing, doll."

"Well, the last time I rode Misty," I say, getting straight to the point.

But he doesn't take his eyes off me or move an inch. "You got a man waiting for ya back in the city."

"What?' I explode.

"You know. A boyfriend." He winks. "A lover."

"None of your damned business," I say through clenched teeth. There are all kinds of bad words clawing up my throat, but I swallow them down. I just want to learn to ride.

"Pipe down, sweet cheeks. It was a fair question. City folk are always runnin' around."

That does it. I suddenly decide I don't like the idea of him training me one bit. What if I fall and he has to catch me the way Lars did the last time?

A) I didn't trust him.

B) I didn't want him anywhere near me, let alone, touching me.

But if I refuse to let him teach me, I'll just get into trouble. Lars could tell Tamara's father. There is a better way.

"This time I want to ride Thunder?" I say.

"Thunder?" he exclaims with a disbelieving laugh.

"Yeah, Thunder," I reply firmly.

He shakes his head. "You want to learn horseback riding on a wild Arabian race horse?"

I nod.

A sly look comes into his face. "You're used to handling big males, huh?"

I know what he is alluding to, but I don't bite. "Don't you think I can ride him?" I counter, knowing instinctively that I can. For the last few days, I've been sneaking carrots and sugar cubes to him and we've become buddies. I think he completely trusts me.

"Oh, baby. I know you can ride a big man, but how about we do your riding lesson on another horse—any other horse." The man with the perfect smile, straight nose, and crystal blue eyes finally shows an imperfection. He's scared of Thunder.

I raise an insolent eyebrow. "Are you trying to tell me that you're afraid of a *horse*?"

"Damn straight, I am? That horse is a hammerhead."

"Hammerhead?"

"A bad horse," he explains briefly.

"No, he's not. Anyway, you won't be riding him. I will."

He shakes his head and takes a step away from me. "Nah, no way. I ain't taking that responsibility."

"It sounds to me like you don't have the balls."

He flushes brick-red with anger and I want to laugh. Men are so predictable. Maybe this is the only way to get what I want.

"You betcha," he snarls. "That brute is damn near two thousand pounds dry, and I ain't stupid enough to put a greenhorn prune picker on it."

"Did you just call me a prune picker?"

"You're from California, ain't you?" he asks belligerently.

I fold my arms stubbornly.

"I was told to teach you to ride. Are you going to make my job impossible?"

"Your job wouldn't be impossible if you'd let me ride the horse I want," I snap.

"Quit your yammerin', woman," he bellows. "That horse deserves to be sent to the glue factory for the trouble it's already caused. I'm telling you now. You're not riding that horse. We can't even get him to cooperate being led on a rope."

"I can lead him," I retort.

"No, you can't," he says, jamming an accusing finger at me.

"Want me to prove it?" I challenge.

"No, I don't. For Pete's sake, just pick another goddamn horse, or I'll pick one for you." His face is nearly purple, and he is irate and completely frustrated at this point. I consider backing off. My dad used to say there are times when pressing to get something you want is a good, healthy action, and there other times when it is downright dangerous and it's best to concede to the whims of your rival. Unfortunately, I've always been bad at determining which situations are dangerous and which are acceptable.

"No," I growl.

"You will get on a damned horse if I have to throw you over my shoulder and put you on the horse myself," he shouts, completely losing his temper with me.

"Screw you," I shout and stomp away from him.

For a second, he is too shocked to respond, then I hear him coming up behind me with the rapidity of a wild animal. I stop dead in my tracks and whirl around. "If you so much as touch me, you'll have a roomful of sharp-suited lawyers come down so hard on your ass you'll wish you never heard of Tamara Honeywell."

And just like that, I unintentionally become Tamara Honeywell's protégée. My sass combined with her money is probably not a good combination.

He blinks as if suddenly remembering that I'm not his equal.

EIGHTEEN
Cass

As I walk away from the barn, my fists are balled and the blood is pounding in my veins, but I revel in my disobedience. It felt invigorating to be able to threaten someone with the force of the law like that, have them quake in their boots with fear, and immediately back down. What must it be like to have that kind of power for real? No wonder Tamara is such a bitch.

As I get to the house, my anger turns toward Lars. That will teach him for setting me up with a complete douchebag. I walk around the side of the house and go in through my patio door into my living quarters. I have a quick shower, change into clean clothes, and go into the kitchen. Emma Jean is just beginning to gather the ingredients for dinner.

"Need help?" I ask her. She looks surprised to see me.

"What are you doing back so early? Aren't you supposed to be having a riding lesson?" she asks with a frown.

"Nope. I'm done for the day. I don't have anything to do but lend you a hand." And it's true. I've already called Jesse and given her a brief synopsis of the day's events. During my lunch break, I contacted Mrs. Carter and begged her to please help me by paying my dad's hospital bill from what I've already earned. She agreed to do it in the morning. I've also called hospice to check that my dad's condition is stable. It is. So, I truly have nothing else to do with my time.

"Do you know how to cook?" Emma Jean asks.

"Not a clue," I admit with a big grin. "But I wouldn't mind learning from you. You're easily the most amazing cook I know."

Emma Jean preens at the compliment. She looks at the ingredients laid out on the counter and then back at me. "Well, then. Neither my son nor daughter ever wanted to learn to cook, and their ankle biters are too young to teach, so you can be my girl for the evening."

"I would love to." A warm sensation fills my stomach. My life would be perfect if I could live here forever on this ranch with her.

"I'm making stuffed shells. Have you ever had 'em?" she asks, tossing me a box full of giant pasta shells. I catch them midair and study the box curiously.

"I think I've eaten them before," I reply slowly. "But it may have been spaghetti and shells."

"There is no mixing up the two. If you've had 'em, you'd know. There's nothing like stuffed shells and pork chops if you know what you're doing." She gives me a big smile. "And I've been known to make the best stuffed shells this side of Montana if I do say so myself." She fills a pan three-fourths full with water. Waving me away, she carries it to the stove, sets it down, and turns the knob to the highest setting. Blue flames spring to life.

"I hope I don't ruin anything."

"Don't you worry, Poppet," she says, tipping salt into the water and covering the pan with a lid. "They'll never notice anyway. They come in so hungry they'll quite happily eat the north end of a south bound bear."

I smile at the description, but there is no way that is true. She's trying to make out they'll eat a scabby donkey, but in the time I've been here, everything I've tasted has been superb. Better than anything I've ever had in Chicago. I licked the plate for Pete's sake.

"Can I dump these in now?" I ask, shaking the box of pasta.

She gives me a sideways glance. "Does that water look like it is boiling yet?"

I shake my head.

"There's your answer."

"Right. The water has to be boiling to soften pasta?"

She looks at me curiously. "Haven't you ever cooked ramen noodles before, child?"

"I stick them in the microwave. Four minutes, max," I say with a grin.

"Oh, Lord help your soul," Emma Jean prays. "Then again, I suppose with your lifestyle there's not much call for cooking. You're probably dining in them fancy restaurants most of the time."

I nod, say a silent sorry for the lie, and don't tell her that far from fancy restaurants, my dad and I lived almost entirely on takeout and frozen dinners. Cooking wasn't our thing. My mom died when I was so young that I have no memory of her at all. All I have are photos of a smiling, fair-haired woman holding me as a baby.

Growing up, people used to look at me with sympathy. I was too proud to let them pity me, so I shrugged and told them it's difficult to miss something you never had. But there was always something missing, and

I'm forever subconsciously drawn to surrogate mother figures.

"I'll be your new teacher, honey," Emma Jean breaks into my thoughts. "By the time you leave this ranch, you'll be an expert on all things culinary."

At the tail end of her sentence, the front door opens and slams shut so hard, the decorations on the walls tremble.

Emma Jean sighs and murmurs, "Oh dear."

"Tamara," Lars roars.

I widen my eyes and bite my lip.

"We may have to wait until tomorrow to teach you to cook," Emma Jean says.

What did I do this time?

NINETEEN
Cass

I hear Lars charging through the house like a raging bull.

My mouth is suddenly dry. I cross my arms in front of my chest in a subconsciously defensive gesture and warily watch the doorway to the kitchen. He soon fills the entire entrance, his straight black hair slightly mussed and his face black as a thundercloud.

"You made my farm hand quit," he yells at me.

I snort and shake my head. "That's a bit overdramatic."

"Overdramatic?" he explodes. "He's packed his bags and gone!"

"Oh, that was quick. I didn't actually expect him to quit," I say with a broad smile. "But it's wonderful to know that I have such a profound effect on people."

"What did you do?" he asks, taking an intimidating step toward me.

I'm usually not easily scared, but my heart rate rises and I have to swallow the urge to move backward. His eyes are spewing venom and a bunch of there-is-no-way-back-from-this vibes, and it suddenly occurs to me that I might have royally screwed up this time.

I shrug. "I refused to ride any other horse other than Thunder."

He looks at me in disbelief. "You what?"

"You spent an entire evening teaching me to mount Misty and ride her around the ring on my own, and I might add, with no problems."

He glares at me.

"While you've been away, I've been sneaking carrots and sugar lumps to Thunder and making friends with him. He trusts me now. Anyway, it's time I learn to ride my horse," I say defiantly.

His breath escapes in an exasperated rush. "First of all, Thunder isn't *your* horse. Second, he is dangerous, and I specifically asked you to choose another."

"I want Thunder and none other," I say calmly.

He walks over to me, every step vibrating with menace and aggression. He is gritting his teeth so hard his handsome jaws must ache. He stops right in front of me, right in my personal space, and my hands itch to shove him backward. I dislike angry people as much as I despise drunk people.

"I thought you said that you wanted this to be an easy month. Weren't you the one who intimated that you wanted to take the easy way out of everything?" he growls, looking at me as if he wants to skin me alive with a blunt cheese grater.

Up this close, he is terrifying, but I lay my hands on his rock-hard chest and shove at it with all my might. He doesn't move an inch. I give up and take a step back instead. "I never said I wanted to take the easy way out. I stated that I didn't want to be here, so don't you dare put words in my mouth you freaking…big…wall you," I spit.

Without warning, his hands shoot forward and grab my shoulders. He gives me a small shake. "You've done nothing but cause trouble since you came here, and I swear, one more cock up from you, and I don't even care if it's not your fault, I'm sending you home. So, you better fucking shape up and fast," he shouts in my face.

"Obviously, you haven't noticed because you're so damned busy," I cry hotly, "but I *have* shaped up. I do all my chores, even though they seem like they are chosen on the basis that they are the most disgusting tasks around. I get hardly any sleep, and I've not complained one single time. All I ask is that you allow me to ride the horse I want. It's not such a difficult proposition, is it?"

'Fucking hell! Am I talking to a brick wall here?"

I don't notice Emma Jean approach, but suddenly she is between us with a hand on each of our shoulders. The little lady has a hard time reaching Lars' shoulder, so she settles for his upper chest. "You two have a lot to talk about. Go take a walk outside and don't come back until you're happy with one another's decisions."

"I-" I begin to protest, but she cuts me off.

"It's not open to discussion. You have an hour until dinner."

I look at Lars and expect him to argue, but he simply nods tersely at Emma Jean. He clearly respects her as a person, but agreeing to her every whim is something I wouldn't have expected from him.

As if we are two bickering children, Emma Jean steers us out the door and closes it with a firm click behind our backs. I'm still tense with anger as we cross the porch and start down the steps. He acts as if I am the worst person who has ever stepped foot on this ranch, but I know for a fact that I am the most hardworking.

When we're on the long gravel road, Lars speaks once again. "Why did you threaten to sue him?"

"He was going to throw me on just any horse, and I was not about to let that happen," I defend.

Lars stops and turns toward me, dragging his fingers roughly through his hair. "He was planning on forcing you onto a horse? He wouldn't have done that."

"Aww…how loyal. It could never be me telling the truth, could it?" I sneer, strangely and stupidly hurt that he'd rather believe that jerk than me.

He scowls. "Are you?"

"What do you think?" I retort crossly.

He stares at me with an odd expression.

I return the stare. "Someone I knew once said, you can't really know anyone until you get them in an unexpected situation and there is no telling what they'll do. He didn't like that I wouldn't pick another horse. And he's a leech. He tried—"

"—What?" he asks, but he has suddenly become very still.

I look at him with surprise.

The change is remarkable. His nostrils flare as he inhales sharply.

"That's right, your precious groom, the one that you'd rather believe than me, came on to me."

"What did he do to you?" he asks, his eyes glittering with a totally different kind of anger.

I shift nervously. I can handle the raging bear, but I don't know what to do with this ice-cold stranger. "Nothing. He found out quickly that I'm not his type. I'm not inflatable."

He exhales audibly, some of the tension seeping out of him.

"He also didn't like it that I said he had no balls," I add, just to throw something into the awkward silence that has descended between us.

He blinks with surprise, then bursts out laughing.

I don't acknowledge the sound and keep marching forward at a steady pace.

"You told him he didn't have balls?" Lars asks, catching up with me easily and laughing loudly.

"Yes," I agree shortly.

"You're something else, you know."

"Are you going to keep pawning me off to rookies who are afraid of a horse, or are you going to man up and teach me yourself?"

His chest rises and falls as he regards me.

If I'm going to convince him, now's the time. "I wasn't sent here to be miserable. I was sent to learn to ride, and I can't do that without your help."

"Tamara, most people take a while to master horseback riding, but you did it in a day. You're already ready to ride. All that's left to learn is barrel jumps," he says.

"But what if I want to find out more? I don't want to have come all the way to Montana only to learn how to sit on a horse's back. I want to know how to live on a ranch, and race a horse over the open ground with the wind in my hair," I tell him. I know it's unlike Tamara to have aspirations that aren't completely materialistic, but this is the real me. I'm kind of done acting and pretending to be someone else. I may look like her and go by her name, but that's all. I'm going to be me.

Lars looks at me in confusion. "You do?"

"Yes, I do," I say sincerely.

117

"You actually want to learn about life on a *ranch*?" he repeats incredulously.

"Yes, Lars. I want to learn about the ranch, the animals, the seasons. Yesterday, I made a garlic braid with Emma Jean and I really enjoyed it."

"It was like pulling teeth to make you do anything a few days ago. What's changed?"

"I guess I just realized that I wasn't acting like the person I want to be."

TWENTY
Cass

Instead of making our way back to the house once the argument is settled, Lars takes me to the horse barn and stops beside Thunder's stall. "If you're going to be his trainer for a month, you need to know his history," he says as he reaches out to pet the horse's nose. Thunder reacts by jumping away and snorting restlessly.

"Why do I need to know his history?" I ask.

"Think of horses like people. If you become best friends with someone, it's best to know who they are on the inside and what forged them into the person they've become. Then you're prepared for any eventuality. It's the same with horses."

I nod and reach out to pet Thunder and he gratefully accepts my caress.

Lars shakes his head in wonder.

"Is there a reason he won't let anyone touch him?" I ask.

"There is, but part of it is still a mystery, especially now that he'll let you get close to him. Thunder is a wild speed demon and he was a great racehorse. In fact, he was legendary. I believe he even set a state record of some sort, which is why we agreed to take him in. He was raised from birth by Catherine, my sister's best friend, to be the best that he could be."

119

He stops to watch Thunder rub his head affectionately against my shoulder.

"But Catherine was bonded so closely to him that only she could get him to ride to his full potential. Her father tried hiring professional riders, but none of them could work Thunder the way she did. Only Catherine could control him the way he needed to be controlled."

"So, he won't let people touch him because of his bond with Catherine? Why doesn't she still have him then?"

Lars pulls a bucket away from the wall and sits on it, his shoulders slouched. He never slouches, so it is odd to see his posture so loose and relaxed. "Catherine died of an inoperable brain tumor at the age of seventeen."

"Oh, I'm sorry," I gasp.

"Yeah, it was a crying shame. She was a wonderful kid."

"But you said Thunder won races. Who rode him?"

"Everyone knew she wouldn't live to eighteen, so they allowed her to enter professional races as a minor. All she wanted was to be the best, and Thunder gave her that gift."

I crouch next to him. How I wish I could put my hand on his shoulder and be a friend to him. "What happened…after?"

"The loss was hard for everyone, she was so special, but especially for her dad. He couldn't live with the reminder that was Thunder. One night after he had seen the bottom of a bottle of whiskey, he took his shotgun to the stables and tried to kill Thunder. Fortunately, he was so drunk he missed, but it scarred Thunder for life. He became so nervous, no one could get near him. The only person he would allow close to him was my sister, Sophia. So, I bought him and she brought him here."

"Do you have any female trainers or farm hands?"

Lars, not understanding what I'm hinting at, shakes his head. "All of my trainers are men. I only have one female farmhand, but she works primarily with cattle."

I stand up and pace the floor restlessly. "Have you ever thought of the possibility that Thunder just doesn't like men? I mean, if he is okay with all the women he has met, what's to say he isn't sexist?"

Lars stands too and looks at Thunder, who eyes him back warily.

"That's impossible. Horses aren't sexist," he states firmly.

"Okay, scrap that. You said that Thunder bonded extremely closely with Catherine, right? Well, it's a proven fact that men and women have different biological scents. When he sees a woman, it's possible that she reminds him of the connection he had with Catherine? Maybe something in your sister and I reminds him of Catherine."

"And maybe he associates men with the man who tried to kill him after his beloved Catherine died," Lars says quietly.

Lars stands and moves away distractedly toward Devil's Ride. He lays his large hand on the horse's neck. It is a gesture that is at once possessive and tender.

"You really love him, don't you?" I ask.

Pride flashes in his eyes and he takes a step closer to the big, impressive beast. "Yeah, he is my boy."

"I can see why you chose him," I say with a chuckle. I know nothing of horse breeds, but this one has to be mixed because I've never seen a thoroughbred with quite so many colors. Unlike Thunder, who has a certain softness to him, Devil's Ride is aloof and proud.

"Why?" he asks.

"Because he's like you."

"Explain."

"He's contrary and difficult," I say with a grin.

Lars takes two long strides in my direction and stops right in front of me. In the stall behind me, Thunder jumps and backs himself against the wall, but I can concentrate only on our closeness. Lars lifts a hand and I follow it with my eyes until his finger brushes gently against my ear. It takes me a moment to realize that I am holding my breath. I exhale loudly.

Lars moves his lips to my ear and his breath sends goosebumps down my spine. His other hand grasps my hip in a tight hold. "We have a lot in common and it's not what you think. We both love to be ridden hard by a contrary, difficult woman," he says in a deep, rasping tone.

My entire body tightens and my breath comes in shallow gasps. I close my eyes and wait, hoping more will come of the moment, but nothing does.

His touch leaves my hip and by the time I open my eyes, he is already walking out of the barn, shoulders stiff and rising rapidly.

"I'll see you at the house." His voice is calm and even, but his body mechanics are the complete opposite. I can't figure out which is more telling.

His muscles ripple beneath his shirt as he walks away, and I can't peel my eyes off him. He is perfect and I hate that nothing can come out of our relationship. If I weren't Tamara, this is exactly the man I would choose for myself.

TWENTY-ONE
Lars

The air is still and the moon is full. Through the open curtains, blue light floods the room. I lie on my bed and find it impossible to sleep. My phone vibrates on the nightstand. I pick it up and look at the screen.

"Where are you?" my brother asks.

"Back at the spread."

"Oh yeah. How's Honeywell's kid doing?"

He catches me off guard so I blurt honestly, "I don't know."

He gives a short burst of laughter. "What the hell is that supposed to mean?"

"I mean it's like dealing with Jekyll and Hyde. One moment she's like this she-devil complete with a rattle in her tail, and the next she's this awesome, intelligent, caring person."

"That's weird."

"I know," I say with feeling. "Half the time I want to tan her hide and the other times…"

"You didn't finish your sentence, bro," my brother mocks.

The rest of the sentence is I want to fucking rip her clothes off and bury my dick to the hilt inside her. "Why did you call?" I growl.

"Just checking up on my little brother, but now that I've scented blood…"

"You haven't scented blood. Nothing is going on."

"Yet."

My brother is a pain in my ass. "Look, I've had a long day and if you've nothing to tell me, I'm going back to sleep."

"Whoa, she's really got you tied up in knots, hasn't she?"

"Back off, Matt. Nothing is going on and nothing will."

"I was messing with you before, but now that I see how raw you are, I should warn you, little brother. Tamara's more she-devil complete with rattlesnake than the awesome individual she puts on to get what she wants. Even if she *was* that sweet, caring person, she lives in LA. There's nothing in it for you. Fuck her if you absolutely must, then put her out of your head. For good. And whatever you do, don't let her sense your weakness or she'll sink her talons into you."

I massage my left temple and sigh heavily.

"I'm serious, Lars. Joking aside, she's trouble. Big trouble. I didn't want to put you off keeping her at the ranch before because it never even crossed my mind that you'd fall for such a manipulative little brat, but now that you are showing a real lack of character judgement, I have to tell you that I have it first hand: The bitch will fuck anything with a dick."

I close my eyes and grit my teeth. I hate my brother talking about her like that. "Thanks for the advice. I appreciate it," I say and quickly end the call.

My brother is right. Of course, he's right. How could I be attracted to her? It makes no sense at all, but it's impossible for me to explain to my brother or anyone else what Tamara does to my insides. I spring out of bed and pace the floor of my bedroom. My heart is banging as if it's about to fucking explode, and my damned dick is rock hard

I'm *aching* for her.

My mind races with all kinds of thoughts. Not just any thoughts, but the kind of filthy fantasies I haven't entertained since I was a horny teenager. I feel as restless as a wolf at full moon. It feels as if something is calling to me and the call is irresistible.

I pinch the bridge of my nose. I still smell the scent of her hair in my nostrils. Fresh. My ears have memorized the sound of her voice, and I don't even have to close my eyes to see that sweet body that just begs to be dominated. I think of her long shapely legs wrapped around my waist. My cock in her stubborn mouth. Oh, that mouth.

I am suddenly rock hard. Again.

I turn on my heel and walk out of the bedroom. The landing is in darkness. I walk down it to the bedroom at the end, open the door, walk through the space, and stand at the window. The moonlight shines soft blue over the open landscape. The mountain range rises like a hulking dark beast against the velvet sky full of stars.

But my eyes don't linger on its beauty. They jerk down to her patio, to the circle of light made by the small candle burning on the little table. My gaze falls on the gleam of her skin. Most of her is huddled inside a blanket, but from here I can see the curve of her cheek and her fingers. When she first arrived, she had long fake nails. Every single one is broken now.

We are two people awake under the same sky.

How can a woman who sits alone looking at stars be all bad? Could it be that all those rumors and ugly stories are all lies and exaggeration? She was caught drinking and driving. That's no lie. Maybe she has changed. Maybe living here has changed her.

A sigh goes through me. A longing I've never known gnaws deep inside me. Tamara Honeywell is poison, but she is proving to be such a sweet poison that I'm finding impossible to resist. I know…

It's crazy.

It's stupid.

It's madness.

It's wrong.

Yet, she's so fucking delectable I want to bite that curvy ass. I want to squeeze those fleshy buttocks in my hands while I…What the fuck is wrong with me. She's spoiled, selfish, annoying, argumentative, stubborn…

Fucking hell, I can't get her out of my mind.

I clench my hands to stop myself from going to her. A dark laugh huffs up my throat. It won't be tonight, Lars. It'll be never if you know what's good for you. Stay away from her. The woman is like quicksand. The harder I try the more stuck I become, and the more my body craves hers, but here's the real kicker. My brother will think I'm nuts if I tell him, but I don't just want to have her body. I want to possess her and protect her and keep her.

When I heard that ass James had horn-dogged on her, I felt boiling fury slam into my brain. I wanted to race after him and rip his throat out. Then watch him bleed out. That's how furious I was. The predatory instinct and aggression in me is something I never suspected I'd have.

It scares the ever-living shit out of me. Even now. Just thinking of him trying it on with her.

A soft snarl rattles out of my throat.

I turn away from the window and go back to my room to lie on my bed, awake, alone, and tormented with images of her for hours. In the end, I give up. Fuck it. What the hell, I'm not going to sleep with a raging hard on.

I fist my hand around my cock and jerk off while thinking of Tamara Honeywell's sweet pussy. I bet she shaves it. I bet it's pink and wet. I close my eyes and visualize her naked. Not one stitch on that beautiful body.

She spreads her legs. Jesus, she's not wearing any underwear. Her pussy is so pretty I want to eat it.

"Let me suck you," she begs, and opens that plump mouth of hers.

Pre-cum drips from my engorged cock.

I feed my cock to her hot, wet mouth. She takes it greedily and moans with the taste. She takes me into her throat. Her mouth is hot and soft and it feels awesome.

I stroke the entire length of my shaft faster and faster.

"Are you going to fuck my tight pussy?" she mewls.

"Oh, yes, cupcake, I sure am."

I pull out of her mouth and lie her face down on the bed. She lifts her ass up into the air and offers her pussy to me. It's all pink and wet and begging for it. I plunge my bare cock into all that pinkness.

"Harder, Lars. Harder," she begs.

"Oh! fuck, Tamara," I groan as my legs stiffen.

The build-up feels like floodwater bursting through a dam. Nothing can contain it. Nothing. I explode, shooting my hot load like a fountain into the air. It covers my hands in a sticky mess. Jesus, it's been so long since I've come like that.

My heart is hammering away and my cock is still hard for her. I just lie there and know... I'm in so much trouble.

TWENTY-TWO
Cass

As I walk toward the barn I realize that today marks my ninth day on the ranch. Despite all the hard work and slanging matches with Lars, I've loved it. I've also started to meet a few of the other employees, and thankfully, not one has heard of Tamara Honeywell. It's been a nice change.

Deep in thought, I nearly jump out of my skin when I hear a man's voice call, "Howdy."

Expecting to be alone in the barn, I take a startled step back. "You scared the bejesus out of me," I say, still clutching my chest.

A sandy-haired, slim man about my age grins widely. "Sorry. Didn't mean to."

"Are you the new groom?" I ask uncertainly. I was expecting Lars to hire a female farmhand after our realization that Thunder doesn't do well with men.

He looks sheepish. "Not really. I'm just supposed to hang around and help you if you need it. Lars says you'll mostly be doing your own thing."

I smile at the eagerness he exudes. "All right, I'll work on doing my own thing, then." Taking a step away from him, I head in the direction of Thunder's stall.

To my amusement, he follows me like a lamb.

"So, is it true that you're famous?" he asks after a moment. His voice is awed and it irritates me.

I'm not famous. I'm just a poor girl from Chicago trying to pay off a nasty loan shark. I put the halter on Thunder and start leading him out. "Yeah, I'm basically a godess in Los Angeles," I say dryly. The phrase is egotistical and I hate hearing it come from my lips.

His brow furrows and I can tell that I have put him off me.

It saddens me a little that I have to behave in such a way, but those are the terms of my job.

"I really don't care if you're famous," he says.

"Then why'd you bring it up?" I ask as I grab hold of Thunder's lead rope and tie him to a post in the grooming bay the way I'd seen the other farmhands do. I notice that Thunder isn't going crazy around him. He only looks slightly weary.

"I was just curious," he says, raising his hands defensively.

I grab the soft bristle brush and begin running it through Thunder's mane. Though I've only ever done it twice before, I've watched how Thunder reacts to each of the strokes and do only the ones he enjoys.

"You're excellent at that," he says from so close behind me that I jump.

I whirl around. "What is your problem, buddy?" I ask irritably. I don't need another James.

He takes a few steps back and looks at me mournfully. "I'm sorry. I didn't mean nothing," he mumbles.

"Just keep your distance, please. You're going to spook the horse." Although, the truth is, Thunder seems all right with him. It's me who's finding his good-natured invasion into my personal space annoying.

"All right. I'll just wait right here then," he agrees amiably.

I sigh. "Look. You can tell Lars I really don't need a babysitter. I've been working with these horses on my own every day for the last nine days, and I haven't done anything stupid or messed up yet."

He tips his hat in that charming way cowboys do. "Pardon, ma'am, but with all due respect, I'm being paid to keep an eye on you, so I need to stay by your side. I really hope you understand."

"What do you mean you're being paid to keep an eye on me?" I demand, my hands on my hips.

I must look fierce because he takes an involuntary step back. "I am technically a farmhand. I repair fences and work with the chickens. I'm good with chickens, but I'm being paid extra to watch you."

"What do you mean by 'watch'?"

"I'm not allowed to leave your side," he admits uncomfortably.

"What?"

His eyes widen. "I'm just doing my job."

"Did Lars ask you to spy on me?" I ask.

He squirms. "No, ma'am. I'm just supposed to keep you safe."

"If he's trying to shirk his own duties by hiring you…"

His eyes widen with alarm. "No, ma'am. He's trying his hardest to be with you, but it's tough for him to find time in his schedule."

"Yeah, because feeding and milking cows take so long," I say sardonically.

His eyes widen. "He does far more than that, ma'am."

It is obvious where his loyalty lies.

"I haven't had one chance to ride my horse yet, so he really needs to get his ass out here."

He clears his throat. "I wish there was something I could do for you, ma'am, but my job is to make sure you don't do nothing...er..." he scratches his cheek, "irregular."

I groan with frustration and turn back to Thunder, my brush strokes ferocious. On the second stroke, I stop and take a deep breath. This is not me at all. I'm never horrible toward perfect strangers. Yes, I'm furious with Lars, but I shouldn't take it out on this poor kid who's just trying to do his job, or this beautiful horse that I love. I kiss Thunder's neck and say a silent apology, then turn around with a smile on my face. "I'm sorry. It's not your fault. Let's start again. I didn't get your name."

"I'm Butch," he says, looking relieved and extending a hand toward me.

"Is that a common name in these parts?" I ask, taking his hand. It's rough with calluses, but his shake is firm and he doesn't hold my hand longer than necessary. I decide I like him. We just got off on the wrong foot. "I've never met anyone—other than a German Shephard—named Butch." I grin to show that I'm not being malicious.

He grins back. "It's way more common than Tamara," he says.

"Oh yeah?" I wonder how common the name Cass is around here.

"I think your accent's real neat," he says bashfully.

"Thank you, but your accent is very different. You're not from around here either, are you?" Except for Lars and Emma Jean, everyone else I've met in Montana speaks with a slight accent that almost sounds like a southern drawl, but less potent. It suddenly occurs to me that maybe Lars is not from Montana either.

"You betcha I'm not from these parts. I've got itchy feet. They've taken me all over the country. I've been in Georgia, Texas, Utah, Kansas, Colorado, Iowa, Wyoming, and North Dakota. I was going to work here for six months then move on, but I kinda like it here and I guess I'll stay on for a bit."

"Me too. I kinda like it here too," I agree with a big smile in his direction. I feel like I have to make up for my previous behavior, more so now that I know that we're in a similar situation. He's not acting like a celebrity to pay off loan sharks, but like me, he's an outsider.

He smiles back.

"You know," I begin, "we should hang out sometime. Maybe we can teach each other something."

For a second, Butch looks unsure of himself. "Yeah, we could hang out," he says as if he's trying to act cool.

I take a step toward him. Crap, he doesn't realize I'm being friendly and not flirtatious. "Butch," I say seriously, "I'm not interested in you in a romantic way."

Butch casts his eyes downward and takes a deep breath. It's clear he's disappointed, but then he chuckles. "That's good," he quips, "because I'm not into high fallutin' city slickers with curves for fuckin' days."

My tense muscles relax with relief. "And I'm not into judgy, douchebags with laughing eyes."

"I'm real pleased to meet you, Tamara Honeywell," he says, smiling.

"Why?"

"I like having attractive friends. And you are hot," he says with a wink.

I laugh and nod my head. "Okay, here's to friends. I need a friend around here anyway. Who's better than a skinny chicken expert who is meant to watch out for me?"

Butch leans against Thunder's stall, and the huge horse reacts by getting onto its hind legs and neighing. Butch jumps away and clears his throat in an attempt to act natural.

I smile and walk toward Thunder. "Are you scared of him?"

"How come you're not?" Butch stands well back and allows me to lead Thunder into the main part of the barn.

"I don't know. This is the first time I've seen a horse in person. I've always thought they were beautiful, but never interacted with them." I pet Thunder's nose and tie him to the fence post outside the barn. "Do you want me to show you what to do? You can't get over your fear from over there."

"I've heard bad things about this horse," he says nervously.

I laugh and extend my hand toward him. "I promise I won't let him hurt you. You're the first man that Thunder has allowed near him, so that's a start. It's good for him." I can't help but wonder if it's because of the gentle, almost feminine vibe to him that makes Thunder tolerate being around him.

He shakes his head. "Nah, I'll pass,"

"Come on, Butch. It's really not that bad. Just try it." I cajole.

When he just stares at me, I pull the guilt card. "Don't you trust me?"

"Of course I trust you, but I don't know about this." His tone is semi-persuaded, but I know I need to go a step further.

"I thought we could be such good friends, but you won't even help me to tame my horse?"

"You know I would if I could," he says, taking a step in my direction.

All that's left is pity. "But you can." I lower my head and drop my shoulders, taking in a deep breath and petting Thunder solemnly. I'm not Tamara, but hell, my acting is top notch right now. "It's fine. Don't worry about it," I mumble.

"Fine." He sighs and cautiously comes toward me.

I look up at him and smile. Thunder doesn't react as Butch approaches, and I bite my lip anxiously. Will Thunder take to Butch the way he took to me?

He comes even closer and Thunder remains stationary, not bothered by his presence. I'm amazed by the fact that Thunder isn't reacting negatively toward Butch. "You're doing great," I say encouragingly. Am I encouraging myself or Butch? I've only been around these animals for nine days, but I feel connected to them. Am I ready to be responsible for someone else as well as myself and Thunder?

"Just pet his snout. He won't hurt you," I promise. I don't know if he'll get anxious about being touched, but he's tied to a post. He won't be able to do any damage while restrained by a rope.

"Okay," Butch mumbles, reaching his hand out. He doesn't touch the horse's head, though. Instead, he hovers for a moment then begins to pull back.

I grab hold of his hand and place it on Thunder's face. He jumps slightly, evidently surprised by the close contact and my forceful gesture, but he doesn't attempt to break free. Instead, he wiggles his fingers on Thunder's snout and the horse snorts nervously and swishes his tail. Butch looks at me and smiles with an awed expression.

"What the hell is going on here?" Lars says from behind us, startling Thunder and making Butch and I leap apart in shock. I jerk my head toward him, baffled as to why he sounds so livid.

TWENTY-THREE
Cass

His jaw is clenched tight and his eyes are narrowed dangerously on both of us. "I asked what the hell is going on here?"

I don't know what he thinks is going on, but the whole situation is quite absurd. A weird giggle escapes from my mouth, but Lars doesn't think it's funny at all. He glowers at me.

"I'm just teaching Thunder not be nervous around men," I explain.

"Oh, you are? And does that involve holding hands and being right on top of one another?"

My jaw drops open. "What's your problem? You hired Butch to hang around me, and now you're here acting as if we've done something wrong."

He strides in our direction, his whole body strung tight like an animal about to pounce. "Leave," he says firmly to Butch.

Butch doesn't hesitate to do as he is told, but he looks back and meets my eyes to ask if I'll be okay with Lars. Brave of him. I smile slightly at him, and he hotfoots it away faster than I can blink.

Lars takes another step toward me and Thunder suddenly goes crazy from his proximity to us. I try to pacify him, but it is no use. He can't handle being this close

137

to another man, especially one who is as angry as Lars. He's probably picked up my angry vibes too.

"Back off, Lars," I say, trying to block his body from Thunder's view.

Of course, it doesn't work, for he is much taller and broader than me. The lead rope attached to the fence is doing its job and keeping him from bolting, but I begin to worry about him hurting himself in his attempts to get away from Lars.

"Lars, back the hell up, please," I shout at him.

Lars leaves my side and Thunder begins to calm down.

"Tamara," he calls, but I'm so furious with him I don't even bother to turn my head. He has been unbearable ever since my arrival. I know I provoked him at the beginning, but I've stopped that now and he still insists on being nasty at every opportunity. I continue stroking Thunder as tears prickle the back of my eyes. It's just anger, I tell myself. It's anger, but I'm hurt too. No matter what I do, it's always wrong.

"Can you turn around and look at me please?" he asks.

"You are the most immature, despicable human being I have ever met," I say in a choked voice. "You don't treat people with respect, or maybe you do, but never me. You treated Butch like shit and all he was doing was the job you assigned to him. I don't know where you go during the day, or why you can't be here, but it's irrelevant at this point." I sniff and wipe my eyes roughly with the back of my sleeves. "And don't for one instant think I'm crying because of you. I'm not sad or emotional. I'm just done with this bullshit."

I hear Lars draw a deep breath and take a step in my direction. I twist around to face him and hold out a hand. "I think you've done enough damage here."

For a brief second, so quickly it feels as if I've imagined it, something that looks like hurt flashes in his eyes. Then it's gone. "I'm sorry I made you cry. I swear it wasn't intentional. I'll teach you to ride Thunder if that's what you want." He sounds utterly defeated.

His tone breaks my heart and instantly, I forget my own anger and hurt and just want to comfort him. Unable to look away from him, I take an instinctive step forward.

"Once I do that, you don't have to see me again," he says bitterly.

My outstretched hand flies to my burning chest. I was just about to embarrass myself. I should keep away from this guy. "I think I can learn to ride Thunder on my own. You won't be able to come near him, anyway," I say sadly. The sooner I accept this man is not for me, the better.

"At least let me stay and make sure you're okay. I can't have you getting hurt," Lars says, taking another step back. "You won't even know I'm here." His beautiful eyes drop to the ground, then rise again to meet mine a moment later, dimmer than before. He takes off his hat and holds it in front of him. A shock of silky dark hair falls on his forehead. My fingers itch to sweep it back.

But I blew my chances with him the same way he blew his with me. I'm ashamed of the way I've been acting, but I had to act like that. I know he was only responding to my rudeness, because I can see the heart hidden beneath his harsh exterior and insufferable arrogance. He's a great man—even if he hasn't acted like one toward me. I wish things could have been different. Maybe—just maybe—we could have worked something out. But now it's too late.

"All right," I say.

He nods and, turning around, walks away.

TWENTY-FOUR
Cass

I tried to avoid leaving the ranch, but it becomes inevitable when I run out of what Emma Jean calls 'feminine items'. When I tell Ms. Moore, she asks me to go get my hair done at the local hairdresser as that is what Tamara would do. To my surprise, she takes the time to book an appointment for me and calls me back to confirm it.

The town is about half an hour's drive away. It is supposed to be tiny, with a population of about three thousand, but I cringe at the thought that someone might recognize Tamara and I'll have to put on another show. It takes me almost an hour to put on my make-up, do my hair, and get into a sundress.

Chance, one of the ranchers, has been designated as my driver, and he is sitting on the hood of a rusty red truck, idly chewing a stalk of grass while gazing out at the horizon. When I come out of the house, he whips his head around as fast as a snake and lets his eyes run down my body like water. As I come down the stairs, he whistles low and long.

"I could squat with my spurs on for a sweetheart like you," he says with a grin that is big enough to split his face.

I just laugh. Chance is harmless, and I like him a lot, even though I can just about make out half of what he says.

Born and bred in Montana, he uses a lot of slang. Someone from Washington is an apple picker. A four-wheel drive is a 4-dig, a horse is a hay burner, sheep are prairie maggots, children are curtain crawlers, a woman's breasts are northern curves, and goodbye is nice speakin' atcha.

He rushes to open the passenger door, and I climb into it as gracefully as I can, considering the truck sits on huge tires and is at least three feet from the ground. As Chance drives me down the road, he tells me about the ranch, the countryside, and the Montana way of life.

I keep interrupting him for translations into English, but overall, he is a mine of information and I absorb it all eagerly. As we come into a town, I start looking around me with wonder. It's like a beautifully preserved time capsule of a forgotten way of life. The main street is a road that runs through two rows of red brick buildings facing each other. There are Mom and Pop stores, a chain dollar store, a gas station that doubles as a restaurant, and a drinking saloon.

"Talk about small," I murmur.

"Heck, this town is so small I went out on a blind date once and found a long-lost cousin," he says, scratching the back of his head.

Chance parks the car in front of a store that says Shoes and More and jerks his chin toward a shop a few doors down the street. "Your hair salon is over there and the grocery store is across the street. I'll be in Steadman's." He points to a hardware store. "Come over when you're done."

I check my pocket to be sure I have my phone.

"You won't need that. No cellphone signal, anywhere, anytime, ever."

"Seriously?"

He nods solemnly.

There are people passing the truck and they look in curiously. Dear God, this is what hell must be like. Maybe if I keep my face covered and head down, I might be able to avoid detection. I turn back to Chance. "Mind if I borrow your hat? I don't want to get caught in a stampede of fans."

Chance laughs and nods. "You know, you're really not as bad as folks described ya."

"Remember what Emma Jean says. Never miss a chance to shut up," I say, plucking his hat from his head and jamming it on my head before jumping to the ground.

"Doggone it, I've been digging for water under an outhouse, haven't I?" he says with a good-natured laugh.

I grin back. "Stop when you smell the shit."

He laughs as I close the door. I adjust my purse on my shoulder and walk confidently to the hair salon. Teri Ann's is done up in shades of pink inside and completely deserted. A woman with permed auburn hair sashays over to me. She has big, inquisitive eyes, but she quickly gives up trying to engage me in conversation when I pick up a magazine and pretend to be completely engrossed in it. When she switches off the hairdryer, I look up at the mirror. She has done a good job and my hair looks surprisingly glamorous. When I go to the little counter to pay her, she tells me the appointment has been prepaid for. I walk out without paying a dime. Having money appear out of thin air is wonderful. If only I could do that in Chicago.

I walk across the street and pull a shopping cart from the pile by the entrance. Ms. Moore told me Tamara will be paying for everything and I intend to take full advantage. She deserves it for insisting on waking me up at two or three in the morning and giving me grief every single time she calls.

It takes only a while for me to fill the entire cart. I buy stuff for Emma Jean, Butch, Chance, and a few of the other guys, and a whole bunch of junk food for me. Once my cart is full, I go through the checkout. One by one, the cashier, a very pretty but unfriendly creature, bags all the junk food and hygiene items before hitting a few buttons and looking up at me with a bored expression. "That'll be three hundred and seven dollars and thirty-nine cents."

I reach for my bag and feel the sides before looking over the brim of my hat at the cashier. Oh, shit! My cheeks feel like they are on fire. I didn't put the credit card Ms. Moore gave me into my purse. It is still in the pocket of my suitcase. How the hell did I do that? I look up and the woman is looking at me with a disgusted expression. As if I'm deliberately trying to cheat her or something.

"I—uh." I try to think of anything to say to make this less awkward, but I draw a blank. "Look, I'm with Chance. He's in Steadman's. If you just put my stuff to one side and wait a few minutes, I'll go get him."

She glares at me. "Haven't I seen you somewhere before?"

The way she is looking at me is as if I've been featured on America's Most Wanted. I shake my head. "Just forget it. I'm sorry I wasted your time."

"Yeah, and who's going to put all the stuff back on the shelves?" She looks mad at the thought that she'll have to do it.

I guess I can't blame her, but if she had only let me go get Chance she would have sold three hundred bucks worth of groceries and I wouldn't feel like a piece of excrement. "Don't worry. I'll put the groceries back myself," I offer.

She puts her hands on her hips. "So you can steal some items while you're at it?"

I stare at her in shock. Did she just accuse me of being a thief?

"Go on, git," she orders rudely.

My face burns with embarrassment.

"Vicky," I hear a deep voice say from a few feet behind me. I recognize the voice almost immediately and realize that the situation really can't get much worse. I am so mortified I can't even bring myself to turn around and see his gloating expression.

"Oh, Lars," the cashier simpers, her demeanor changing so fast it's enough to give you whiplash. "What can I do for you?" She shakes her hair even more dramatically than Tamara Honeywell could. Twirling a lock around her finger, she gazes up at Lars with wide, doe eyes. I can't decide if I want to puke or go across the counter and show her why it's important to be kind to everyone, not just drop dead gorgeous people of the opposite sex.

"What was the total again?" he asks tightly as he slides a card across the counter.

Her eyes widen with shock then fill with jealousy. "What? You...you want to pay for her?" she stutters, throwing me such a venomous look I nearly laugh at her bewildered expression. I wonder if she and Lars have history. Sure feels like it. The thought makes my insides twist suddenly. My hands clench so hard my nails bite into my flesh. I can't believe it. I'm jealous!

"Looks like it, doesn't it?" he says coolly.

"You know her?" she asks as if she can't believe.

"Not that it's any of your business, but yes," Lars replies.

Vicky glares at him in a way that would send chills down a lesser man's spine. "You're right. It's not important to me," she snarls, as she swipes his card.

I know that I'm missing something between them, so I take a step back as Lars signs his slip. Silently, he helps me fill the shopping cart with my bags.

"Say hello to your mother," he says as he pushes the cart out of the store. I follow closely behind.

"Well, that was awkward," I say as soon as we are on the sidewalk

He spares me an impatient glance.

"Where is Chance?" I ask, looking around and not seeing his pickup.

"I sent him back," he replies shortly.

"Oh. Why?"

"Get in," he orders as we approach his flat-bed truck. "We need to talk."

"Do we?" I ask doubtfully.

TWENTY-FIVE
Cass

We've been kind of avoiding each other since our conversation two days ago. Anyway, Lars has hardly been around at the ranch and I've come to the conclusion that it's better that way. We pull ourselves into the truck and sit side by side. Just being in the same space with him is doing things to my insides, and I wring my calloused fingers. They used to be soft, but I'm fine with them being rough, since I prefer my new stronger, firmer body.

"Take that damned hat off," he says irritably.

Confused, I take Chance's hat off and place in the space between us.

"What were you doing buying groceries?" he asks. "You have someone who does that for you."

I shrug casually. "I needed some personal items."

"Chunky monkey ice cream is not a personal item," he says dryly.

"Stop, stop, if I laugh any harder I'll rupture my kidneys," I retort sarcastically.

He takes the sales receipt out of his pocket and quickly runs his gaze down it. "You bought three hundred dollars' worth of junk food, Tamara."

"Okay, I might have gone a little overboard, but I deserve it. I've had a rough eleven days."

"Oh, I'm sorry that the princess had to work for the last eleven days. It must have been such a foreign concept to you."

I scowl and turn to face him. "Oh, for God's sake, change the freaking record. Stop patronizing me all the time. I thought we got past this the last time. I've had it up to here," I wave my hand over my head, "with you. Why am I on your shit list now? I've done nothing wrong."

"You put yourself on my shit list by acting like an entitled bitch. Who goes to the grocery store and spends hundreds of dollars on snack food?"

"I don't know why you came to my rescue. Let me tell you, I would much rather have put back all the groceries than have to watch the checkout girl fawn all over you or listen to your arrogant crap."

"You are wasteful and have no concept of money or hard work," he snarls.

My face is flushed and I have trouble finding words to adequately describe how angry and frustrated I am. "I don't know who you think you are? I can buy myself whatever I please with my own money."

He raises his eyebrows.

"I forgot to take my credit card, but—"

"—Figures," he says so knowingly I want to slap his smug face.

"I'll make sure to pay you back," I continue as if he had not said anything. "And while we're at it, I probably have a better concept of money than you. And another thing. Do *not* call me a bitch ever again or I'll tell my father."

His eyebrows rise. "Go ahead. Call your father. Tell him," he challenges.

He turns that sword back on me. I swallow hard. "I would, but there's no reception in this damned town."

"Right, let me get you back to the ranch where there will be plenty of reception." He starts the engine and the pickup roars onto the street

I chew my lip. Oh, hell. What have I gotten myself into now? There's no way I'm going to be talking to Tamara's dad. I sit stewing for about ten minutes, until the better part of my anger cools. Surreptitiously, I sneak a look at him. His face is a dark mask of rage. I decide to swallow my pride and sort this out before I end up blowing everything. I clear my throat. "Are we going to keep fighting just because you like the idea of hating me? Because I don't hate you, and I am trying hard to see your good points. In fact, I was beginning to think you're a decent person. Apparently, I was wrong."

"You know what," Lars says through clenched teeth, 'I've had enough of this bullshit from you." Jerking his wheel to the right, he comes to a screeching stop at the side of the road. I place my hand on the dash in front of me to stop myself from banging my head on the windshield. My seatbelt bites into my chest painfully and I wince.

"What is your problem?" I shout. "You could have gotten us killed."

"You think I like the idea of hating you? Why the fuck would you think that?" he asks, voice calmer than before.

"Is that a serious question?"

"Humor me."

"Because all you ever do is criticize me. I don't work hard enough. I don't have any concept of money. I picked the most difficult horse in the barn, which of course, makes

149

me a selfish *bitch*. It may have escaped your notice that I was sent to the ranch to learn to ride a horse, work, and learn respect, but you aren't teaching me any of those things. You're teaching me that I'm just not good enough to do anything except shovel animal dung all day. If not for Emma Jean, I'd still be doing that twelve hours a day, wouldn't I? So, you tell me, why do you hate me?"

I'm out of breath by the end of my fiery monologue, and he just stares at me with a weird expression that infuriates me even further. I wrench open the door to his truck and before he can grab my hand, jump outside.

The midday Montana sun burns my bare shoulders. Even my newly scrubbed scalp protests at being in such heat, but I ignore it and start walking down the road in the direction of the ranch. It will be a long walk—maybe a day if I push myself—but I am not getting back into his truck without a damned good explanation from him.

"Tamara, get back in here," he shouts at me.

"Not in a million years," I yell back.

"I don't hate you at all."

In the still hot air, the sound is no more than a whisper, but it stops me dead in my tracks. I turn and face him. He is standing in front of the truck.

"I don't hate you," he repeats louder.

"Well, in that case, you obviously need to work on your manners."

"Tamara," he begins, and I have a crazy wish that I could hear my name coming from his lips instead of hers. "I wanted to hate you."

"I noticed," I say with a scowl. "You did a really good job, too."

"Will you shut up and let me finish? I'm trying to apologize."

"Has anyone ever told you that you suck at apologies?"

He sighs elaborately then continues. "But you're not what I expected. At first you were someone I couldn't tolerate, but I realized that wasn't you. It was a façade, and now that I've seen who you really are, I find it hard to believe that you are the person the media tears apart, or the one who wreaks havoc everywhere she goes. You're down to earth, strong-willed, clever, intuitive with animals, and kind to Emma Jean. I wanted to hate you, but I don't."

I stare into his gray eyes. The sun is burning down on my head and shoulders, but shivers spark up and down my spine. I look at the ground, suddenly unsure of myself. "I wish I hated you too," I mumble.

Lars takes a step toward me and pulls my chin up to face him. His face is even more beautiful up close. He has scruff that lines his jaw and wind-tossed black hair curling out from under his hat. His molten eyes pierce mine and I can't look away. Is he going to kiss me? He looks like he is. How did this go from pure hatred to passion in a split second?

I feel my body involuntarily leaning toward him, and he pulls my chin further upward until my neck is almost uncomfortable. I arch my back to accommodate his height, close my eyes like the heroine in some romantic drama, and wait.

And wait.

His hand loosens around my chin. I open my eyes reluctantly and see him standing with his face centimeters away. "Jesus, Tamara, what the fuck are you doing to me?"

he groans. Suddenly, he steps away from me. "Get into the truck."

I obey immediately, my legs like jelly.

What the hell just happened between the two of us.

TWENTY-SIX
Cass

"**W**hat do I do, Jesse?" I ask, lying back on my bed and opening the box of Sour Patch Kids that I bought at the grocery store yesterday. This morning, I've decided to eat junk food for breakfast.

She giggles at the other end of the line.

I scowl. "This isn't funny. Do you understand the gravity of what's going on here?"

"Oh no, I understand all right. It's pretty straight forward. You're busy drowning in a puddle."

"Thanks, I'm so glad I called you for advice," I say, popping the candy into my mouth. "Ooh," I say, scrunching my face at the sourness. It's been years since I've had one and I've forgotten how strong they are.

"He's not there doing something to you, is he?" Jesse asks.

"Ha, ha, very funny. I've just popped a Sour Patch Kid into my mouth."

"I think you should have sex with him. He wants you. You want him. Go for it," she says. I can hear the smirk in her voice.

I spit the sour candy onto my hand and swallow a few times. It's unbelievable how quickly my tongue feels raw and burned. "I can't just go and have sex with him."

"Why not?"

I look at the ceiling and clear my throat. "Because he's so…contrary."

"Contrary men make for hot sex."

I put the candy on a piece of wrapper and survey the rest of the packets of sweets and chocolates. "I hardly know him."

"Even better. Stranger sex is the best kind. More sexual tension," she counters.

I laugh. "You're crazy, you know?"

"Don't you want a piece of that cowboy?"

"I don't know. It's complicated. I can't get my head around the idea of sleeping with someone while being someone else."

"Treat it as a fling."

I lick my fingers. "I can't do that either."

"Why not?"

"I kinda of like him, Jesse."

She pauses. "What? As in like, like?"

"Yup. He makes me feel things no one else does. Most of the time I want to rip his eyes out, but sometimes…"

"Here's the thing. You're supposed to be Tamara, right?"

"Yeah," I say cautiously as I unwrap a Hershey bar.

"She would be all over him by now, so logically, by sleeping with him you'll just be staying in character."

I bite into the bar. "Be honest with me. Would you sleep with him if you were in my shoes?"

"I'd freaking throw myself at him," she gushes immediately.

"Liar."

"I so would," she insists firmly.

"Well, I'm not going to throw myself at him and end up getting attached. After this month, I'll leave and he'll never see me again. It's just not worth it." I'm saddened by admitting such a thing, but these are the hard facts.

"Are you really going to pass up this opportunity?"

"You make it sound like this is a once-in-a-lifetime break. We're talking about sleeping with my boss. As tempting as it may be, I'm not going to do it."

"Don't come crying to me when you're back here in the suffocating smog and soot and you're all regretful and sad that you didn't get naked and ride the cowboy."

"Stop being disgusting."

"How hot is he, anyway?"

"You've never seen anything like it in Chicago."

"Really?"

"Really."

"Aww...come on. Do it for me," she urges.

"No."

"Girl, I'm living my life through you. You need to do something worthwhile for once. Just have some spontaneous, passionate sex then act like it never happened. You won't get attached and neither will he. We all do it."

"Jesse, you're engaged." I laugh.

"I lived it up in my glory days," she defends. "Don't judge."

"I wouldn't dare. Anyway, I have to go and take care of Thunder now. Lars is expecting to meet me in the barns soon."

"At least think about it," she says persuasively.

"Okay, I will."

"That's my girl. Bye, Cass. Much love."

"I love you, Jesse."

I end the call, spring to my feet, and gather up all the wrappers from my bed. It's already quarter past nine and I need to be in the barns by nine-thirty, but I've already eaten, showered, dressed, and talked to Jesse.

I wave goodbye to Emma Jean and make my way down the hill toward the barn. I expect to be alone for a while before Lars joins me, but my expectations are crushed again when I find Butch is waiting inside for me. Does this mean that Lars is planning on blowing me off again? I shudder with barely contained rage and strut into the barn with a scowl.

Fine, I'll learn to ride Thunder without him.

TWENTY-SEVEN
Lars

I stand at the window of my office and watch as Tamara gently strokes Thunder's head and talks to him in a low voice. He rubs his head affectionately against her. Gently, she leads him to the ring. She has an unexpected and completely natural gift when it comes to animals. I've always been a good judge of character, and every fiber of my being tells me that her bitchy façade is a hoax. She's someone else entirely, but why on earth would she hide her true personality when it is so beautiful and appealing?

It's incredible to think that she came here a little under two weeks ago. Feels as if she's turned the place upside down, and not in the way I imagined either. All the men are fuckin' half in love with her, and Emma Jean gives me looks blacker than the inside of a cow if I say anything about her that is not a downright glowing compliment.

I watch her saddle Thunder the way I taught her.

"Good girl," I find myself whispering.

Then she mounts him. Her right leg is clumsy. Automatically, I hold my breath and silently pray that she doesn't make any sudden moves that spook Thunder. Me praying? That's a laugh.

Thunder stays still.

I sigh with relief when I see the happy grin on her face once she's seated firmly on top of him. She says something to Butch, but I can't make the words out. He raises his clenched fist high into the air to signal victory and she laughs. The musical sound wafts over to me.

I can't help but slide my gaze down her body. It's one helluva bod. That small and perky ass trapped inside tight jeans, and those breasts. They're not huge, but they aren't small by any means. I remember seeing a photograph of her in a magazine a few years ago, and I could've sworn they were much bigger. Very much bigger. Maybe she's had the implants out. What I see now is a sight for sore eyes.

Round, full, ripe.

With the tip of her tongue slightly extended, she gives her total concentration to riding Thunder. Watching her becomes my entire world. It's amazing how a single person can be so damned beautiful. She's beyond beautiful. It hurts when a nasty voice in my head reminds me that all that buttercup and honey real estate I'm gawking at ain't for me.

Her life is in LA.

She completes a circle and waves to Butch. He does the chicken dance and she laughs joyfully. Their obvious closeness irritates me. My gut burns with possessive fury. As if she's mine.

How did a fucking scrawny kid like him get closer to her than me?

Fuck, I picked him deliberately, knowing that he isn't exactly popular with women. With jealous, lustful eyes, I watch her stop Thunder next to Butch. The stallion stays calm, even though it is near a man, which surprises me. She has tamed him. She has actually tamed Thunder. She slides off the horse and they hug and dance around like a couple of idiots. I can't even watch. I turn away and take a deep breath. I remind myself that she was never mine to begin with, which angers me even more.

Even though I try not to, I can't help swiveling back to look. To my immense relief, they are no longer joined and are just standing two feet apart talking. I watch her get back on Thunder before I leave the window and exit the room. I know if I stay, I'll end up doing or saying something I'll regret later. When I'm around her, I don't seem to have even the sense God gave a damned goose. I told her that I'd leave her alone from here on out, but I know I can't honor the agreement.

I can't seem to stay away from her.

As I walk back to my truck, Matt calls me on my cellphone.

"How's the dick rider?" he asks.

I feel something tighten in my chest. I don't want Matt to be disrespectful about her. "She's riding Thunder as we speak," I say to divert the conversation in a different direction.

"Whoa. Can you run that by me again? What the actual fuck do you mean she's riding Thunder?"

I smile. "She's sitting on Thunder and Thunder is moving."

"You'd better be kidding me."

"Nope."

"What the fuck, Lars?" my brother swears. "Do you want a dead celebrity on your hands? Her old man will have a heart attack if he knew we put her on that bone breaker."

"Calm down. Tamara figured out that Thunder will only accept females." I think of Butch. "And it seems, feminine men too."

"Right, that makes perfect sense, but I still can't believe you risked it."

"It wasn't much of a risk. Thunder took to her instantly, and she's got natural talent with horses. She'll be okay. Besides, I've asked one of the guys to keep an eye on her while she practices."

"You did what?"

"Just to make sure no harm comes to her. We don't want old Honeywell breathing down our necks, right?"

"Right. Great move, bro."

"I'm on my way out. Call you later?"

I end my call and walk to my truck parked not far from the barns. The first thing I do when I jump inside is to look in my rearview mirror. I see Thunder trotting around the field with Tamara seated straight and firm on his back. I've seen so many women ride horses, but Tamara is the second person who looks as if she belongs on the horse. As if the horse is an extension of her. The first person was Catherine.

My phone buzzes in my pocket and I pull it out and look at the caller ID. "Sophia," I greet with a small smile. I put my truck into drive.

"What's going on?" my sister asks.

"What do you mean?"

"Don't play dumb with me. Who is she?" Sophia asks. I can't understand how she has determined that there is a girl in the picture from a single word.

"No, seriously. What are you talking about?" I insist.

"Lars, you've lost two trainers in like two weeks, and you haven't called me to help with Thunder once. Thunder doesn't take well to anybody, and I know you didn't hire someone new to work with him. And just now, when you answered the phone, you had a lilt to your voice. You better tell me. I'm not asking you again, Bubba."

I scowl at the nickname. "There's nothing to tell because there's nothing between us," I growl.

"Us?"

"You're making wild assumptions again. There is no us. She's just here for a month then she's gone."

"Did you do that thing where you treated her like she was an inconvenience just by existing? Because you always do that when you don't know how to act."

I despise how well my sister knows me. "That may be why she hates my guts," I admit.

"Oh, Lars. Ask her to dinner and bring her flowers. If she absolutely hates you, she'll laugh in your face and turn you down. If you have a chance, she'll accept. So, what's she like?" Sophia asks.

Beautiful, smart, caring. "It's Honeywell's daughter."

For a few seconds my chatterbox sister is struck dumb. "Which Honeywell?" she asks cautiously, even though she knows exactly which Honeywell.

"The Honeywell you're thinking of."

"Oh, my God! No. What are you thinking, Lars?"

I smile to myself. "What happened to ask her to dinner and bring her flowers."

"That was before I knew it was Tamara. She's horrible."

I stop smiling. "Look, I gotta go."

"Fine, but this conversation is not over," she says seriously.

TWENTY-EIGHT
Cass

"**H**ell, Tamara, what the fuck are you doing to me,'

he growls, his eyes shimmering with a bright supernatural hue like a wolf's.

The last time he said those words, he walked away from me, but now he grabs my face in his hands and swoops down on my mouth. My heart stops beating. The kiss is rough and possessive, like a man claiming his woman. My whole body starts humming as dormant desires wake up and an insistent throbbing begins between my legs.

My fingers slip into the waistband of his jeans. His skin is like warm silk. I feel the round metal button cool against my thumb. Deftly, I slip the button out of its eye.

I use both hands to drag his jeans down and I feel his shaft, so hard and ready for me.

"Oh, Lars," I whisper, "I've wanted you for so long."

He grasps my button up shirt at the front opening and rips it in two. Buttons fly and ping against the wall. My shirt hangs open as his hungry eyes devour my body. He reaches behind and works the fastening of my bra. He flips the straps and it falls to the ground with a soft whisper.

"Jesus, you're exactly how I dreamed you would be,' he says, his big manly hands cupping my breasts.

Then we both hear this odd buzzing sound.

"Just ignore it," I groan.

"What is it, though?" he asks, his voice curious.

The noise gets louder and louder, and I suddenly wake up. It was only a dream. Disorientated, I look in the direction of the noise. My phone is vibrating against the nightstand. For a second, I do nothing. Remnants of the dream still cling to me. It felt so real. I take a deep breath, hit the light switch, and press the green circle on my phone. Tamara's tanned face flickers onto my screen.

"Hi," she says brightly. She is sitting on a black leather chair wrapped in a fluffy white bathrobe with a towel tied like a turban around her head. A dark-skinned woman seems to be doing something to her. I can see her head and a bit of her face bobbing at the bottom of the screen. She is obviously getting a pedicure or a foot massage.

"Hello, Tamara," I say, rubbing my eyes.

"You look sleepy. What time is it over there?"

"It's 1:30 in the morning here." I keep my voice neutral and completely devoid of the intense irritation I feel.

"Have you learned to ride yet?"

"Yeah."

"Oh good. Has everybody there seen you riding?" she asks eagerly.

"Uh...not yet. Only Butch."

"Butch? I thought your trainer was someone else."

"Ah…well. Lars didn't have the time."

She frowns. "A mere trainer didn't have the time for me?"

For crying out loud. She is insulted because someone didn't drop everything to put her needs first. "It's not that he didn't have the time. We kind of fell out and I decided to practice on my own with just Butch to watch over me."

"You fell out?"

"It's a long story."

She rocks her butt as if she is settling in for a good story. "You better tell me everything then. Because I don't want to trip up and say the wrong thing to the wrong person when I get there."

Me and my big mouth. God, why did I ever mention Lars? "It's actually nothing. I wanted to ride a particular horse, but he thought the horse was too wild."

Her eyes become saucers.

"It all worked out in the end," I say quickly. "He was wrong because the horse was fine with me."

"Oh, my fucking God. He's on your *To Bang* list, isn't he?"

Every vestige of sleep deserts me, and I feel a shaft of unease go right through me. "What?"

"Don't worry, you can tell me everything. I'm no prude. I love sex," she says in an overly saccharine tone.

"No, no. You're completely wrong. I don't think of him like that at all."

"Yes, you do. You've gone all red," she cries triumphantly.

"Tamara, it's not what you think. We're just friends who—"

"—Have fallen out," she interrupts slyly.

"I—"

"—Send me a photo of him," she orders bossily.

I clear my throat. "You want me to take a photo of him and send it to you?"

"Exactly."

I swing my legs to the floor. "Why?"

It seemed like a reasonable thing to ask, but it sends her into a frenzy. I mean, she totally loses it. She goes

164

ballistic. It's the most incredible thing how she can go from normal to this ranting and raving monster. Her hands fly out and smack that poor woman crouched at her feet. The woman screams and I hear a clatter as if she has fallen to the floor. Frozen with horror, I stare open-mouthed as she curses me for daring to question her order.

"Okay, okay. I'll take a photo," I cry, recovering from the shock of seeing her incredible transformation.

"You better," she screams furiously, and breaks the connection.

I stare at the blank screen. Wow! That was unbelievable. No wonder her staff is terrified of her. I put the phone down and lie back down, but I'm wide awake now. My sleep is completely ruined.

Why would she want a photo of Lars? It can't be just curiosity. Just because she thinks I want him? The more I think about it the more I realize that she could be one of those women who will take their friends' boyfriends simply to show that they can. I stand up and pace the floor uneasily.

I *don't* want to send a photo of Lars to her.

She'll take one look at Lars and want him for herself. I know it in my bones. I toy with the idea of sending a photo of Butch, but then I know that if anything at all goes wrong, she will try to find some way to punish me financially.

Anyway, it's not like Lars belongs to me.

I suddenly remember my dream and goosebumps scatter across my skin. I stand at the window and stare out into the night, wishing I had never mentioned Lars to her. At traumatic times like this, the only thing that can make me feel better is ice cream.

TWENTY-NINE
Cass

Barefoot and in my pajamas, I pad out of my room and head toward the kitchen. Everybody is asleep and the house is still and quiet. I switch on the light, get ice cream from the freezer, sit down, and slip a spoonful into my mouth.

Chunky Monkey ice cream.

Yes.

A big middle finger to Tamara and her lawyers and Lars and the whole world. Except of course for Jesse, Dad, Thunder, my mom, wherever she is. And Emma Jean too. And Butch. He's a sweet guy. Well, maybe Chance as well. Okay, make it all the animals in the barn. Might as well include all the animals in the world. They're innocent too.

I take another spoonful and hear a noise.

I turn my head toward the door, and sweet Jesus! Lars is standing there in a pair of old jeans and a white T-shirt; exactly the way he was dressed in my dream.

"Couldn't sleep, huh?" he says.

I shake my head.

He nods and, coming into the room, takes a spoon from a drawer and then sits opposite me. I give the ice cream tub a push and he catches it as it slides toward him.

"What's bugging you?" he asks, digging into the ice cream.

"Nothing."

"Don't ever play poker. You'll lose your shirt." He looks up at me. "Although, that would be a sight."

My eyebrows rise. "Are you flirting with me?"

He slides the ice cream back toward me. "Isn't that obvious?"

I catch the carton and frown. "What's bugging you?"

He pulls a clean spoon out of his mouth. "Nothing,"

I fill my spoon with ice cream, push the carton toward him, and say, "You should stay away from the poker tables too."

"I'm actually a very good poker player."

I catch the tub that he passes back to me. "Are you saying I shouldn't trust you?"

He grins, a wolfish, totally feral grin. "I wouldn't trust any man with you, let alone me."

Suddenly, the air in the room becomes thick. Confused and certain that we are talking about two totally different subjects, I gulp the ice cream in my mouth and blurt out, "I rode Thunder today."

"I know. I saw you."

I'm so shocked, I almost don't catch the tub barreling toward me. "You did?'

He looks at me strangely and nods.

"Where were you?"

"In the study. I was wrong. You did very well."

My cheeks heat up with pleasure." I did do well, didn't I?"

"Yup, you're good with him. He'll miss you when you're gone."

The atmosphere in the room changes again; fills with tension. He stares at me, his eyes like molten silver, his body rigid. I want to smile or say something, but I can't move a muscle. He is like a magnet...or Dracula. Then he blinks and I look down into the ice cream tub. What the hell is going on here?

"You've set a record," he says softly.

I dig into the ice cream. "For what?"

"You've gone nearly ten minutes without insulting me."

I look at his smug expression and act instinctively. I flick the ice cream on my spoon in his direction. Bingo. It smacks him on the nose.

I can't believe my aim is so accurate. He looks so shocked I start laughing and can't stop. I clutch my belly and bend with laughter. He gets up and starts to come around to my side, but I am up on my feet and running. I run to the other side of the table and face him, still laughing but wary. He tries to chase me, but I am super-fast. We do two circles around the table. Once he changes direction, but I was prepared for it, and he gained not one inch on me.

"I'm sorry," I say.

"I might believe it if you said it without cackling like a witch."

That makes me laugh even harder.

He rips a couple of pieces of paper towel and holds them out to me. "Show me you're sorry by cleaning up your mess."

I lick my lips. All my laughter is gone. Like a robot, I walk toward him. A foot away from him, I take the bunched-up wad in his hand and lift it toward his face. He catches my wrist halfway and pulls me toward him. I look into his eyes. Oh, my God, he's going to kiss me. Just like in my dream.

Suddenly, his eyes narrow.

"What?' I whisper.

"Your eyes are green."

It's like a slap in my face. I feel my blood draining down to my toes. Oh, crap. What the hell am I up to? It's that time of the night when men want some easy sex, and I've fallen right into it like a complete fool? I can't believe I'm that stupid. Not after I just witnessed how batshit crazy Tamara really is.

I could have ruined everything just because Lars woke up wanting to get his dick wet. I blink as the horror of what would happen if I am unmasked hits my lust induced brain. Mrs. Carter has paid my dad's hospital bills on good faith that I will complete this job successfully. Dangerous loan sharks are circling and I'm thinking about sex.

"Yeah," I say as casually as I can. "My eyes turn color when I'm tired, or I don't get enough sleep." I force a smile onto my lips. "And that must be my cue to go back to bed." I tug my arm out of his grip. "Goodnight, Lars."

He doesn't say anything, just watches me with a strange expression on his face. My body feels stiff and I know my movements are robotic, but I make myself walk away without turning back. When I get to my room, I close the door and lean against it.

That was a lucky escape, Cass. Don't ever put yourself in that kind of situation again.

THIRTY
Lars

I open her bedroom door softly and in the shaft of light from the kitchen behind me, I see her asleep in her bed. Quietly, I walk to the side. For a few seconds, I don't do anything. I can't. I just stare at her. In sleep, with her blonde hair spread out around her, she is like an angel. This moment when I found her asleep is precious beyond words, and my mind takes a picture of it. For later. For when I am old and sitting on my porch smoking my pipe.

I reach down and gently shake her arm. "Tamara," I call softly.

"Daddy," she mumbles in her sleep.

That moment of vulnerability makes something inside me shift, and I feel as if I could give my life up for this beauty. I long to stroke her silky golden hair.

"Wake up, Tamara," I say.

She opens her eyes and for an instant, she smiles at me. An open, childlike, innocent smile. Totally without guile. "Lars," she whispers.

I stare at her. How different it would be if this sweet creature was the real her, but as I watch, a veil comes into her eyes and she jerks back.

"What are you doing in my bedroom?"

"Bessie is in labor and Emma Jean said you wanted to see a foal being born. Do you still want to?"

Her eyes widen with surprise. "Yes," she says nodding her head. "Yes, I do."

"Okay, get ready and join me in the kitchen."

I go into the kitchen and stand by the table. My heart is pounding in my chest. There is a saying around these parts. *Don't go in if you don't know the way out.* I don't know what's happening to me. I've never wanted a woman so badly in my life. I thought it was just lust, but it is more. So much more.

"I'm ready," she says from behind me.

I whirl around. She is dressed in a plain blue sweatshirt and black jeans. Her hair has not been combed and it makes my fingers itch to run through it, fist it, and turn her face up to mine.

"Come on," I say, picking up the lantern from the kitchen table.

We walk quickly out of the house into the darkness of the night. The night air is cool and we go quickly toward the barn. I don't switch on any of the lights to avoid disturbing the other horses. I lead Tamara to the stall thickly laid with hay. It is larger than all the others and designed to give a laboring mother plenty of room to move around. I've already tied her tail and she is pawing the ground restlessly. A gust of wind slams against the side of the barn, but inside the stall, the world is warm and humid.

"How do you know she's ready?" Tamara whispers.

"I've been watching her all night."

"You've been up all night."

"Yup."

The lantern casts a gentle glow over the mare's smooth, tan hide. She snorts and tosses her head then slowly comes to a stop. Painfully, she lowers herself to the straw and rolls onto her side, breathing hard, her big belly rising in the light.

It's almost time.

I point to the milking stool at the corner of the stall and Tamara goes and sits on it. She pulls her knees up to her chin and stares at the mare with wide eyes. I know she's trying to play it cool, but inside she must be quaking with the same something I felt when I saw my first foal being born. It's a blend of discovery, fear, joy, and worry, all rolled into an emotion so sharp and strong, it stings your eyes.

I sit back on my heels and watch as the mare turns this way and that, her restless hooves kicking through the hay. She huffs hard through her nose, lifts her huge head, and looks first at Tamara, then me, before she lays back down with a soft groan. Her sides heave with the effort of breathing, and her belly is hard as she bears down, preparing to bring her foal into the world.

"Is the baby coming?" Tamara asks, her voice hushed.

"Nearly. It won't be long now."

"Have you seen many births?" Her eyes gleam wetly in the yellow light.

"Many, but the magic never dies," I tell her.

At that moment, the mare rises to her front knees and rocks back and forth, obviously in the throes of pain. She gets back down on the straw and lies on her side. This time, she pushes long and hard. Suddenly, a bulge appears between her legs and then it is gone. Liquid seeps out.

"Come. You can see it better from here," I whisper.

Tamara creeps from the stool to sit on her knees next to me. I look over to her and our eyes meet. For a long, excruciating moment, our gazes remain locked. I take a deep breath and it hurts deep at the bottom of my lungs, just as if I'd sucked in a cold blast of mountain air.

Our gaze breaks when the mare kicks at the straw and rolls. This time, the bulge takes more shape. Little hooves wrapped in a white sac appear. I stare intently, ready to jump in and help if necessary. I had to help Bessie once before. I hope I won't have to again. Tamara creeps closer still.

"What can I do?" she whispers.

"Nothing. Just watch. We'll intervene if things don't go smoothly." We stand guard as the mare pushes again with a long drawn out sigh, this time revealing not only tiny hooves but the nose of her foal as well.

"Oh, my God," Tamara squeals, her hand clasped over her mouth.

Another gust of wind rattles the old barn. I settle on my knees, a little bit closer to the mare. I look at Tamara and tears are slipping down her face.

"Why are you crying?" I ask, making my way to her side

"She's in pain and I can't do anything to help her. Can she even do this on her own?" She sniffs, wiping her tears with the sleeves of her sweatshirt.

I stare at her in amazement. It never crossed my mind that she could feel so much for another creature. How I longed to take her in my arms and comfort her.

"She has to do this part on her own," I say softly.

She hugs herself. "She's hurting though."

"Giving birth hurts, but she's done it before. It shouldn't take her too long this time."

Tamara nods and tries to creep even closer to the mare, but I reach out to her.

"Come back here with me. She might kick out and you could get hurt. Give her plenty of room."

We sit side-by-side against the wall, watching the mare as she labors to bring her baby into the world. She pushes, then pauses, then pushes again. Each time she pushes the baby a little further out.

"Does it always take this long?" Tamara asks.

"It's only been fifteen minutes," I tell her.

"It feels like hours."

Finally, the baby's head pops out of the birth canal so suddenly that Tamara gasps. I grin at her.

The mare rests for a bit then pushes again. A sudden gush of red liquid soaks the straw underneath the mare, and the foal begins to slide out, covered in a glistening sac. There's a small popping sound and the sac rips away. There is nothing left inside but the foal's hind legs. Bessie lays her head down as if she is done.

The foal lies on the ground, lifeless. I wait for a moment then pick up a piece of straw and gently poke at the baby's head.

"What are you doing?" Tamara cries, her face a mask of fury. I know what she feels. She is overwhelmed with the need to protect the new baby. She thinks I'm messing with the miracle in front of us.

"I'm making him breathe," I explain as I tickle the baby's nostrils with the straw.

The foal suddenly heaves, his whole body shaking as he coughs the tiniest cough imaginable, then his chest rises with a small breath. The second breath is much bigger and a moment after that, the mare pushes one last time and the little one is free.

The foal lifts its head, lays it back down, then tries again.

Tears run completely unheeded down Tamara's face. I look at the city girl, the painted butterfly who has spent her entire empty life fluttering about in the glare of the media, and all I want to do is wipe away those tears and never let her go again.

I reach out and take her hand.

A spark of static electricity shoots up my arm, heightening everything that is already coursing through my mind. She feels it too, because she jumps. Then she grips my hand hard and together we watch as the foal begins his clumsy journey of standing on his own legs. For almost ten minutes he flops around, trying out his spindly legs, failing, and trying again. Finally, when his exhausted mother reaches her nose out to him, it is as if he takes strength from her. This time when he stands, he stays up.

"It's the most beautiful thing I've ever seen," Tamara murmurs.

"Yes, it is," I agree, but I wasn't talking about just the foal.

Her cheeks become pink with confusion. "I like it here at the ranch," she whispers. "I like everything about it, but I especially like the way it smells. It's so crisp and clean that it almost hurts my lungs when I take a deep breath."

Then she holds her breath, because she's opened the door to her heart the tiniest little bit, just enough to let in a sliver of light, and if I throw it back in her face, she will slam it shut forever.

For the longest time, there is silence because I can't find the words. For the first time in my life, I'm at loss for words. "I was going to ask you on a date. I mean, it doesn't have to be formal if you don't want it to be. It can be an apology or an actual date. It's up to you." Fuck, I sure messed that one up.

The horse neighs loudly and she jumps back and almost hits the foal. I shoot a hand out and catch her by the wrist and pull her toward me. She slams into my body.

"I'll go on a date with you," she says, her body molded to mine.

I smile. "Good."

"So you don't hate me?" The unguarded words tumble out of her mouth. Her lashes sweep down and she looks up at me through them.

"I never did."

"I don't hate you either," she says, a small smile trembling on her lips.

THIRTY-ONE
Cass

I thought hell would freeze over before I received a day off work at the ranch, but I was wrong. It's well past four in the morning before we leave the mother and her new foal, so Lars offers me a day off.

I try to go to sleep for a couple of hours, but I am too excited. After fifteen minutes of tossing and turning, I hurriedly get dressed and run back to the barn. I spend most of the day gawking at the new baby. He is so cute and sweet, I can't stop kissing him and petting him. Bessie puts up with me while I take hundreds of photos of her.

Under the guise of taking photos of the horses, I also surreptitiously manage to take a few of Lars. I'm hoping there will one or two bad ones of him, but he looks awesome in every single shot. I send Tamara the one where the shadow of his hat makes his eyes look like they're not piercing, but kind of dull. Even so, you can see that his shoulders are strong, his hands broad and powerful, and his jaw chiseled. As I gaze at the photo, my heart swells high and tight. Everything about him draws me in a way that nothing else ever has. I say a little prayer and hope that Tamara will not be interested in him.

I spend an hour with Thunder in the yard before I go back to my living quarters and have a shower. It's about seven when I open my suitcase and look through the stuff that I am supposed to wear if I go out anywhere as Tamara Honeywell. Tamara's wardrobe is not something I would ever be comfortable in, but I'll have to tough it out tonight.

I separate the clothes into three piles—tolerable, unacceptable, and absolutely not. Sixty percent of the clothes fall into the absolutely not range and the rest fall into the unacceptable pile. Only a few low-cut tops make it into the tolerable pile, but none of them are worthy of being worn on a proper date.

I look at the clock and get a shock. I never realized how much time I've wasted strutting around my room in a bra and an uncomfortable thong trying to figure out what to wear. I quickly put on some make-up. I know I'm supposed to pile it on, but I don't. Tonight, I want to look as fabulous as I can for Lars. Then I turn back to the pile of clothes and groan. I just can't bring myself to dress in my Tamara-approved gear. Not tonight. I don't want him to look at me and think *city slut*.

In a moment of pure weakness, I FaceTime Jesse. Jesse can put together three rags and make it look like it came from a fashion runway. She picks up, looking flustered, so I look at the background of the frame. Before I can speak, she says, "Hey. Just give me a moment," and starts moving out of the room she is in.

As soon as she is in another room, she grins. "Howdy, partner. You're wearing make-up. What's going on?"

"I'm going on a date with Lars."

She shrieks loudly.

I ignore her and carry on. "And I need help picking an outfit. I have a suitcase crammed full of expensive clothes, but I can't wear any of it."

"Back up. Back up," she says. "I need more details. What kind of date is this? Where is he taking you? Will you get a little action afterward?"

"It's just a first date. I don't know where he's taking me. Nothing will be happening after," I say, but I don't know if I'm being entirely truthful with the last statement. Do I want something to happen?

"Then why are you wearing sexy underwear?"

"Look, can you save the interrogation for later. I only have," I look at the clock once again, "fifteen minutes and I need your expert help."

"Okay, flip the camera."

I do as she asks and place the camera on a pile of clothing. I avoid the dangerously inappropriate pile and show Jesse the other two.

"Nope, nope, nope," she mumbles, rejecting each garment that I lay down on the bed. She comes close to the camera. "I see a third pile. Let me see that," she demands.

I know not to argue with her, as I turn the camera to the pile of clothes that I planned to never wear.

"That's the one," she says triumphantly. "Grab that yellow belly shirt."

"I thought you told me never to wear yellow?" I say, not reaching for the top. Besides it's not a typical belly shirt. It is full of artfully placed holes throughout the fabric.

"That was before you became all lovely and tanned. Yellow is a fantastic color for you now. Isn't it scalding hot in Montana right now? A belly shirt will be tactical and cute. You can wear it with the black mini skirt."

I wince. "The top has holes all through it," I state.

"Your point?"

"People, country people, will be able to see my boobs," I say, looking at the yellow top doubtfully.

"You're wearing a bra, aren't you?"

"But—"

"No, buts. You'll never see those country people again. It will get him going."

"I don't want to get him going," I argue.

"Lie to yourself all you want, but don't lie to me, Cass. You know and I know you want to get him going."

"I called you for fashion advice," I remind.

"The tummy top is my advice," she says firmly.

"Please, just choose something else," I plead, flipping the camera back to my face.

She pouts. "Fine, go with the blue halter top and the black miniskirt. That's my final decision. Take it or leave it. I've got to go. Guests. Call me tomorrow and tell me how hard you rode him. Much love!" Jesse makes loud kissing noises and hangs up.

I survey my three options: wear what she suggested, wear something that I choose on my own, or wear the sundress again. Lars has already seen me in the sundress, and I don't have the time to press it, anyway. Option two really isn't an option since I have about ten minutes left and no other ideas.

That leaves option one. It looks like I'll be wearing a halter top on my date with Lars.

With that thought, a knock echoes through my room. I didn't anticipate him being early, but I should have known.

"Tamara, are you about ready?"

"Nearly," I call back. Throwing my clothes on quickly, I go to my door.

THIRTY-TWO
Cass

I open the door and come face to face with…

Whoa! Oh boy, oh boy. My eyes widen.

Gone are the mud-stained jeans, the worn shirts, and the dusty hats. He looks dangerously—no, make that mind-blowingly—dazzling in a silky black shirt open at the throat; a pair of low-cut, made-to-fit-at-the-hips, ultra-sexy, black jeans; a tan hat, and black cowboy boots.

"Hello," he says, his eyes stuck to my skimpy outfit.

"Um…uh…I can go change. I didn't realize we were going somewhere so gorgeous…oh…I mean…so formal," I say, waving my hands around and trying to hide how flustered I am by his appearance.

"No, you're wearing that," he growls.

My eyebrows fly up at his tone.

He looks down at me, a possessive, dominant expression etched into his handsome, sensual face, and something happens between my legs. "Okay," I whisper. My lips are suddenly dry and I lick them. His eyes become focused on my mouth. The mood changes as strange vibes surround us.

His expression suddenly changes. "Shall we?" he asks thickly.

I blink. What? What the hell just happened? Is he angry? Why? All I did was open my bedroom door.

Dumbfounded by the sudden change in his behavior, I nod. Immediately, he starts taking big strides away from me. I tilt my head and watch as he puts as much distance between us as quickly as he can. Okay. This is obviously going to go down as one very strange date. And there's Jesse expecting me to tell her how good the sex was.

Lars opens the front door and stands beside it, his back tense. "Ladies first," he says, motioning for me to go forward.

I stop next to him for a few seconds, then shaking my head, I obey him in a rush. I get to the car, wrench open the passenger door before he can reach the truck, scramble in, and slam the door shut. I'm furious. I swear I don't understand him at all. I did nothing wrong, but he's angry again. Roughly, I pull my short skirt down as low on my thighs as I can before he jumps into the driver's seat.

It is then that I notice that the interior of the truck looks freshly cleaned. It also smells of lemons. Compared to the mud-stained seats I saw yesterday, it's a nice change, and it makes me aware that he did make an effort after all.

"Did you clean your truck?" I ask with a smirk.

"It needed it," he responds tersely.

That's it. I've had it. I angle my body toward him. "Come on. Out with it."

He frowns. "Out with what?"

"You're angry with me. Just spit it out. There's no point going out on a date like this?"

He looks startled. "You think I'm angry with you?" he asks incredulously.

"Aren't you?"

"Tamara, where did you get your reputation as a man-eater from?" he asks, shaking his head in wonder.

"What?"

"You seem to have no clue about men and what they're thinking or feeling."

"What do you mean?"

"Forget it. I'm not angry. With you or anyone else. I was just…thinking of something else." He forces his stiff shoulders to relax and smiles at me. "I'm sorry. You didn't do anything wrong. I'm just a big fool who wants to drag you off to my bed. Let's just have a nice dinner, okay?"

Desire stirs low in my belly. He wants to drag me off to his bed? How caveman. How hot. He smiles at me. Oh God, that lower lip. I could suck it into my mouth. Thank God, people can't read minds. I return the smile. "Okay. Where are we going?"

"You'll see," he says.

He switches on the radio. I stare out at the scenic landscape while country music plays in the background. Periodically, I notice him glancing at me from the corner of his eye. Sometimes, our eyes catch and I blush like a schoolgirl. His eyes dart away as if he's shy or awkward. God, how can someone be so adorable while being robust and masculine at the same time?

We drive through a town and I gaze at the old-fashioned buildings. Nearly an hour later, we stop at a quaint establishment surrounded by an empty parking lot.

"Is this it?" I ask, looking around me curiously.

"This is it."

I grin at him. "It's really cute."

He smiles, jumps out of the truck, and is around to my side before I have a chance to open my door. I hold onto his hand and get out of the truck.

"I know you're used to bigger and fancier restaurants, but this is the best one in these parts, so I hope it will do," he says.

"It will make a nice change to what I'm used to," I say and I'm not lying. I've never been to a fancy restaurant in my life or one outside Chicago, so this is very different and special.

I follow him through the doors and the delectable scent of meat barbecuing assaults my nose. I can almost decipher which meats are being cooked at the time, and I can barely contain my excitement. Would Tamara appreciate being brought to a steakhouse? Probably not, but I feel almost sick with happiness at being in this warm, rustic place with Lars.

I can tell Lars is trying to gauge my reaction as we walk through the joint, so I allow my expressions to show on my face—my fascination with the lovely scents, my love for the open brickwork, the wild west decor, the cowboy memorabilia, and my pure delight in being out on a date with such a magnificent man.

We are shown to a candlelit corner seat by a very friendly woman who addresses Lars by name, and though her eyes do slide down my body in surprise, she calls me honey and her smile is genuine enough. While we are looking at the menu, she brings us beers.

Lars orders a burger, but I restrain myself from ordering the largest, juiciest burger on the menu and ask for a strip of grilled chicken instead. I've never been a fan of grilled chicken, but old habits die hard. Even as the waitress is taking the menus away, I start to feel the first pang of regret. I should have gotten the bison burger. I push the regret aside and let myself be drawn into a conversation about the new foal until the food arrives.

"What's on your mind?" Lars asks, chewing his first bite.

"Nothing," I say with a polite smile. Since when do I hold my tongue?

He doesn't respond immediately and I continue to look at my dry, unappealing chicken. My attention jerks back in his direction when his beer bottle settles with a firm thud on the table in front of me.

"You have always been open and blunt about what's on your mind. You're looking at your chicken as if the damn thing's been dipped in a toilet. You're eyeing my burger as if you'd like to murder it, I'm sitting here watching all kinds of unpleasant thoughts swim across your eyes, and you're telling me nothing's wrong," he exclaims.

Obviously, I can't tell him I didn't order the burger because it was twenty bucks, and it was force of habit that made me choose the cheapest thing on the menu. "You're right," I say, peeling my crop top away from my stomach. "I hate grilled chicken. Your burger looks amazing, and I wish I had ordered that instead."

He opens his mouth to comment, but I don't stop there. I've held my tongue all night and I'd like to discuss some of my issues. "And another thing is bugging me. You never specified if this was a date or an apology, so I don't quite know how to behave."

"I've already apologized. This is a date, so feel free to behave like you're on one."

I nod slowly.

Lars shoves his plate across the table, takes mine, and puts it in front of him. Now, instead of chicken I have almost all of a juicy burger at my disposal. He takes a bite of my chicken and chews it slowly, pretending that it isn't one of the blandest things he's ever eaten.

I laugh. "You're a pretty cool dude when you aren't being a pig, you know. Here," I say, cutting the burger in half and giving him the larger half.

He lifts his hand and the waitress comes back. "Can we have another burger, please?"

As soon as she walks away, Lars turns to me. "Actually, you've surprised me. I expected you to have dry chicken and salad. Isn't that what most celebrities in LA exist on?"

I shrug. "I guess I'm different."

"And that, Tamara Honeywell, is exactly why I like you."

And with those words, my spirit feels crushed. I wonder if he will still like me if he knows that I'm not a millionaire heiress. That my name is Cass Harper and I'm in debt to the tune of thousands of dollars.

I've got the lemons. I don't know where to find the sugar, water, and a stand.

THIRTY-THREE
Cass

Dinner is long finished and our dessert, wild huckleberry swoon fudge pie and white chocolate sauce with two spoons, arrives. The restaurant closes in an hour and I know we'll be leaving soon, but I don't want the night to end. The wine, the candles, and the good food have done the trick, and for the first time, Lars and I have been relaxed with each other.

Of course, it is not a perfect night. He tells me about his brother Matt, his sister Sophia, and his parents, but I am constantly forced to pepper all my stories with lies. The other thing that bugs me is when he occasionally uses Tamara's name to address me. It reminds me that none of this is real. It's not Lars and Cass, but Lars and Tamara, the spoiled celebrity with enormous boobs and a bad attitude.

"Am I going to start, or are you?" I ask.

"It may be poisoned. You go first."

"Careful. I might start to think you don't like me very much," I retort as I take a spoonful of my pie. Wow! I nearly moan.

"That good?" Lars asks, that odd look back in his eyes.

I swallow the delicious concoction and nod. "I'm practically dying with happiness."

He grins.

I dig my spoon into my gooey dessert and take it toward his mouth. He opens it and the spoon slips between those sensuous lips. His gaze never leaves mine. I withdraw my spoon. Something strange is happening inside my body. Breathlessly, I watch his eyes darken. My spoon clatters back on my plate.

"Your turn," he says.

He brings a spoonful of pie and ice cream toward my face. I open my mouth and I think he does it on purpose; the spoon misses my lips slightly so some of the ice cream smears around my lips. Before I can lick it back into my mouth, his fingers are on my face, tracing the ice cream, pushing it into my mouth, lingering on my lips.

This time I can't help it. A moan escapes. Slowly, he takes his fingers to his mouth and sucks them. I stare open-mouthed. It must have only been seconds, but it seems like time has stopped and we are just staring at each other hungrily. Then the waitress comes to ask if everything is fine and I snap out of my trance. He says something, but I am so flustered I don't even make it out. The waitress goes away.

"Have you been up the mountain?" I ask. It's totally unrelated to anything, but it is the first thing that pops into my confused, over-heated head.

"When we were kids," Lars says, leaning back in his chair. "we used to spend our holidays up there in Dad's cabin. We were practically the only people within miles of that place. Us kids were all hardcore with our walkie-talkies that had a twenty-mile reception radius. The only rules we had were to stay out of the way of bears and mountain lions. So, we ran wild."

I laugh and shake my head. "That sounds amazing."

"It was great. And you've spent your whole life in the city?" Lars prompts.

"Yeah," I say with a smile. That, at least, is the truth. I grew up in Chicago. There were no bears or mountain lions. Just apartments, unhappy people, and crowded streets. In certain areas, I had to hold my dad's hand tightly when we went down the street.

He draws his brows together. "I've never liked cities."

"You're not the only one. This is the most beautiful place I've ever been," I say, thinking about the wide-open, lush landscape of the ranch.

"You don't have to leave, you know," Lars says quietly.

I look into his blue eyes as if they're a television screen, shining my future before me. If I stay here, I would learn to be a horse trainer, and learn to live off the land. I may one day even meet the owner of the ranch, and maybe he'll hire me. Then Lars and I might make it. Who knows what will happen if I can stay.

But I can't.

I look at the wooden table and take a deep breath. Then I look up. "I can't stay, Lars. My life is not here."

Lars's expression falls faster than I thought possible. He looks so vulnerable and hurt that I want to hold him and comfort him, and tell him...

If I'd met you any other time, I'd stay without a second thought. You're a beautiful person and this ranch is fantastic. I've learned so many things here on the ranch, and sometimes I fantasize about staying forever. About just tossing away all the things I know

189

and never going back to the city. I'd love to work here, but I can't. I have problems at home and I need to take care of my father. I'm not allowed to come back. I just want to be Cass with you, but I can't.

Of course, I don't say any of those things. I'm just building castles in the air with dreams of a life with him. I look into his hurt eyes and force myself to bite my tongue and remain silent.

"We should probably leave. It's about closing time," I murmur.

He pushes his chair back with a loud scrape and stands. I look up at him, worried that I have ruined the night, but his expression is soft. "You're right," he says far more gently than I was expecting.

I follow him and wait while he goes to pay for our meal.

We ride home in awkward silence. I try to think of something—anything—to say, but nothing comes to mind. I know I've initiated this new bad vibe, but he must know I can't stay. When we pull to a stop in the driveway, I turn to him in the hope of remedying the situation, but instead of waiting for me to speak, he throws himself out of the truck. I can only watch in distress at the way my date has flopped.

His disappointment, or possibly anger, doesn't stop him from coming around and opening my door for me. I guess at heart, he's a gentleman. I avoid his extended hand and jump down on my own. I know that his gesture is an empty formality. He'd much rather avoid touching me after what I said.

I stand beside the truck sorry that I'm not Tamara, sorry that I don't have a choice in what I do this month. It makes me feel sick to my stomach. I guess it all comes down to whether I will accept what I feel for him and allow it to last a measly month, or deny my heart what it truly craves—him.

I watch him reach to close the door and suddenly feel a flash of anger. It's not fair. No, I'm not going to let the night end this way. Why should I let us suffer? It won't matter to Tamara what I do with the ranch hand. To hell with the NDA. I'm going to trust him and tell him the truth, confess my part in it, and beg him not to ruin it for me. I grab his arm.

"Lars," I begin. "I need to tell you something-"

At that moment, my phone rings. My first thought is something has happened to my dad. He's taken a turn for the worse. Then, I look at the caller ID and the blood runs cold in my veins. It is as if the universe has spoken. *Don't be so freaking stupid.* The number has a Chicago area code, and even though I don't recognize it, I know exactly who is on the other end.

I look at up at Lars. "Sorry, but I have to take this call."

He shakes his head and begins walking away from me. It was nice while it lasted, but that's the end of me and Lars.

I turn my back on him. "Hello?"

"Where the fuck are you? And where the fuck is this week's money? You trying to swindle T-bone, little bitch?" a man's voice yells.

"I told you I had to go away. I'm working on getting the money right now. At the end of the month, you'll be paid in full," I respond, my voice shaky.

I turn slightly and notice Lars stop in his tracks and become still. It's obvious that he is trying to listen in on the conversation. I press the phone to my ear and start walking away, but the screaming at the other end of the phone deafens me and I have to hold it away from my ear. "End of the month? That's not what our agreement was," I whisper nervously. "I spoke to Fingers before I left. He agreed."

"Fingers?" he scoffs "Fingers is not in charge. You're asking for your debt to be doubled again, little girl."

"Doubled?" I cry in horror. I'll be able to afford ten thousand dollars once this job is concluded, but I was hoping to have twenty grand to help my father. If he doubles the figure, I'll only have ten grand left for my father, which will mean I can afford the medicine, but not the caretakers or house bills.

"Did you just fucking yell at me?" T-bone snarls.

"No, no," I say quickly.

"At this rate, you'll be working your debt off on your fucking back."

"I know exactly what I owe you, and I'm not agreeing to pay double for no reason," I argue. I'm trying my hardest to hold my tears at bay, but I feel so helpless. I can't even run away from this problem. If I run, they could hurt, or even kill my father. They could find me and do the same.

"You stupid bitch," the man spits. "Don't you think-

Suddenly my phone is snatched out of my hand. Lars holds the phone to his ear and gets an earful of the man ranting and raving on the other end of the phone before making his presence known.

"Listen to me, and listen good, you little shitbag. If you ever dare threaten her life again, this debt will be the least of your problems. We can work out a way to pay what she owes, but if you even think about contacting her again, I'll rain hell down on your ass," Lars says quietly.

I stare at Lars with a mixture of shock and fear. Even in his angriest moments, he has never spoken to me in such a dangerous and menacing tone. This low, controlled voice is far scarier than T-Bone's enforcer yelling threats at me. Lars almost sounds like a psychopath.

Still holding the phone to his ear, Lars glares at me before walking away. I try to follow him, but he holds up a finger and I stop. Usually, I'd argue, but in his current state, I'm unsure if I want to press the issue. I stand still and watch him go out of earshot then I cross my fingers and hope that the guy he is talking to won't address me by my name. But how likely is it that two strangers won't say my name while talking about me?

It takes less than two minutes before Lars comes back to me and hands me my phone.

"I've taken care of it. He'll never bother you again, but if he does, let me know immediately."

He's taken care of it? "What? How did you do that?"

There is something distant and cold about him. "What put you in debt with these people?" he asks softly.

"Drugs," I blurt out. It's the first thing that pops into my mind.

A light dies in his eyes.

"I borrowed money for drugs. That's part of the reason I was sent here, but I've quit now," I add quickly, but the light doesn't come back into his eyes.

"So why does he refer to you as Cass?" he asks warily, staring at me as if I've hurt or betrayed him.

"Fake name," I throw back smoothly. Lies flow from my lips far too easily, and I detest it. "Didn't want them to know who I was."

Lars looks suddenly tired. He simply nods.

"I'll pay you back," I say.

Lars closes his eyes for a second. When he opens them, they are expressionless. "Don't do anything. Just go to bed."

I open my mouth to argue.

"Please," he says between clenched teeth.

I whirl away from him, run up the steps, and through the front door. When I get into my own room, I throw myself on my bed. I can honestly say I have never felt so small, sad, or ashamed in my entire life.

THIRTY-FOUR
Cass

I shove the last bit of horse manure into a wheelbarrow and wipe the sweat from my forehead. Amazing how the smell no longer bothers me. In fact, I don't even notice it anymore, but the relentless heat wipes me out. I go and sit on a bucket beside Thunder's stall. It's so much hotter here than it ever was in Chicago, or even Los Angeles. I'm dying for a long, cool drink from the refrigerator, and a shower, but I know Lars is around and I dread going back to the house and risk bumping into him, so I stay in the humid barn in a funk of self-pity and cowardice.

The tension between Lars and me is so thick now you'd have trouble cutting it with a knife. I desperately want to diffuse it, but I don't know how to handle the situation, which is unusual for me.

I always have a plan.

Maybe there is another solution, but I'm just too tired to think clearly. I hardly slept last night. Tamara called in the early hours and disturbed my sleep again. She was extra friendly, which made me even more wary and distrustful. She asked me a bunch of personal questions about Lars, but she mostly seemed to want to know how I feel about him and if he likes me back.

I'm not stupid, so I didn't confirm her suspicions. I lied and told her I wasn't interested and neither was he. I could tell she didn't believe me, but the weird thing is, I also kind of got the impression that she saw it as a challenge and that she was plotting something.

She ended the call by reminding me that the terms of my contract mean I have to behave in a way that does not tarnish her reputation, so I am not allowed to sleep with anyone. There's no one here I want to sleep with, I told her.

"Why is this so much harder than a regular job?" I ask Thunder wearily.

Thunder snorts and looks at me as if he's contemplating my question.

I laugh. "You're a really good listener, you know."

Oh, my God, it's happened. I've finally gone mad. I'm talking to a horse as if it's my best friend. I stand, brush the dirt from my jeans, and stretch my limbs. The action makes me lean back into Misty's pin. She neighs and presses herself as close to me as possible.

Aww...I do love her. I hug her and plant a noisy kiss on her nose. We've become really close. Because she's so placid and easy going, I'm more relaxed and can learn quickly while riding her. I've practiced barrel jumps and a few other training techniques with her that I hope to use on Thunder once I've mastered them.

Giving her a last pat, I leisurely make my way toward the entrance. Halfway through, I come to a dead stop. Lars is standing at the entrance of the barn. The light is behind him and I can't see the expression on his face.

"Finished for the day?" he asks quietly.

Unable to speak, I nod.

He takes a few more steps into the barn and I see the gleam of sweat on his skin. His clothes are dusty and his hands grimy. He has obviously been working on the land.

He takes his hat off and runs his hand through his hair. Motes of dirt slide from the dark strands and fly in puffs away from him.

He scowls, looking at the fans that whirl above each of the horse's stalls. Chance told me that it's important to keep the horses cool, but even the fans are simply stirring the blistering air.

"Why is it so hot?"

"It's Montana," I say with a slight smile.

He returns my smile, which makes me feel better. Maybe it will be all right between us. "Montana's summers aren't usually one-hundred and five degrees at dusk."

"Emma Jean was telling me about a pond beside the cow pasture," I say, rubbing the sweat from my own forehead.

His eyebrows rise. "You want to swim in there?"

If he is feeling anything like me, he must be looking forward to that refreshing body of water just waiting there. "I'm game if you are."

"Sure you don't mind swimming with fish and cow manure?" he asks, watching me to gauge my reaction.

"After these past two weeks, I would be ashamed of myself if a little shit scared me away. As for swimming with fish, I can handle that." I laugh. "It's just like swimming in a lake or the ocean, right?" Not that I have ever swum in the ocean, but I took a dip in the Chicago River a few times as a kid.

His lips curve and his eyes dance mischievously. "I'm always game, cupcake."

He has no right, no goddamn right to be so gorgeous. I put out a hand. "Truce."

He covers the space between us in three strides and puts his hand into mine. Our grimy hands touch. A thrill runs up my arm and his eyes become hooded. I retract my hand as if burned.

"Let's go," he says huskily.

Outside, the sun is beginning to set, but the sky is still lit with an assortment of bright colors. The scenery is beautiful in an innocent, simple way. The field looks recently mowed and hay lays on the ground in stripes. We walk together, not touching, but every nerve in my body is vividly aware of his next to mine. As we near the pond, I see a large oak, branches sticking in every direction, growing beside it. The setting sun makes the surface of the water glimmer. The top layer is probably as hot as the air around us, but the depths will surely be cooler. I bounce a little in between my steps and halt at the water's edge.

I turn to look up at Lars. "Do we just hop in?"

He gazes into my eyes with an indecipherable expression. Then he shakes his head slowly and steps away from me. Maintaining eye contact, he peels his shirt over his head and hangs it on a branch of the tree. I stare at his abdomen in shock. His abs are toned and his midriff is twice as wide as mine, but he's all muscle.

He bends down and takes off his boots. While I watch wide-eyed, he unbuttons then unzips his jeans and yanks them down his big thighs. My eyes veer to his boxers. They cover him far more than a bathing suit would, but I feel my temperature rising.

In nothing but his boxers, Lars walks into the water until it covers his stomach. He waits for my move.

"Shit," I whisper under my breath. Can I do it? I know that if I do this, it will show him how I feel in a way that words can't.

I take a deep breath. *I want to do this.* Keeping my eyes on the ground in front of me, I tug my shirt over my head and hang it on the same branch that he hung his. Thanks to Tamara, I'm wearing a lacy pink bra and matching panties. If it weren't for her undergarment choices, I would be dressed in a sports bra and granny underwear.

I lift my eyes cautiously to find him staring at my chest. Bending from the waist, I peel my sweat drenched jeans from my body as smoothly as possible, but obviously, nowhere near as seductive as his stellar performance. I leave my jeans in the loose dirt and take a step into the pond. As I suspected, the water is warm on the surface, but as I get deeper, it is shockingly cold. Goosebumps spread across my body. I suck in a breath of sweltering air.

Despite the coldness of the water, I continue walking toward Lars until I am standing chest to chest with him. I'm down to my bra and underwear and he's in his boxers, but I can't help the need to outdo him. I bend my knees so I am neck deep underwater, reach around my back, and unclasp my bra.

Lars can't yet see what I'm doing, but his eyes are full of a feral hunger. Once I hold my bra above the water and drop it beside me, our taunting game is over. I know what's coming before he reaches with both hands for me. Nothing can stop this moment from happening—neither man nor animal. Being close to him is a long overdue necessity,

In one fluid movement, he lifts me out of the water and holds me up higher than his head while he stares at the water sluicing off my naked breasts. With a strangled groan, he presses my freezing body against his. Our lips are centimeters apart and we share the same breath. I want him closer than he is even now, and I can't help pressing into him as tightly as I can. He feels big; shockingly big, hot, and hard.

My breathing is heavy and his mimics mine. Suddenly, his lips crash into mine, rough and possessive. I follow him blindly, allowing his tongue to penetrate my lips and his hands to massage my breasts. I wrap my legs around his abdomen and my fingers become claws that rake through his hair. A sound emanates from the back of his throat and I tug at his hair, unable to control my reaction to his hot mouth devouring mine.

I don't know how long we remain in that position; closer than I would have thought it possible for two human beings just greedily eating at each other's mouths.

I never want to let him go, but he begins pulling away and I allow a small sliver of distance to form between us. My breath comes in shallow, fast pants, and my lips feel swollen and hot. There is a needy pulsing between my legs. The coolness of the water invades the heated space between us, and I realize what we are doing.

In Lars' silvery eyes, I see nothing but raw emotion, the pupils so enlarged they make his eyes appear almost black. In the space between us, I feel him wiggling around beneath the water. When he holds his boxers above the water, I reach for my panties. Peeling them off effortlessly, I hold them up. I see him take a sharp breath.

With a triumphant smile, I fling the scrap of material away.

Slowly, much slower than before, he reaches for my body. His eyes depict a serious warning that I should take heed, but I don't. Instead, I lean eagerly toward him. I think he is going to kiss me again, but he avoids my mouth and goes for the base of my throat, peppering barely felt kisses all the way to my ear. When he reaches my ear, he takes the lobe between his teeth and bites down, and I shake like a leaf, almost unable to hold myself on my two feet.

I pull back and whisper. "What now?"

His hands grab my waist and pull me against him—close enough for me to feel *all* of him press into me. His cock jerks impatiently against my belly. "I'm going to spread you open and make you mine. I'm going to sink so deep inside you, you won't be able to walk for days," he whispers thickly into my ear. "Not yet. But soon. Very soon."

With a growl, he turns away from me and exits the water wearing nothing but his dignity. I watch him dress.

"Come on out. I won't watch," he says, turning away from me and giving me the opportunity to come out of the water and dress without being seen.

I can't decide if I want him to be a gentleman, or if I'd rather he watch as I exit the water. Either way, I leave the water, leaving my bra and underwear at the bottom of the pond, likely never to be seen again. The water laps around my knees when he turns around. I freeze. His chest heaves up and down and his eyes glow with a fierce hunger.

'You said you wouldn't watch."

"Why wouldn't I look at what's mine?" he asks.

I take the last few steps to dry land and dress quickly. Then I follow him back to the horse barn, neither of us speaking, as if nothing had happened.

But something did happen, and I can't help but feel as if this is the turning point of our relationship.

THIRTY-FIVE
Cass

After skinny dipping with my boss, I thought it would feel uncomfortable, but it isn't. What I really feel is antsy. Lars has initiated close contact and a bone-melting kiss, but he has deliberately left me flustered and craving more.

I FaceTime Jesse as soon as I reach the house. As soon as she answers, I lay back on my bed.

She squints at me. "You look…hmmm…what's that look? Aroused. Oh, wait. Is that drool? Have you been reading smut? Or have you been opening the big book of Lars the Cowboy," she teases.

"Jesse, I don't know what to do," I wail.

"So you *have* been opening the big book," she pounces.

"I might have glanced at the first page."

She laughs. "Remind me again what's on the first page?"

"We skinny dipped in the pond and kissed."

"This sounds like a very interesting book," she says with a mischievous grin. "Why don't you see what's on the next page?"

"I want to, but it's such a bad idea."

"Why is it a bad idea?"

"Because—"

"—Yeah, yeah," she pretends to yawn hugely. "I remember how this soap opera goes. You like him, but you don't want to like him, because you'll never see him again after this job. I think it's bullshit. You should just sleep with him and be done with it."

"Well, I just wish I hated him more than I do. Then maybe I could do what you say. Go to bed with him, enjoy the sex for what it is, and walk away without a second glance."

"You only have like ten days left. Just do it. You'll be fine," Jess encourages.

"Nine days," I correct.

"Even better. Fuck like rabbits at night...dirty, sweaty, flesh slapping flesh, meaningless sex, and keep your distance during the day." Jesse is making it sound like a walk in the park, but that's partly my fault. I've been seriously under-exaggerating my feelings for Lars

"Jesse, I have feelings for him," I finally admit with a sigh. "And they're growing. A lot."

She sits up straighter. "Oh, mistake! Since when? I mean, the guy doesn't even know your real name."

I bite my lip. "I know he doesn't. Okay, I just needed to talk this out and hear you say the words. Thank you, Jesse. I love you," I say and hang up. She can't give me good advice in this situation because there's no good advice to give. My phone continues to ring as she tries to call me back, but I put it on silent.

I stand from my bed, walk toward my dresser mirror, and stare at my reflection. I would have never guessed that being someone else could be so difficult. It was meant to be just a job and nothing else, but now I'll be leaving a piece of my heart behind in Montana. My phone rings again and with a sigh, I go and pick it up, thinking it is Jesse—but it isn't.

Strange, Tamara has never called at this time of the day. I accept the call and she comes on. She is still in bed.

"Hello, Tamara," I say politely.

"Don't you know how to take a good photo?" she asks sourly.

"What?"

"That photo you sent of that Lars guy. It might as well be the backside of a fucking rhino."

Holy purple cows! This woman is unbelievable. "Well, I didn't want him to know that I was taking his picture," I explain.

She yawns. "Take a couple more and send them to me this morning."

"It's already evening here and I won't see him again today. I'll do it tomorrow," I promise.

"All right. Get me shots that show his body."

A steel claw grips my stomach and I try not to show any emotion on my face. "Okay," I whisper. Thank God, the screen goes black. She disconnected the call. Slowly, I put the phone down on the dresser.

Oh God. She wants him for herself. When I leave, he's going to think I'm her, and he's going to sleep with her. An imagine of her bouncing on the blond man flashes into my mind. The blond man morphs into Lars and my heart hurts. I lean on the dresser and lower my head. Nine days. I have nine days to lose the feelings I have for a man I shouldn't have fallen for in the first place.

I don't know how long I stand in my room and try to brainstorm ways to stay away from Lars, but I know there is no way I'll be able to do it. On top of that, I don't even *want* to stay away from him.

Finally, I rouse myself, and begin peeling the clothes off my body as I walk into the bathroom. I have plenty of time to take a hot shower and clear my mind before dinner, so I do. When I get out, I feel no better. Maybe I'll take a walk around the ranch, I think as I get into a pale pink, low cut T-shirt with a shredded back. It's cute and not too revealing, with a tank top underneath. Then I throw on a pair of frayed light shorts. They are inappropriately short, but there is not much choice.

Quickly running a brush through my hair, I go into the kitchen to look for Emma Jean.

THIRTY-SIX
Cass

The counters are lined with appetizers and food designed for large gatherings, and Emma Jean is wrapping a large glass bowl of potato salad with cling wrap. She sends a big smile in my direction.

"What's going on tonight?" I ask curiously.

"Lars didn't tell you?"

I shake my head.

"We have barn parties every few months for the employees who live on site. There are a bunch of them, so the party is usually quite large."

"A barn party?" I ask.

Emma Jean turns the stove off and moves a large pot off the burner.

"Yup. They're quite fun. There's music and dancing."

"Will…will Lars be there?"

"He hasn't missed one yet."

"Right."

"Lars throws the parties, so he makes sure to be at all of them," she explains.

"Are the employees the only ones who will be there?" I ask with a frown. I haven't had to act like Tamara in front of too many people yet, but if I'm surrounded by people who know more about her, how am I supposed to be convincing while acting like myself. For the most part, I've been able to be myself lately, but that's all going to have to change in a crowd.

"No, dear. All the employees will be here, but it's not limited to staff. Often, they'll bring family members and friends along with them."

I bite my thumb. "Maybe I shouldn't go."

Emma Jean turns her full attention to me. "Why would a pretty little thing like you not want to go to a party?"

I shrug. "I don't know how everyone expects me to act," I admit.

"No one expects you to be anything but yourself."

I hesitate. She doesn't know the real reason I don't want to go.

"Honey, listen to me. You're a great person. I don't know what you're like when you're in the big city, or what you've done over there, but I've never seen you be disrespectful toward me, and I can tell you are a fine person. We're all simple country folk here and ain't nobody here gonna expect anything from you. You just be yourself and they can damn well like it, or take a hike," she says passionately.

I smile and wish I could be honest with her.

"Personally, I think you've changed a fair bit since you've been here."

"Really? In what way?" I have tried to gradually become less like Tamara as the days progressed, so if they believe I have changed, I have done my job. That also means that I will be able to act like myself.

"When you came here, you looked like you had your head on the chopping block waiting for the hatchet to drop, but over the last two weeks, I've seen the cares drift away from your eyes and you've blossomed like a flower."

I grin at her. "Why, Emma Jean, I don't think anyone has ever referred to me as a flower before."

"They will when they see you now," she says with a firm nod.

A door across the kitchen shuts with a click, and I turn toward the entrance. Footsteps grow closer then Lars fills the kitchen door, looking as fine as hell. My heart skips a beat. Only he can make a flannel shirt and jeans look sexy.

His eyes widen as his gaze travels down my body. I realize his choice of clothing is a major contrast to my pale pink top and beach shorts.

"Should I change?" I ask.

He rubs his chin thoughtfully, a faint smile playing on his lips. "I don't know. You're making me sweat like a sinner in church in that getup, buttercup, but you probably should wear something warmer. Once the sun goes down, it's going to get cold. Do you have a sweatshirt or a shawl?"

Of course, there isn't a shawl in my suitcase. I doubt Tamara has even heard of such a thing. She probably thinks it's one of the ingredients in rat poison. All Tamara's servants have packed for me to wear when I am around people is small, barely there clothing. There are no sweatshirts, hoodies, or jeans without strategically placed rips. I shrug. "I don't really have anything warmer."

Lars looks me up and down once more, his eyes lingering on my legs. Then, he begins unbuttoning his shirt. My eyes get pulled to his chest, which surprisingly, isn't bare. A white wife beater clings tightly to his frame as he extends his flannel in my direction. "I can't do anything about the shorts, but at least I can warm your top half."

My heart lurches at the smoldering expression in his eyes. I take the flannel shyly. "You have another one, right?"

Lars chuckles. "Of course. Be right back."

After he leaves the room, I strip off my pale pink over-shirt and slide the large flannel over my black tank top. It's still warm from his body and smells heavenly. I smooth it down and it falls to halfway down my thighs. It's at least triple my size, but it's a nice change from the tight clothes I've been wearing lately.

"Here, let me," Emma Jeans says, coming over to me and grasping the two front ends at the bottom of the shirt. Expertly, she ties them into a rose-shaped bow at my waist.

"Wow, that looks cute!" I exclaim.

"Let me go get a pin," she says and leaves the kitchen.

Lars struts back into the kitchen dressed in a gray and black flannel. He whistles low and long. "You sure give flannel a good name, Honeywell," he drawls as he approaches me. I allow him to take my hand and guide it to his chest while he rolls the sleeve up to my wrist.

I smile up at him, mesmerized by his piercing gray eyes and dimpled smile.

A small click echoes from across the room and both Lars and I turn our heads simultaneously. Emma Jean is standing on the other side of the kitchen counter with a camera pointed directly at us. Lars turns back, calmly finishes rolling the sleeve, and lays my hand gently back at my side with a slight squeeze. Was it intentional, or was it merely a friendly gesture? Then he blanks his expression—

possibly for Emma Jean's sake—and turns to look at her. "What are you going to do with that?" he asks with a light-hearted tone.

"I'll keep it with all my other memories," Emma Jean says with a smile. Carefully slipping the camera back into her pocket, she comes up to me and fastens a pin into the rose bow. "There you go. You'll be the belle of the ball," she declares, standing back and looking at me with satisfaction.

"Yes, she will," Lars agrees.

I swear I blush to the roots of my hair.

"Right, I guess I better load everything up into the truck and head out," Lars tells Emma Jean.

"Careful not to tip the containers," she cautions.

"Yes, ma'am," Lars says, carrying out the first batch of food. I grab two trays and follow him. When we get back inside, Emma Jean is standing over a pot still bubbling on the stove. She stirs the contents and looks up at us. "You can take everything else but the chili. It isn't ready. I'll drop it off at the barn when I head out for the night."

"You don't have to do that. The pot's heavy. I'll come and get it," Lars says.

"It's no bother. This is not heavy for me."

"No, I have to insist that you don't carry it yourself," Lars says.

"All right. I'll call Chance or Barry to come get it."

"Fine. Do you or Jack need anything?"

"Nope. We're good. You kids don't wait around. Go on and have a good time."

"How is Jack doing anyway?"

"Honey, don't act like you don't call him a few times a week to see how he's doing."

I turn to look at Lars and a dull flush of embarrassment stains his cheeks, making him look utterly adorable.

"He's healing up nicely, but I don't know if I want him training horses anymore. A man of his age shouldn't be jumping on and off wild horses, but he's a stubborn mule and won't back down."

Lars inclines his head and listens quietly.

Emma Jean clasps her hands together. "He doesn't want to let you down, but it's about time for him to retire," she says quietly. I can tell that she feels awful about her opinion, but I understand why she's saying it. Her husband is too old to be doing such a physically exerting job.

After having worked with horses for less than a month, I can categorically say that I've gained muscle in places where I never even knew you could have muscles. The job is not only physically, but also mentally trying.

"Hey, don't feel bad, Emma Jean. I completely understand. You two have worked for me long enough, and if either of you wants to retire, it's okay by me. The pension will kick in as soon as the paperwork's done. I'll get Steve to explain the whole process to Jack so he has a better understanding of it all."

Emma Jean looks at him gratefully, her eyes brimming with tears. "You're a dear, Lars. Thank you."

I look at Lars' handsome profile and realize that his ways are brash and arrogant, but his heart is big and generous. When it feels as if he can't get any more perfect, he surprises me yet again.

THIRTY-SEVEN
Cass

We drive the short distance toward the brightly lit, huge barn, capable of holding hundreds of people. Will there be that many, I wonder nervously.

"What should I expect at a barn party?" I ask.

He turns to me with a crooked grin. "A hog-killin' time."

I crinkle my nose at the description.

Lars laughs. "That's country talk for a blast."

"Oh yeah?" I say doubtfully.

"I swear, it's just good clean fun. Food, beer, and a bit of dancing."

I chew my lower lip. "What are the chances of anybody in there recognizing me?"

He stops smiling and throws me a serious glance. "Do you want to be recognized?"

I shake my head vigorously.

He grins. "I can't be a hundred percent certain, but it's a pretty safe bet that no one in there has heard of you."

A great weight falls from my chest. No one in there knows about the bad reputation Tamara has in L.A. I can just relax and be myself. "How many people come to these parties?" I ask as Lars parks and kills the engine.

There is music coming from the massive building and shadows dance across the ground. I have yet to see any bodies, but judging from the pickups parked all around us, I know they're all inside. Lars comes around, opens my door for me, and offers a hand to help me down from the truck.

"It's hard to say. I never really know what to expect. This party should be smaller than most, since five families are on vacation and some folks couldn't make it. I expect around seventy-five to turn out, but I could be wrong. There could be a lot more, or less, depending on the guests they bring."

I go to open the truck's back door, but Lars gently tugs me in the opposite direction.

"The food. We need to carry it inside," I remind, turning to look up at Lars.

The shine of his eyes halts me in my tracks and my jaw drops. That simple gaze from him does something amazing to me. I'm seriously in trouble of falling hard for this man.

"Since we brought the food, somebody else will come and get it," he explains, but his voice is much deeper than before and his eyes are dark.

"Okay, let's go then?" I say slowly, trying to make sure I don't stutter or skip any words.

"In a minute." He reaches behind me and pushes the door closed before sandwiching me between it and his body. His hard thighs brush against my naked legs.

"Yo, Lars!" someone yells from the barn.

A small, growl-like sound emanates from Lars' throat.

"Saved by the bell," I croak, and push at his chest lightly, but my fingers want to curl and clutch his shirt.

He takes a respectful step backward and raises his hand to the man walking in our direction.

"Who is that?" I ask.

"I have no idea. Must be a guest of one of the men," he says.

"Man, you threw a real banger this time. This might be one of the biggest yet," the man shouts, slapping Lars drunkenly on the shoulder. Lars' easy expression makes it look as if he knows the man, but the way he stands angled directly in front of me as if he is shielding me from him, tells a different story.

"Are there a lot of people in there?" Lars asks.

"Barn's packed to the rafters."

So, the party is a lot bigger than Lars was expecting.

"Well, why don't you go tell them that the food's in my truck and needs to be carried inside?" Lars asks.

The man grins, then tips to the side before overcorrecting his movement and flinging himself in the other direction. He just barely stays on his feet. Laughing, he chugs the rest of his beer before discarding the empty bottle on the ground and smiling glassily at us.

As the man staggers into the barn, Lars turns back toward me, wraps his arms around my waist, and plants his lips directly on mine. The kiss is sweet and gentle, and I melt as the delicious warmth of his body seeps into my skin.

He raises his head reluctantly. "You're staying by my side all night. No exceptions and no questions, understood?"

My head is swimming and I don't think I am able to deny him anything. I simply nod and allow him to pull me toward the barn. How strange. I feel like I *belong* in his grasp. As we get closer, the sounds grow louder and the smell of alcohol and hay grows thicker.

Lars opens the barn door and a dozen laughing people file out. They are on their way to get the food and carry it inside. They wave and greet Lars and he returns their greetings. Inside, there are groups of people gathered around, drinking and talking. The middle space has been reserved for dancing, and I see Chance leading a dark-haired girl in a long skirt and cowboy boots in a country style dance. He looks up, spots us, and waves. I wave back.

Lars moves through the crowd with ease, all the while keeping a tight grasp on my hand. Soon, we stop to talk to a group of guys in Stetson hats almost identical to Lars. Of course, none of them have hair as nice and well-maintained as his, or look as handsome as he does. A man with a long gray beard and red cheeks tips his hat to me and grins.

"Well, I'll be a billy goat. I'm thinkin' Lars jes' found himself a sweet huckleberry to marry him. What's your name, sweetheart?"

I feel my ears begin to burn. "Tamara."

The man nods sagely. "That's a mighty fine name for a purdy gal."

"Cut your wobblin' jaw, Chester. She's with me," Lars says, pulling me into his side.

He just told everybody I'm with him. Something inside me leaps with joy.

Chester laughs jovially. "Don't dig for your cannon, son. I'm not one to go milkin' my neighbor's cow."

"Hold up," one of the other men in the group interrupts, "ain't you that celebrity? Tamara Honeydew or something?

I can feel my brain swirl as I try to find words. Even though I hate the idea, I am Tamara Honeywell for another nine days.

Lars chuckles. "What would we do with a hot shot celebrity on this ranch, Vernon? Get her to clean out the horse pins?"

I almost crack a grin. Cleaning horse pins is *exactly* what I've been doing and Lars knows it. Is he hiding my identity to protect his own reputation, or mine?

"Great, you guys just carry on talking as if I'm not here," I say.

Chester's eyes twinkle as he cackles heartily. "You got yourself a live one here, son,"

"Don't I know it?" Lars says and pulls me even more snugly into his side. I look up at him and see pride in his eyes. My heart swells with happiness. He is proud of me.

"See you later, guys," he says, not taking his gaze off me. With me glued to his side, we walk away from the group of men.

"You look so sexy," he breathes into my ear.

My spine straightens involuntarily and I turn my eyes to his. He's trying to look innocent, but we both know that he is the furthest thing from it. Daringly, I reach up and pull his head down until his ear is inches away from my lips. "Guess what?" I whisper.

"What?"

"I look sexier without my clothes."

He is still trying to assimilate my words when I break from him and move into the crowd. I'm not typically a tease, or overconfident, but I feel like I can be anything with him. I turn back to look at him and he is still staring at me with an intrigued expression. "Where are you going?" he mouths.

"Wait there. I'll get us a couple of drinks," I mouth back.

As I turn back to walk toward the bar, I bump into a huge, burly man. He has a receding hairline and beady black eyes. I apologize swiftly. He looks at me funny but doesn't say anything, and I continue pushing through the crowd. Suddenly, a large hand latches onto my arm. I whirl around. It's the same man I bumped into seconds earlier.

"Well, I'll be darned. You're Tamara Honeywell, aren't you" he says, his eyes full of admiration.

"Oh, uh, yeah."

"I'm Steven. Steven Robert Hallivel." He shakes his head in wonder. "I can't believe it. I come to hillbilly country on a visit and meet you here. I'm a huge fan of *everything* you do. I might even be your biggest fan. I've seen both your movies, and I'm looking forward to the one you have coming out soon. Don't be surprised if I'm the first one in the theater."

"That's great. It's really nice to meet you," I say nervously. I did not count on meeting one of Tamara's fans here. I didn't even know that Tamara was working on a movie. This man obviously knows more about Tamara than I do, which is a dangerous situation, to say the least.

"It sure made my year," he says heartily.

I chuckle politely. "Yeah, I love all my fans too. Enjoy the party." Flashing a big, fake smile, I turn around to leave

The man grabs my wrist once again and pulls me closer into him. He smells of sweat and cheap beer and it causes my gut to tighten even though I know I have nothing to fear. It's not like he's going to try anything in such a big crowd. He's just an over enthusiastic fan of Tamara's.

"Hey, what's the rush?" he asks.

I jerk my head back. "I'm here with friends and they're waiting for me to join them."

He moves his mouth closer to my ear. "I've seen every part of you in your sex tapes," he says, looking me up and down.

I try to pull my wrist from his iron-tight grasp, but he doesn't budge.

He smiles and locks his gaze on my breasts. "They looked bigger on the screen, but no matter. I know you like it kinky. So do I. And that scene with that Chinese chick? Whoa! That was epic, man," he says and groans. I can tell he's getting turned on by his own dirty thoughts. I'm so embarrassed and humiliated that I just want to run away and hide from everybody, but he tightens his grip on my wrist. I glance around wildly to look for a means of escape.

Everyone around us is oblivious to my distress, and I've gone too far from Lars for him to see me. I was told to stay by his side, and I should have listened. Now I have to deal with this big pervert on my own. I take a deep breath. I didn't come this far to allow someone like him to make me feel like a worthless slut. I'm not Tamara, and I wasn't the star of the sex tape he watched, so I've nothing to be ashamed of.

"Let me go right now or I'll scream," I grate through clenched teeth.

His eyes flash with even more interest. "Why don't we get out of here? I promise you I can fulfill your every fantasy."

I realize that his alcohol-induced brain is telling him that I'm game. He is so utterly convinced that my reluctance is a prelude to sex that I might have to knee him in the nuts or something equally painful to get out of this one.

"Look, buster. I'm *not* interested," I shout over the noise. If this doesn't work, it will have to be the knee, but if at all possible, I'd like to avoid a scene.

"I know you're interested," he insists. "You wouldn't have bumped into me if you weren't."

"It was an accident!"

"Let her go," I hear from behind me. I've only ever heard this cold tone one time, and I thought then that I'd be happy never to hear it again.

THIRTY-EIGHT
Cass

"**W**ho the fuck are you?" Steven barks aggressively.

"I'm her man," Lars states quietly.

I am acutely conscious that people have started making a circle around us.

Steven grins. "You and a whole bunch of out-of-work Hollywood actors moonlighting as porn stars."

Lars blinks with shock.

"Looks like you didn't know about her starring role in Beauty and the Fist, huh?" the man mocks.

I cringe and Lars blanches. "If you don't let go of her right now..." he threatens.

The man tightens his hold on me. "You'll what?" he taunts.

"Let go of her and I'll show you," Lars snarls.

The man releases me suddenly, and I stumble backward and fall into Lars. Instantly, he winds his arms around me protectively, while his narrowed eyes quickly scan my face and body. "Are you hurt?" he asks urgently, and I can feel the dangerous anger throbbing in his voice.

I shake my head. "I'm fine. Let's just go. Please. He's just a pig," I say, rubbing my sore wrist. In the grand scheme of things, a bruised wrist is nothing to complain about, but in one quick movement, Lars peels my left hand from my wrist and touches the sore part. I yelp, pulling it back to my chest.

Suddenly, his eyes become pitiless chips of gray ice. At that moment, he is the most coldly aggressive man I have seen in my life, and I feel a tight knot of fear inside me. Taking his hat off, he places it on my head before guiding me a few steps backward and away from the man. Looking me dead in the eyes, he says, "Don't. Move."

I stare at him in confusion as he turns to the man who is as broad as he is and just as tall. The man puffs out his chest and makes a beckoning gesture with his fingers. Lars stands still. He doesn't move a muscle. Like a bull readying itself for a matador. He doesn't look at the crowd surrounding him; his whole focus is on his opponent.

In the next moment, he swings his fist and slams it into Steven's jaw. I gasp and take a step back, covering my mouth with my hand. I would have *never* guessed that Lars was a violent man. Even at his angriest, he's always been gentle and kind toward me. Even on the phone with the loan sharks he wasn't violent. He was assertive and angry, but totally in control.

The man's arms flail as he hurtles toward the ground. He lands with a loud thud. An angry howl is torn from him. He cups his jaw and scrambles to his feet. For a second, he sways unsteadily then throws a wild punch at Lars. Lars ducks and in flash, lands a jab to Steven's unprotected stomach. The fight is noticeably unfair. Steven is drunk while Lars is not only stone cold sober, he is also clearly an experienced fighter. When the man gets lucky and lands a blow that catches Lars on his eyebrow, I know I can't just do nothing.

"Enough," I yell and rush in their direction. I lodge myself right in between them. Lars immediately unclenches his fist and steps back from the punch he was about to throw.

Steven, on the other hand, maddened with fury, grabs me by the waist and throws me out of his way. I fly through the air for what feels like forever before I crash to the ground, knees first. Just as I am about to face-plant into the concrete floor, a set of arms encircle my chest and pulls me up.

I'm too shocked to even cry. I look up at the man who caught me and Chance grins at me. He turns toward Lars and gives him a thumbs-up sign before looking back at me.

"For a yellow belly, that was one hell of a throw," he comments coolly.

I stare at him in disbelief. "Lars is going to get hurt," I shout.

Chance chuckles and turns me around so that I'm sitting on my butt. "Lars is a little rusty from years of sitting behind a desk, but he can take that green horn no problem."

"Will you help stop the fight?" I beg.

He shakes his head. "I'd be fixing to do the same if someone disrespected my girl. It'll teach that fancy city slicker a lesson." He grins. He is about to say something when he looks down and notices the state of my scraped and bleeding knees. He pulls a face. "Oh, my own Aunt Mary, that don't look good. I reckon Lars is gonna be hoppin' mad when he sees that. Might as well let him get his pound of flesh off that tenderfoot now."

I have no choice but to sit and watch as Lars rain blows on the man's body so quickly and so relentlessly, the ferocity of the attack overwhelms him.

"Fast is good, but accurate is better," Chance chuckles approvingly.

One power punch from Lars catches Steven flush on the chin and he flies backwards, landing on one of the hay bales. The crowd hoots as if this is entertainment. Blood is pouring from the man's nose. He pulls himself to a sitting position and looks around him with a dazed expression.

Lars stands over him, his chest rising and falling quickly.

"Lars, don't," I scream.

He turns toward me, his eyes instantly connecting with mine, and I freeze. His face is clenched tight and his eyes cold and bloodshot with murderous rage. He looks like a crazed bull. I don't even recognize him. I gasp with horror.

"Please don't," I whisper again.

He turns back to his opponent, grabs him by the collar, and drags him up. The man looks terrified. Then he punches him so hard in the jaw it sends him flying backward in an arch. He crashes into some bales of hay stacked in one corner of the room and lies unmoving in a tangle of limbs.

Lars turns toward me. There is a cut over his eyebrow and it is bleeding. I open my mouth to speak but no words come out. I close it and open it soundlessly like a fish.

He strides toward me. "Heck, Tamara. I told you not to move."

I'm trying unsuccessfully to keep my tears at bay, but it's getting impossible. "You were getting hurt," I whine. My knees have started to sting, but they don't hurt too bad. I'm sure I'll be able to walk. I try to stand and my legs buckle under me. Lightning fast, Lars catches me around my waist. His eyes flicker up and down my body. Cursing, he lifts me into his arms and carries me out of the barn. Everybody is staring at us. Outside, the night is balmy.

"I'm sorry," he grates.

"It's okay," I mumble, but I'm horrified by what has happened. Everybody in there has heard what the man said. Everybody in there thinks I was the main star in a sex tape. A tear slides down my cheek.

"Oh, fuck," he swears.

"I'm not really crying. It's just the shock of it."

"It's all right, baby."

"I'm sorry I embarrassed you," I sob.

"You didn't," he says, looking at me with sad eyes. "I don't give a flying fuck what anybody thinks about you."

I want to hug him and apologize for the fight, but instead, I simply lay my head on his chest and allow him to carry me to the car.

THIRTY-NINE
Cass

"It's nothing. I just scraped my knees," I say softly as Lars pulls his entire medical kit from his bathroom closet. He lays every possible antiseptic spray and ointment on the counter along with gauzes, splints, and bandages.

"I don't want it to get infected," he says, frowning.

"Lars, I'm okay," I persist, even though the sight of my knees all bloody and filled with hay and dirt fills even me with disgust. One knee looks worse than the other, but I can tell that they are both shallow. It's not my physical wounds that hurt. It is what everyone must now think of me that really pains.

"I'm cleaning your knees. It's my fault you got hurt and I can't even do anything about your wrist."

I look at my wrist, which is becoming blue.

"How is it your fault?" I ask. "I'm the one who ran from you and jumped in between you two."

"I shouldn't have let you walk off. Instead of listening to that fool Gary talk my ears off about his stupid tractor, I should have stayed with you. But I messed up and now you're hurt." His beautiful eyes look at me sadly.

I stare at him, unsure of how to convince him that he's wrong. This situation is entirely my fault—or rather, Tamara's.

If she hadn't starred in those sex tapes, that man wouldn't have recognized me. If Tamara wasn't such a bitch, my life could be so much simpler.

"You ready for this?" he asks, holding up a bottle of hydrogen peroxide. My eyes and mouth pop open when he pours it on my wounds. I watch it clean out all the dirt and hay from my cut. It hadn't hurt much up until now.

"I'm so sorry," he whispers as he wipes the excess from around my leg.

I shake my head and take a deep breath as the pain subsides. "It's not your fault," I repeat.

Lars places a bandage with two different ointments over my less severe knee and sprays another antiseptic on the more damaged one. This one doesn't hurt nearly as bad. Instead, it cools the pain temporarily. I watch as he works nimbly at retrieving a much larger bandage and gauze tape. He puts a few ointments on the bandage and carefully covers my knee with it. Once it's covered, he wraps the gauze tape around the bandage to hold it in place.

"Thank you," I whisper. He nods his head and continues looking at the floor. I notice a small cut on his eyebrow where he got punched. I grab a small antiseptic wipe from the counter and dab it over his brow gently.

He jerks back and I scowl sternly. "Hold still."

I gently tend to the cut and place a small amount of Neosporin on it. Lars continues staring at me, but I ignore him and finish by sticking a Band-Aid on it. He leans his head into my hand and his hair falls over my fingertips. The urge to grasp it in my fingers…

I pause, trying to gain the control I need to finish the task at hand, but we both know that my control is gone.

"I'm such a fucking pervert," he whispers against my palm.

"Why do you say that?" I ask curiously.

"Because I'm horny as hell even after I've seen you look like you've been attacked by a fucking shark."

I giggle. "I scraped my knee, Lars."

"It looked far worse. I hated seeing you get hurt. I wanted to fucking kill him."

I bite my bottom lip. "About the sex tape-"

His finger lands against my mouth and he shakes his head. There is some great hurt in his eyes. "I don't want to know, Tamara. I can't take it. Not now. Not tonight."

I nod. "Okay."

My heart is beating so fast I hear it booming in my ears. I know what I want. Even if it is just one night. I want it. I'll keep it in my heart for when I'm old. For when I am sitting in a rocking chair. That one night when I went to bed with the most beautiful man who ever walked God's earth.

Lars stands to his full height and lifts me from the sink. I wrap my arms around his neck and my legs around his midsection as tightly as possible and meet his lips. He walks me backward and out of the bathroom into his bedroom.

His lips drown all reasonable doubt.

Lars carries me to his bed and lays me gently beneath him. "I can't wait any longer. I need to have you," he groans, pulling his shirt over his head and leaving nothing to my imagination.

I pull his bare chest into mine and say something that I know he won't be able to resist. "I've needed you on top of me for weeks."

With an animalistic sound originating from the back of his throat, Lars grabs the hem of my tank top and pulls it over my head. The flannel top falls over my arms and leaves me in nothing but a bra.

I groan at the pure bliss I'm feeling and my small sound seems to excite him even more. He arches his back and presses himself into me, which causes a louder, more frenzied noise to escape my lips. I wrap my arms around the back of his neck and pull at the tips of his hair while simultaneously pressing his head more tightly into mine. I can't get close enough to him and closeness is what I need.

FORTY
Lars

I kiss her lips again, unable to resist the fullness of them. "You feel so damned good."

I slip my fingertip underneath the lace of her bra. The nipple hiding under there is hard and full. I touch it gently and she arches into my hand, looking for more.

I unbutton her little shorts and pull the zipper down slowly, teasing us both with the reveal. Sure enough, the panties match. My sister once said if a man undresses a woman and finds that her bra matches her panties, he's played right into that woman's hands. Fuck, I never wanted to play into a woman's hands more.

I lick along the top of the panties, right where they meet her skin. She gasps and clenches my hair with her hands. I pull her shorts down more and she wiggles her hips until they are down to her thighs. Carefully, I slide them lower without letting the material touch her knees. When I finally get them off, she lifts those long, smooth legs and teasingly, provocatively, spreads them wide.

Hell! She's showing me the sweet, wet heat at the center of her.

I stare like a man transfixed at the wet patch as she lifts her hips until her sex is inches away from my nose. The heady scent of her arousal fills my nostrils.

Like a wolf scenting the air, I inhale in quick bursts.

She pulls back and my nose moves forward, following the intoxicating trail of her scent. Her hands skim lightly over her ribs and linger over the tops of her satiny breasts. She cups her breasts. I stare at her utterly riveted. Keeping her legs straight, she opens her thighs so her long, long legs make a fabulous V. The position is obscene and bewitching.

She is good enough to eat.

She holds the pose while I kiss and lick my way up her spread thighs. The crotch of her panties is completely soaked and I can see the puffy lips through the transparent material. I push my hand against it and the moan that comes from her almost makes me come in my pants.

I pull the material to one side–I need to see all of her–and look at her pussy. Fuck me. I can't take my eyes of it. So goddamn pink and sweet. God only knows how many pussies I have seen in my lifetime, but hers takes my breath away. I stare at the pink glistening whorls of wet flesh. In that position, the hole gapes, as if begging to be filled, taken, fucked. Enticingly thick nectar drips out of it.

Like an uncivilized heathen, I stick my watering mouth right where it was dripping.

She groans at the first stroke of my tongue along her swollen folds. Her pretty little pussy is as soft as the petals of a flower and as sweet as nectar. My tongue delves deeper as I eat her out greedily. I can't get enough.

My hungry slurping draws even louder moans from her as I hit on the spots she loves the most. She pushes her fingers through my hair and arches her hips up to me, giving me more access.

I begin drawing designs all over her with my tongue. When I hit a spot that makes her shiver and go tense with pleasure, I hold her tighter to my mouth and keep at it, rubbing, licking, sucking, worshiping until I find a rhythm that makes her moan with ecstasy and her body squirm.

"Don't you dare stop," she begs, driven purely by pleasure.

I suck the engorged button hard. It takes less than a minute before her body becomes a hard bow. She pushes her clit even deeper into my mouth. She lets out a long wail that bounces off the walls as she collapses underneath me. Limp and completely sated, she lies panting...but not for long. Sticky-sweet honey is all around my mouth and I lick it clean.

"You've got a sweet little pussy," I tell her, and lick her all over again. Her poor clit throbs under my tongue.

When she comes clawing and grasping at the sheets, I lie down beside her and rub my palm on her nipple, over the lace of her bra. It's as hard as a little stone. It doesn't take long for her to catch her breath and rise on her elbows.

She grins at me. "Now it's your turn."

Her searching hands find the button of my jeans and slide the zip down. She fumbles a bit so I help her push my pants off. As soon as they get to my ankles, I kick them away.

Now there's nothing between us but a pair of boxers. I lift my hips and she hooks her fingers into the waistband and pulls the thin material down. My dick jumps to full attention.

"You're so huge," she gasps in wonder.

I look down and my dick is pulsing so crazily to get inside her silky warmth it actually hurts. "That's right, and you're going to take every inch of me inside your tight pussy, baby."

She slides her hands up my thighs and my cock jerks at her touch. One hand curls around my upright dick. I groan at the sudden thrill of her small hand fisting my cock. Her fingers are cool and sure as she slowly slides them along the shaft and over the pulsing veins as she feels every inch of me. It is as though she's memorizing me, testing the texture of my skin, exploring me.

"Your skin is like silk," she murmurs.

Leaning forward, she wraps her red mouth around my cock and starts sucking it in. I want to say something, but I lost the power of speech. I dig my hands into her hair as she takes my cock deeper and deeper into her throat.

"I won't be able to last long," I warn.

She looks up at me with wide open eyes and bobs her head up and down my shaft.

"Spread your legs, Tamara. I want to see what's mine."

Obediently, she readjusts her body and allows me to see her wet, open pussy. I stare at her flesh and lick my lips thinking of how sweet she tasted earlier. Suddenly, I can hold it no longer. I try to pull my cock out of her mouth, but she clamps her hands around my hips and starts making a swallowing motion.

I explode in her mouth while she moans and milks every last drop from me.

FORTY-ONE
Cass

I am tempted awake by the delicious smell of bacon. With my eyes still closed, I roll over in bed lazily. Mmm…Emma Jean is making breakfast. I should get up. Wait, I shouldn't be able to smell bacon from my room. My eyes snap open.

I'm naked and alone in Lars' bed.

My immediate and first thought is he's done a runner because he regrets sleeping with me. But that insecure thought doesn't last. The way Lars worshiped my body last night is not what people do to their one night stands. A secretive smile curves my lips to think of all the things he did to my body. I've never met anyone who did the things he does, or who made me climax so hard. I guess he must be very experienced.

We did it so many times I'm sore this morning.

I stretch deeply, and it makes both my knees and wrist ache. I examine my wrist gingerly. It hurts, but it's bearable. I sit up and look around the dim room. Last night, I had no eyes for anything but him, but today, I'm curious. It's surprisingly bare. A couple of watercolor paintings of horses, a wardrobe, a dresser, and a daybed with some olive-green pillows. It's almost as if he lives here, but it's not really his home.

The sheets reek of sex so I quickly strip them off the bed and bundle them up. Picking up the flannel shirt I wore last night off the floor, I slip it over my head. As I pass the mirror on the dresser, I glance at it. Yup, I look like a dirty stop over, but I can't stop grinning at my reflection. Nothing can be done about my swollen mouth, but I run my hands through my hair to put it to some kind of order before I turn away.

Still wondering where Lars is, I quickly gather the rest of my clothing, add them to the sheets, and carry the wad out of the room. Pausing at the top of the stairs, I listen. Everything seems still until I hear clattering sounds coming from the kitchen.

I briefly think about exiting through the front door and accessing my living quarters through my patio, but I don't like the idea of sneaking about like a thief, and I certainly don't want to tell an unnecessary lie to Emma Jean. She's been good to me and I respect her.

Clutching the dirty laundry against my body like a shield, I go down the stairs and head toward the kitchen for my walk of shame. The door is not closed, and I can hear Emma Jean moving around. For all I know, she has probably already heard about the sex tape and the ensuing fight. It'll be embarrassing, but I'll just have to brazen it out.

Cautiously, I put my head around the kitchen door, expecting to see Emma Jean's cheerful face. But what I see is a stripped to the waist, totally edible Lars presiding over a big mess. There are pots and pans on the fire and in the sink. The table is littered with broken egg shells, cans of beans, bread, a bowl of pancake batter, packets of open bacon, and sausages. For a second, I stare at him blankly.

"You okay?" he asks, cocking an eyebrow.

I nod, still too bewildered by the sight of him cooking to form actual words.

"Well, I'm most definitely not," he says.

I frown. Is this where it's supposed to get awkward? I can act cool about last night if that's what's needed. Straightening my spine, I step into the kitchen. "Why aren't you okay?"

He places his hands on his lean hips. "Here I am busting my gut trying to make and serve breakfast in bed to the most beautiful, naked woman God ever created, and she's ruined it all by stripping the bed and getting back into clothes."

I grin with relief. "The sheets reeked of sex."

"What's wrong with that?" he asks, genuinely surprised.

I laugh at his expression. "I think your beans are burning."

He turns around, grabs the pan off the fire, and to my surprise, deftly and with the great flourish of a top-Chef, pours them into two plates that are already loaded with food parked on the warmer.

"Voila! Now, tell me that wouldn't make an award-winning photo," he boasts proudly.

That reminds me of Tamara's order to send a picture of him this morning. I force a smile to my lips. "You're absolutely right. It is photo worthy. I want to take a picture of it."

He looks at me strangely. "You do?"

"Yeah, the first breakfast you ever made for me." I lift a shoulder. "It can go into the Lars and I album."

His eyes twinkle. "You're going to make a Lars and I album?"

I nod guiltily. It never even crossed my mind to make one. "Give me a minute to get my phone. It's in my room," I call as I flee from the kitchen. I drop the bundle of clothes into the wash basket before going into my room to get my phone.

I see that Jesse has called three times. I text that I'll call her soon then return to the kitchen. I notice that Lars has brought in a vase of flowers from the dining room and put it by the plates. Something tugs at my heart. How amazing it would be if this was real. That I'm taking a picture for a Lars and I album. I start clicking and sweeping the camera around to get a few shots of the chef. I try to take a few head shots too. There's no way I'm sending Tamara pictures of a half-naked Lars.

Lars pours coffee into a mug. "Do you want milk or sugar?"

I shake my head and he sets the mug in front of me

"Where's Emma Jean?" I ask, picking up the coffee.

"She never comes in the day after the party. Everybody is usually hungover in their beds, and no one comes around for food."

I take a sip and nearly spit it out. Forcing myself to swallow it, I look at him. "What the hell have I just drank?"

He grins. "Cowboy coffee. Strong enough to float a horseshoe."

"Ugh, it's how I imagine battery acid would taste." I stand up and walk over to the fridge. Getting a carton of orange juice, I pour myself a glass of it and walk back to the table. As I pass by, Lars' large hand curls around my thigh. I look down at him.

"I never got my morning kiss, sugar pie," he drawls.

I bend down and lightly place my lips on his. His other hand comes up and winds into my hair. His tongue forces its way into my mouth. I suck it and his other hand slides up my thigh. My stomach becomes jelly. His mouth leaves mine, but his eyes watch my face avidly as his fingers run along my wet seam.

"Are we really going to waste all this food?" I ask in a shivery voice.

"I'll make us more," he mutters.

I look deep into his beautiful eyes. "Do all your hook-ups get this treatment in the morning?"

His fingers still. "What's that supposed to mean?"

"I mean you've had a lot of experience, haven't you?"

"I've had my share," he says with a slow, cocky smile.

"Do you make breakfast for them all?"

His smile widens. "Sometimes I give them such a good time they give me breakfast in bed."

Arrogant pig. I keep my face totally straight and my voice solemn and slightly apologetic. "I know you tried, but I didn't have a very good time last night."

It's water off a duck's back.

"What if I told you I don't believe you," he replies.

I run a finger down his straight nose. "You're very, very sure of yourself, aren't you?"

His hand caresses my butt cheek. "I am. Are you very, very sure of your assertion."

I nod slowly.

"Care to test out your theory?"

I put my glass of orange juice on the table. "How?"

He shrugs. "If I'm really awful, you should have no problem resisting me, should you?"

I pretend to consider. "That's true."

"You should be able to say no, no matter what I do."

I pick a sausage from his plate and lick it slowly.

His eyes widen. "What are you doing?"

I look at him innocently. "Nothing. Haven't you seen a girl lick a sausage before?"

"No. Has anyone ever told you what happens to girls who lick sausages?"

"No. What?"

"They usually get thrown on a table and end up begging for more."

"There's more evidence of your caveman techniques," I say before gently sucking the tip of the sausage.

"Right. I'm going to get you to admit that I'm the best you've ever had, or I'm never eating another sausage in my life."

I want to giggle so bad. "You can try, cowboy," I say in my sultriest voice.

He stands up and sweeps all the plates of food to the floor. They smash and food flies everywhere. My jaw hangs open. "I can't believe you did-"

He grabs me by the waist, lifts me up, and sets me on the edge of the table. "Hey," I exclaim as he grasps my knees and pulls them apart. "What are you doing?"

"Haven't you ever seen a man lick a pussy?" he asks.

I place my palms on his chest and crinkle my nose. "You're not seriously going to do that, are you? Not after all the sex last night?"

239

"Why not? Day old muff. Heaven sliced up," he mocks.

My mouth drops open with shock. "You really are irredeemable."

"Now, have you got any other excuses, or are you ready to submit?"

"Do your worst," I throw at him.

It takes him only seconds to tear an admission out of me. "You are the best I ever had."

"And the sex?" he asks with his tongue poised inches away from my tormented clit.

"The greatest," I pant. And I wasn't just saying it either. As Chance would say, "Damn if that shit don't take you to another place."

FORTY-TWO
Cass

While Lars cooks breakfast again, I clean the mess on the floor, saving the bacon and sausages on a plate. Then Lars whistles for the dogs and they come running in to lick the plate clean. After we eat, we agree to go to our separate rooms to shower and change before meeting again in the hall. Lars wanted me to shower with him, but I knew I had to send his photo to Tamara or she would be breathing fire down my neck.

I go to my room, crop the photo, dim it a little with a filter so he doesn't look so blindingly sexy, and hit send. With a sigh, I put my phone down on the dresser and turn toward the bathroom, but before I get to the door, my phone rings. I turn around and look at it in astonishment. It can't be. She never calls at this time. I walk toward it and look at the screen. It's her. This time, I know she isn't drunk dialing me from a beach.

"Hello," I answer politely.

A totally photo-shopped version of me fills my phone's screen. From the background, I can see that it is nighttime and she is propped up in bed. "How's cleaning up horse dung coming along?" she asks with a big, fake smile.

"Could be worse," I say lightly. I'm not going to let on that that she can never make me feel bad about being

241

here. I'm having a whale of a time. Far better than she is on her private island in whatever part of the world she is.

She scowls suddenly. "What's wrong with your face?"

Instinctively, my hand flies to cover the lower half of my face. "Why?"

"You look…red faced and…odd."

"Oh, I must have gotten sunburned yesterday."

"Does everyone really think you're me?" Obviously, she still thinks I'm not anywhere near her level of beauty.

"Don't worry, there are only a few people here and none of them have heard of you."

"You're in Montana, not outer Mongolia. There must be people who've heard of me," she snaps irritably.

It's like walking on a minefield with her. "What I meant to say is, I've only been dealing with ranch hands. They're not worldly. They spend all their time with animals doing filthy work. God knows if they even know what a celebrity magazine is," I explain patiently.

That seems to pacify her somewhat. She twirls a piece of her hair on her finger. "What about Lars then? Is he a ranch hand too?"

"Yes, he's a ranch hand," I agree warily.

"Well, he doesn't look very filthy. Maybe he's filthy in the sack." She laughs at her own joke.

My belly tightens, but I make a show of pretending to laugh.

"Do you spend a lot of time with him?"

"Not really."

"Define not really."

I word my reply carefully. "Well, I guess whatever interactions I have with him are those that happen while carrying out my duties." Sleeping with him is probably not part of the job, but Tamara definitely doesn't need to know that little detail.

"You like him, don't you?" she asks slyly.

"No," I say, but I must have either taken too long to deny the question or been too emphatic, because she purrs. "Cass, I know that you do. You can tell me. I'm your boss, but I'm also your friend."

Yeah, right. She must think I fell off a turnip cart to believe that. The mess of baked beans I scooped off the floor and threw in the trash would make better friends to me than her. "You're mistaken, Tamara. I don't feel anything for him other than gratitude for teaching me to ride." I pause, thinking of something that would make sense to her. "He's just a ranch hand. He has no money or future."

But she is on to me. "You don't have to hide from me, Cass. I completely understand how the heart works. It doesn't matter how much money someone has if you have feelings for them. I've been there, you know."

"I don't have feelings for him," I mutter, but Lars chooses that very moment to knock and call from outside my door. Damn.

"You about done, baby?" he asks.

"I'm just on the phone. Can you give me a minute?" I reply, turning away from the phone because I can't look Tamara in the eye.

"Right, come to the living room when you've finished," he says through the closed door.

"Will do," I reply. His footsteps move away and I turn back to the screen. My heart is beating like a drum, but I keep my face totally expressionless.

Tamara's eyes glitter as she moves in for the kill. "That was him, wasn't it?"

I don't even try to lie. "Yes."

"You don't have to be ashamed. I don't think having feelings for a ranch hand is a bad thing." Her tone is both wheedling and conniving.

"I don't have feelings for him," I insist.

"Come on, just admit it." Delicately, she shrugs one shoulder. "It's not like it's a crime or anything. You're a grown-ass woman. So fucking what if you do?"

I realize that she's not going to give up. She'll just go on and on until I admit it. Sometimes, you gotta take the bull by the horns. "Okay, yes, I do."

She smiles triumphantly, a cat-got-the-mouse smile. "There. That wasn't so difficult, was it?"

"No," I say softly.

"So, you're actually happy there?" she says in a wondering voice. "You found yourself a drop-dead-gorgeous man and you're not miserable even though you're shoveling shit all day with a bunch of laborers?" To my surprise, a tinge of bitterness creeps into her voice. For all her money and fame, she is a lonely, sad woman.

"I guess so. I enjoy being with horses. Learning to ride is fun and everybody here has been really kind to me." Maybe I was responding to that wistful tone in her voice. Maybe, I thought I could ignite some spark of empathy in her, but it was a stupid move.

"But you know you can't sleep with him, right?"

My eyes pop open.

She grins. It's not an evil grin. Just the kind of smirk you would give someone when their Monopoly token lands on your heavily built up properly. A smirk that says, gotcha. "It's in the contract you signed," she says sweetly. "You can't act in any way that besmirches my good name."

Her words jar my brain. Who would have thought her name and the words *good name* could ever be uttered in the same sentence? "What?"

She fake sighs. "Here's the short version. You can't fuck him."

For a second, the image of how wantonly I opened my legs last night and exposed my bits to Lars' hungry gaze flashes into my mind.

"You've already slept with him, haven't you?" she pounces.

I frown, not knowing where she's going with this. I can play nice up to a point, but if she ever tries to shaft me, or get out of paying me for this job, she'll see another side of me. The side that has nothing left to lose.

"I'm waiting for an answer," she prods impatiently.

I straighten my shoulders and flick my hair. "Yes, I have, actually, but I'm not in breach of my contract. I was *categorically* instructed by Ms. Moore to act like you, and I figured that if you wanted a man, you would take him."

She seems to find my outburst funny. She laughs. "That's the first bit of bitch-spine you've shown. I like it. You're absolutely right. When I see something I want, I take it. And that's exactly what I intend to do now."

I look at her in disbelief.

"However, you may carry on sleeping with him. Keep his dick hot and hard until I arrive," she orders haughtily.

I blink. Is she serious?

"Just remember that you're not to reveal your true identity to anyone, especially him…or you won't get a cent from me. If that's not enough of an incentive, I'll get Daddy to make sure your little fuck-friend loses his job too."

I stare at her in horror.

She pretends to yawn. "Right. Carry on as you are. I'll be in touch to let you know what changes there are to the original plan."

Her face disappears from my screen.

FORTY-THREE
Cass

Tamara's call leaves me in a state of mental turmoil. On autopilot, I have a quick shower and dress in jeans and a T-shirt. I don't know what she can or will try to do. All I know is whatever it is, it will hurt me. I go out to the living room and flash a bright smile at Lars.

He looks at me with narrowed eyes. "What's wrong?"

I shake my head, my smile in place. "Nothing. Everything is just perfect."

"Something is wrong. Tell me what it is, baby."

God, I want to confide in him, tell him the whole sordid story, but now I have another sword hanging over my head. Telling him could mean he'd lose his job. I know he loves being here, and the last thing I want to do to him is to part him from his beloved mountain. I walk up to him and rub my hand against the bulge in his pants. His face changes as I knew it would. His cock jerks instantly to attention.

He groans. "Hell, Tamara. You're going to make me come in my pants."

I take my hand away. "What have you got planned for us today."

He gives a slow smile. "We could start by finishing what you just started."

I put Tamara out of my mind and grin at him. "That's just to keep you keen and mean for when I show you my cherry pop routine."

"I am keen and mean." His eyebrows fly into his hat. "Wait! Your what?"

I wink. "You'll just have to wait and see, won't you?"

"You expect me to wait after telling me about your cherry pop routine?"

I stand on the tips of my toes and nibble at his earlobe. "Trust me, it's worth the wait."

He runs his hand through his hair. "Jesus, woman. You sure know how to drive a man crazy."

"What's the plan for today?"

"Come on. We're taking the horses out," he says, picking up a bag.

"What's in the bag?"

"Let me in on what a cherry pop routine is and I'll tell you what's in the bag."

"No way. Only a fool would accept a cow in exchange for magic beans."

He throws his head back and laughs, the sound warming my heart and saddening it at the same time.

We go to the horse barn to get our horses. If I thought the sexual tension was bad before, it is ten times worse now. I just want him inside me all the time. I force myself to stop thinking about sex and concentrate on saddling Thunder.

I set Thunder's saddle in almost the same time frame as Lars saddles Devil's Ride, which makes me really proud. We go through the barn doors and out into the sunshine,

"So, what are we doing?" I ask

"We're going on a picnic."

"A picnic? Really?" I feel my heart lift.

His dimples show. "That's the plan. But we don't have to if you'd rather show me your cherry pop routine instead…"

"Nope, that'll keep. I want to go on a picnic," I say with an easy smile as I prepare to mount Thunder.

"Shame," he replies, swinging his leg over Devil's Ride.

Lars leads us beyond the horse pasture where the rest of the horses are roaming freely for the day. Dismounting from his horse, he opens the fence and waits for me to ride through before closing the fence and getting back on Devil's Ride. We change from a canter to a gallop, but Lars lets me decide the pace I am comfortable with as we cross the open grasslands. The wind tears through my hair and I bend forward and laugh with exhilaration as I urge Thunder to go faster. It is one of the most amazing sensations I have ever experienced. The power of the animal beneath me makes me feel one with nature and fantastic speed makes me feels as if I'm flying.

Soon, Lars gives me a hand signal and we drop to a trot. My face feels flushed as I look at him. He smiles encouragingly at me. I pat Thunder's neck and start to notice the scenic landscape around me. More than once, I find myself silently praying that one day I will have the chance to live in a place as beautiful as this, doing something as fun as this. Eventually, we arrive at an Aspen grove.

We follow a narrow trail that winds between the majestically tall trees and to my delight it opens out to an enclosure of vibrant green grass. There is a stream running through it with mossy stones at its banks and the air is lovely and cool. Red flowers sprinkle the ground and there are lilies growing in amongst the Aspen.

"Like it?" he asks.

"I don't think I've ever seen anything more beautiful," I reply, gazing at my surroundings in amazement. How can one place be so beautiful in so many different ways? I never thought that a ranch would be my favorite place on earth, but it truly is. I haven't been many places, but this is by far the most magnificent.

We dismount and let the horses drink the fresh, cool water before we tie them to a tree. Lars unloads the bulky bag from his horse and walks to a shady patch. He pulls a blanket from the bag, lays it out on the ground, and signals for me to sit on it. I take a seat and watch as he unpacks the basket he brought with him. Inside, it is filled with food.

"Mini sandwiches and turkey and ham. I also brought the condiments because I don't know what you like," he says, unveiling a packet full of small sandwiches and a whole bunch of condiment bottles.

"Chocolate covered strawberries," he adds, extracting a long Tupperware container of the fruit from his basket.

"And," he finishes, "a bottle of champagne."

"My, my," I murmur, widening my eyes.

Ignoring the sandwiches, I take a chocolate covered strawberry from the bowl. "You could do one more thing to make it better," I say, taking the entire strawberry in my mouth and biting off the stalk. It is just as juicy and sweet as I expected.

"What?" he asks, leaning back.

"Kiss me."

"I can do that." He pushes himself against me, eating the rest of the strawberry from my mouth. I groan and allow him to finish the chocolate flavored kiss with a sweep of his tongue.

"Now it's perfect," I whisper.

But it wasn't truly perfect until I undressed and, unmindful of a couple of peeping tom wild pigs in the grove, showed him the cherry pop routine that I stole from Jesse and he had slurped champagne from my breasts.

FORTY-FOUR
Cass

By the time we return, Emma Jean is in the kitchen preparing dinner. I tell Lars I want to speak to her alone and he goes off down to road to see to some other chores. When I appear at the doorway, she is busy mixing something in a big bowl.

"Hey, Emma Jean," I say awkwardly.

"Hello, Poppet," she says with a big smile. If she has heard anything, she certainly is not showing it.

I walk over to the table and lean my hip on it. "What are you making?"

"Chicken pot pie."

"Oh."

"I see someone raided the fridge," she comments innocently.

I blush. "Yeah, we went for a picnic. The strawberries were delicious."

"I always said Albert's strawberries are the best."

I follow the grain of the wood on the table's surface with my finger. "Uh…I don't know whether you heard." I lift my head. "About last night…"

She snorts. "I'm not one for gossip, but I did tell Mabel Hawthorne that just cause some greenhorn troublemaker put his boots in the oven, that don't make them biscuits."

I look at her gratefully. "Thank you for defending me."

"Aww, honey. I wouldn't mind her. That woman never did know whether to check her ass or scratch her watch."

I smile. "I just wanted you to know that I'm not some porn star. I've never been in-"

"You don't have to tell me that, Poppet. I know exactly what you are. You're a real lady. From the top of your head to the soles of your feet."

I feel tears start pricking the back of my eyes. "Thank you, Emma Jean, for believing in me."

"I know what I know, child. Now you run along and go get into something pretty for dinner. I believe you might be having it in the dining room tonight."

****

That night I get dressed in one of Tamara's sexiest outfits and join Lars in the dining room. The plan is to have dinner, but Lars pushes me up against a wall and rips my panties off.

"It's your fault," he whispers in my ear. "You wore that damned dress, got me rock hard, and now you can take the consequences.

Our chicken pot pie is cold by the time we get to it, but I must say, the consequences were worth it. Afterwards, I get into my comfy pajamas while Lars makes a big bowl of popcorn. Then we curl up on the couch and watch a horror movie. It isn't very good and before long Lars stands up and, scooping me up from the couch, carries me upstairs.

253

I wrap my arms around his strong neck. "I've never been carried to a man's bedroom to be ravished before," I whisper.

"And I've never carried a woman to my bedroom to be ravished."

****

To my surprise, Ms. Moore calls me the next morning.

"Can you talk?" she asks.

"Sure. There's no one here."

"What did you say to put a bee in Tamara's bonnet?"

"Why do you say that?" I ask anxiously.

"Cass. Can you please tell me what you said to her to get her all riled up?"

My shoulders sag. "Nothing. I didn't say anything. She just found out that I like one of the ranch hands."

Ms. Moore goes silent for a couple of seconds. Then she sighs heavily. "I see. That's a shame."

"Why?" I ask worriedly.

"Because there is a change to the plan."

My stomach feels funny and I lay my hand on it.

"The original plan was for you to hurt yourself badly enough that you could bow out of riding or attending the masked ball, but you'll have to pretend to hurt yourself badly enough that you're too frightened to ride, but you are still able to go to the ball."

I start to feel sick. "What is her new plan?"

"In a nutshell. She wants to go to the masked ball herself."

"Oh," I gasp.

"I'm so sorry, Cass. You shouldn't have told her."

"I didn't. She forced me into admitting it." My fists clench as angry, helpless tears start running down my face. I am glad that Ms. Moore cannot see them. I swallow hard and try to get a hold of myself, but in spite of my best efforts, a sob tears out of my throat.

"Oh, Cass," Ms. Moore says. "Come on, be a brave girl. You couldn't have kept him anyway."

That makes the tears fall even faster. I take a deep, shuddering breath. Just because she has money she is just going to come down here and steal my man and there's not a single thing I can do about it. My heart feels as if it is breaking into a million pieces.

"Stop crying, dear."

"Goodbye, Ms. Moore," I sob.

"Just a minute. Wait."

I dash the tears away with the back of my hand. "What?"

"Look, let me see what I can do for you, okay?" she says.

"Thank you," I choke out and cut the connection. Then I rush to my bathroom, strip my clothes off, and get into the shower. I switch it on and ugly cry for a long time. I never dreamed when I took this job that I'd be asked to step aside and let Tamara take away the man I fall in love with. The tears mingle with the water rushing away down the drain.

****

That night, Lars has to go to New York on business. I sit alone on the patio. Part of me refuses to believe that in five days, I will be back in Chicago, to my old life. I can't get it out of my mind that soon, all this beauty will become just a memory. A dream I once had. I will never see Emma Jean, or Chance, or Butch, or Lars ever again.

I pick up the wine bottle by the neck and refill my glass. I have already had two glasses and I feel very, very drunk. But I've cried a lot and I need to replace the liquid. My phone rings. At first, I consider not picking it up. It's probably just Jessie and I don't want her to see me looking so down, but then I think what the hell. I need to talk to someone. I lurch unsteadily to the phone and find it's not Jessie. It's Ms. Moore.

"Hello," I say.

"Can you talk?" she asks.

"Yes. I'm alone."

"Cass, do you want to go to the ball?"

I grip the phone hard. "Yes."

"But you do know that you cannot have that man, right?"

"I know." She is right. The sooner I accept it, the better it will be for me.

"This is what I will do for you. I'll send you an exact replica of the dress that Tamara will be wearing. You will wear that and go to the ball. Dance with your ranch hand and have fun, but as soon as I call you on your mobile phone, you must go to the bathroom where you will exchange places with Tamara."

"Tamara agreed to this?" I ask incredulously.

"She doesn't know yet. I will work it in such a way that she gets delayed, and it will seem as if you are doing her a favor to appear during the first half of the ball."

"Thank you, Ms. Moore."

"Though you cannot let on to him who you are, you can say a private goodbye from your heart. Remember why you're doing this. When you get back, you can start again with all your debts paid. You are a beautiful girl and there will other men for you, okay?"

"Okay."

"Now, go take a couple of headache tablets and go to sleep. You might escape waking up with a hangover. Oh, and switch your phone off tonight. You don't need to deal with her until tomorrow. She's only going to call to gloat."

"I will switch my phone off. Goodnight, Ms. Moore. You've been very, very kind to me. I just want you to know that I really appreciate it."

"Goodnight, Cass," she says softly before the line goes dead.

****

I go and lie down on my bed. The room is swimming. My life feels empty and sad. I close my eyes and try to think of me galloping across the grasslands with Lars. I was happy that day. I feel a hand stroke my face and open my eyes to see Lars sitting on my bed. In the silver moonlight, he is incredibly beautiful.

"What are you doing here? Aren't you supposed to be in New York?" I whisper.

"I couldn't stay away. I missed the feel of your skin."

I turn my cheek to his hand. The alcohol has made me emotional and I just want to cry.

"Hey," he says, a frown on his face. "What's wrong?"

"Nothing."

His eyes narrow. "Have you been crying?"

"No."

He switches on the light. "You have been crying. Why?"

I remember that I don't have my contact lenses in and immediately reach over and switch the light off. Oh, how I wish I could tell him. That I could stop lying to him. How I wish I didn't have to go back to Chicago, back to my dreary life. How I wish he could be mine.

He strokes my hair. "Tell me, Tamara. Please? Whatever it is, we'll sort it out."

My eyes fill with tears and run down my temples.

"Is it something I've done?"

"No."

"Are you hurt?"

I shake my head. Lord, men are so stupid.

"Has someone else upset you?"

"No," I say quickly.

"Then what is it?"

"I've been drinking and sometimes when I drink, I get emotional. Nothing is wrong."

"Bullshit," he growls.

My phone starts ringing. I forgot to turn it off. He frowns. "Who's calling you at this hour?"

"No one important," I say. I'll deal with Tamara tomorrow. At this point, there's nothing more she can take from me. Rising on my elbows, I kiss his mouth. At first, he is too distracted by the identity of the caller to respond, but then he makes a muffled curse, wraps his hands around me, and kisses me back as if he is a man who has been lost in a desert for a long, long time and has suddenly come upon a creek full of sweet water. After a while, I don't hear the phone ringing either. All I feel is his tongue, his hands, his body, his cock. As if he can feel my desperation, he makes love to me frantically. Our fingers clawing at each other, our bodies pushing against each other as if trying to meld together.

When it is over, I start drifting to sleep in his arms.

He murmurs something in my ear, but I am too drunk to make it out. My mind and body are too tired. I want to tell him I love him, but even that is too much effort. It is a relief when the blessed darkness comes to claim me.

****

I wake up with an electric sledgehammer inside my head. I should have taken those pills before I went to bed. The sun is high in the sky, throwing squares of light onto the wooden floor. I roll over and groan. There is only the indentation in the pillow next to me to show that I did not dream last night. Lars did come to me.

I stumble into the bathroom and stand under the spray of hot water and give myself a stern pep talk. You've got to stop with the self-pity. You've got Dad to think of. Be strong. Finally clean and feeling a bit more human, I get dressed and go over to the kitchen. There is a note under a magnet on the fridge door for me. Lars is out mending fences with the boys, and Emma Jean has gone to town. I am directed to the fridge where I find a ham sandwich inside.

I take a couple of headache tablets and eat the sandwich. Then, I go out to the stables. For the last few days now I have not been expected to shovel horse dung or patrol the grounds picking up dog poop or trash. In fact, Lars has made sure that I have so little to do, I now spend most of my time grooming the horses or riding them. As soon as I enter the barn, Thunder neighs and calls to me. I stand in front of his pin and hold out the lump of sugar.

"I will miss you," I whisper sadly against his sleek face.

FORTY-FIVE
Cass

There are only two days left before I have to leave the ranch. Before lunch, a courier brings my ballgown in a massive cardboard box. I sign for it and take it to my room. My fingers are shaking when I break it open and carefully take the dress out of its tissue.

It's a stunning peacock-blue, floor-length, full skirted affair that looks like it has been plucked from the pages of a fairytale. With a sweetheart neckline, a crystal embellished bodice, and yards and yards of organza, silk, and tulle, it is quite simply the most beautiful and dreamy dress I have ever seen.

I try it on and it fits perfectly.

Inside the package, there is also a pair of designer shoes that look like they are made of rainbow-hued glass. I could never even have dreamed of owning something so gorgeous in my other life. I step into them, stand in front of the mirror, and stare at myself in amazement.

I hardly recognize myself. I'm not the same girl who came to this ranch. I came here, desperate for money but strong and confident, and I am leaving a broken woman defeated by a selfish, rich whore. Still, it's a funny ole world. I came here to impersonate Tamara and now she's coming here to impersonate me.

I turn away from the mirror and carefully take my dress off.

Yesterday, Lars told me that I could take the day off and do anything I liked on my last day here. He smiled when he said it, but he had no idea how much my heart hurt to hear those words. We both know I'm leaving tomorrow, but I'm the only one who knows that I won't ever come back.

I know Tamara only wants him because she knows I want him. After she has taken him away from me, she won't want him for long. A ranch hand won't fit in with her plans. I saw how rude she was to the blond man. She won't be able to do that with Lars.

But none of it will matter by then. I'll be gone, never to see Lars again. I'll be back in Chicago. He'll stay here, doing his job, and eventually, he'll forget about me.

I know I won't ever forget him.

I hang the dress up carefully and go back out to the house. Lars is just coming in from outside. His face breaks into a grin. "Guess where I'm taking you?" he asks.

I smile softly up to him. "Your bedroom?"

He grabs my ass. "That's where I want to take you, and probably where I should, but I'm actually taking you to the Dairy Queen."

"That sounds great." I try to look happy.

He looks at me strangely. "So, what are your thoughts about the day after tomorrow?"

"What about the day after tomorrow?" I ask more specifically. I don't want to talk about anything he isn't talking about. I don't even know if I *can* talk about leaving without bursting into floods of tears again.

"You know what I'm talking about. You'll be leaving and we need to talk about it."

"Can we not talk about it?" I ask, my voice cracking slightly.

"You're just not going to talk about it at all? That's your plan?" he asks.

"Would it be so bad if we just let things roll and see where it goes."

He stares at me and I find I can't hold his gaze.

"This discussion is not over, but I'll leave it for the moment. Let's go," he says quietly. We walk to the car in silence.

Lars has no idea how hard this is for me. This isn't my decision, yet I have to act like it is. I wish with all my heart he could know the truth. If only there was a way I could tell him without getting him into trouble.

We almost don't speak at all in the car. Lars seems preoccupied as he stares straight ahead, and I am too sad to pretend to be happy. I try turning on the radio, but he turns it back off, explaining that there is never any proper reception around that area. We pull into Dairy Queen after almost an hour of dead silence. As always, he opens my door for me and leads me in like a gentleman.

It is small and rustic and nothing like the one in Chicago. There is no one inside except the staff and a man with his hat pulled low over his eyes. There is a girl with pigtails standing behind the counter, who smiles at us.

"We're getting ice cream to go, Sophia," Lars tells her. "You know my order."

She looks at me and I ask for double chocolate chip.

Sophia gets the ice cream in record time and Lars pays, leaving her a ten-dollar tip.

Once we're back in the car eating our ice cream, Lars speaks again. "You may not want to talk about it, but I need to. You can't just leave here without some kind of discussion of how we go forward."

"I have a life and it's not here," I say, staring miserably at my ice cream.

"Have I ever asked you to move up here?"

"No, but…oh, I wish I could explain the situation I'm in, but I can't."

"I accept that long distance relationships are hard, but we'll work it out."

I set my ice cream in the cup holder of the car and scoot over to him. He wraps both of his arms around me and rubs my back. "There is no future for us, Lars," I whisper.

He tightens his hold on my body. "I can't accept that. How old are you?"

I rack my brains. Has anybody mentioned Tamara's age to me? "You're not supposed to ask a woman her age," I say.

"Do you realize how rare what we have is? You're young so you think you can find what we have under every rock you pick up, but I can tell you now, what we have is precious. I'm twenty-nine and I've never found what we have with anyone else. My brother is older than me and he doesn't have it either."

"I'm sorry, but I've made up my mind."

He takes a deep breath of frustration. It makes his chest rise against my cheek. "There has to be a reason for your decision. Are you afraid of what your dad will say? Because I can talk to him if you are."

"No, Lars. I'm not afraid of that."

"Is it something to do with the loan sharks?"

"No."

"Then it just doesn't make sense. Did I do something wrong? Tell me, because I can change for you."

I feel the tears start streaming from my eyes. "No, I never want you to change anything. You're perfect. Nothing about you needs to change. It's not you, it's me. I wish I could explain, but I literally can't. This is so hard."

"Well, I'm not fucking giving up. I'm going to get to the bottom of this if it's the last thing I do," he growls stubbornly.

I don't know what to do anymore. The man I want more than I want anything else in the world is asking me to stay and I can't. I never knew life could be so cruel. I start sobbing into his chest and he just holds me.

Our ice cream melts and eventually, he starts the truck and pulls away. I don't bother looking up or moving away from him. I can't move away from him. I never want to. If only I didn't have to.

My tears stop. He takes one hand off the wheel and plays with my hair. All I want is for him to understand, but he can't because I can't tell him the truth. Money may not be as important as happiness, but I need this money to help pay for my father's medical bills. That's why I'm here, and that's why I can't quit now.

We arrive at the ranch, but my hands refuse to let him go. Instead of pulling away from me, he sweeps me into his arms. Leaving our ice cream cups in the truck, he carries me gently into the house and into my bedroom. Carefully, he lays me on my bed and pulls the covers over my body. He doesn't understand that what I need is him.

"Please stay," I whisper as he turns to leave.

"Is that what you want?"

I don't tell him that I need him to love me the way I love him, because tomorrow, he won't be mine anymore. Tomorrow, Tamara will probably get him drunk and bounce on him. Even that passing thought makes me feel sick to my stomach. I just want to live out tonight like I'll never leave. "I want us to play out this night as if I'm not leaving. I want you inside me and all over my body."

"I can do that," he whispers, climbing under the covers with me. "Because you're not leaving. Not ever."

How I wish that were true.

We don't have the hot passion that we had before. What we have this time is so much more intimate and profound. We work slowly and diligently at taking off our clothing and lay together for the longest time, skin touching skin.

I stare into his silver eyes as he enters my body, and cry for the person that I may have become if I could have stayed with him. He is the man I can see myself making a family with and growing old with. I can see us surrounded by a whole bunch of curtain biters. My future could have been so bright here, but I have to leave it all.

Sometimes, life throws you slices of happiness, but it quickly balances the bliss with sadness. That has been the story of my life. Lars is that shining slice. Now it is time for balance again.

Finally, after what feels like hours of being caught in my own head, Lars gives me exactly what I asked from him. A climax so deep and long I feel as if I have broken into a million pieces. Like star dust, I float away, weightless and uncaring about what tomorrow brings.

FORTY-SIX
Cass

I feel as if I am walking around in a daze. There is so much activity around me, and everyone seems to be so excited about the masked ball happening tonight. Apparently, it happens only once a year and is attended by the governor. Even Emma Jean has gone to town to get her hair done. Tamara's father is supposed to arrive at the ranch to watch me ride just before the ball starts.

This morning, I must somehow engineer my fall from a horse and feign injury; if I don't actually sustain a real injury. I decide I'd rather fall from Misty than Thunder. Not only is he more unpredictable, but I will also be a lot higher off the ground. My plan is to take Misty out in the morning and fake a fall when no one is watching.

Unfortunately, the opportunity for me to go out on my own with Misty doesn't arise, since Lars insists on warming up Thunder before I ride him in front of Tamara's father. Of course, he has no idea that I have absolutely no intention of riding for Tamara's father, or even being anywhere near the man.

I glance sideways at Lars and can't decide how he'll react when I pretend to hurt myself.

I lead Thunder into the horse pasture and Lars leads Bessie. It's been a while since she's been mounted due to her pregnancy, but Lars thinks it's time to ride her again.

"So, are we just going to trot them?" I ask. "Or are we sprinting?" My performance will be more believable if we're sprinting, but it will be much easier to fall at a slower pace.

"We shouldn't sprint with Bessie just yet. She's still healing from giving birth," he says.

We each mount our horses and begin trotting through the field. There aren't many options of places to fall off inside the horse pasture, but I'm afraid Thunder will spook and run if I fall, so I would rather it be in an enclosed area.

"How is the new baby doing?" I ask, referring to a foal that was born in the early hours of the morning. Neither Lars nor I were present. Only Chance and one of the other men were there to guard and help if necessary.

"She's funny. She likes new people." Lars laughs and I memorize the sound. I love hearing him laugh. "Just like her mama."

"Will I get to meet her?" I ask with a smile.

Lars doesn't respond for a moment. "You can see her if you stay a couple more days," he says. The tone of voice is heartbreaking, and I know I have to jump now. There aren't any bushes near me, and I don't know how safe the fall will be, but if I don't finish this job, I'm afraid I won't ever leave Lars' side.

I slide from the saddle and push myself to the side while reaching upward, as if I'm trying to get hold of the reins. A small screech escapes my lips as I fall backward. Then everything happens in slow motion. My senses become extra sharp. A clear thought flashes into my mind. *You idiot. You don't even have insurance.* I see the ground approaching fast and remember to turn myself midair so the brunt of the force will not be on my head.

"Damn, Tamara," I hear Lars curse as I land on the hard ground.

I feel my ankle pop and an intense pain shoot through my leg. My brain goes into disbelief mode. Oh god, did I just break my leg?

Thunder bolts across the field. It takes less than five seconds for Lars to be at my side. I lie on my back and grind my teeth together, not needing to fake the pain radiating from my ankle.

"Where does it hurt?" Lars shouts urgently, crouching next to me, his face pale under his tan.

"I think I broke my ankle," I groan.

"Don't move," he says, grasping my foot with both his hands.

"Oh no," I cry, looking worriedly at my booted leg. "What are you doing?"

"Getting this boot off."

Tears swim in my eyes as he takes the boot off and tosses it away.

"Shhh…I'll take care of you. It's okay," he says as his cool fingers gently and quickly move over my skin. He looks up at me, relief etched in his face. "It's not an obvious break." He takes a deep breath. "God, Tamara, you need to be more careful. You nearly gave me a heart attack," he says.

"Gave you a heart attack? I'm the one who's hurt."

"You can't imagine how fast my heart is beating. Fuck, when I saw you go down… Thank God, it's only a sprain or a fracture."

"It hurts like hell."

"Sometimes a sprain can hurt more than a fracture."

"Whatever it is, I won't be able to ride for my father."

"Of course not. You can ride for him another time."

"No, I don't think I ever want to get back on another horse," I say quickly.

He looks at me strangely. "We'll see how you feel later. Can you stand?"

"I don't know."

He stands up and helps to pull me up. To my surprise, it doesn't hurt as much I thought it would. Maybe I got lucky. "I think I can still walk on it," I admit.

"It's good that you can stand on it, but let's get some ice on it straight away." He sweeps me into his arms and carries me back to the house. Lars wants to call a doctor, but I refuse. I know by how little pain I am feeling that I haven't done any real harm and it's more fear than anything else that made me panic before.

I lie on the couch with an icepack on my ankle for the next hour. It is badly bruised, but that is only because I bruise easily. The swelling itself is minimal. After a while, I realize that I can walk quite well on it. I still want to attend the ball and have a dance with Lars. He comes in with some bandages and wraps my ankle. He also brings a pair of crutches.

"Do you want to give the ball a miss? We don't have to go."

I shake my head. "No, I want to go."

"All right. I have to go meet the governor so I've asked Chance to bring you. I'll see you there, okay?"

"What if you don't recognize me?"

"Baby, there's not a mask in the world that can hide you from me."

"I'll see you at the ball tonight."

His eyes pierce into mine and my tears begin stirring. I broke my ankle—or greatly injured it—and I didn't cry. But as I watch him suffer with the same turmoil I have been for weeks, I want nothing more than to curl into a ball.

FORTY-SEVEN
Cass

I take two Vicodin and hobble into the bathroom. I may still be in shock to think that I have done the dreaded fall and that it is all coming to an end tonight. I take a shower and am cautious not to get my bandage wet. When I get out, I find Selene, Tamara's hairdresser, standing on the patio.

"Hey," Selene says. "Ms. Moore sent me to make sure you have exactly the same hairstyle as Her Highness."

"Okay, where do you want me?" She points to a chair and I go sit on it.

For the next forty minutes, she works on piling my hair into a complicated updo. When she is finished, she picks up her bag and walks toward the sliding doors. "Right, I'm off. You look amazing, by the way."

"Thanks."

I stand up and walk to the mirror and take in the sleek beauty of her work. Cautiously, without ruining my hair, I get into my dress. The dress is comfortable and feels like silk on my skin. I slip into the heels and feel a twinge of pain, but when I walk, it doesn't feel too bad.

I paint my eyes dramatically as I know Tamara would and apply a layer of Cherry Lush lipstick. The last piece of the outfit is the mask. I cross the bathroom and grab the mask before bringing it to the mirror. It's a stunning black half-face mask with sharp edges and teal and blue designs that make it both pop and match my dress.

I slip the plastic over my face and look in the mirror with wide eyes.

Tonight will be the last time I'll ever see Lars.

FORTY-EIGHT
Lars

I usually avoid public gatherings like the plague, but Tamara has changed everything. I can't wait to see her, dance with her, and then take her home and make love to her all night.

Realizing that she is on the verge of leaving, I finally admit to myself that I love the woman. When she fell off her horse and got hurt, I felt as if a part of me had shriveled up and died. At that moment, I knew I'd give my own life to save hers. I have never loved anyone the way I love Tamara, and I won't lose those feelings. I plan on being with her forever. I don't understand what's going on with her, but I know she's hiding something. I can see how cut up she is about leaving, but she insists on going. I know she loves it here, so I can't understand why she wants to run away tomorrow. I must find a way to convince her to stay.

I will tell her everything about myself tonight. There are so many things she needs to know, and once she does, I won't let her go.

I will do whatever I have to do in the few hours I have left to get to the bottom of this mystery and convince her to stay.

I stand on the balcony and scan the crowd for Tamara. The entrance is above the ball itself, so I am able to look over everybody inside. From above, they all look unidentifiable in their strange costumes and masks, but it only takes me a second to find her. Her head of bleached blonde hair stands out beyond everyone else's as she arrives on Chance's arm. I see that everybody has turned to watch her. She is, without doubt, the most beautiful woman in this hall. My heart swells with pride even as I curse every man who lays eyes on her and thinks a dirty thought.

I walk down the steps and as I near Tamara, I notice her wince in pain and my heart drops. She's gotten so many injuries since being here and I couldn't stop any of them.

"Tamara," I call out.

She turns around and I stare at the bright blue dress that hugs her body in every area. It's a body I've seen up close, sucked, licked, bitten, and entered many, many times, but I can't help but gawk at how beautiful she is.

"It's you," she whispers coming in my direction and smiling with the same, shy smile that got me up all knotted up around her little finger.

"Of course, who else would it be?" I ask, handing her a glass of champagne.

She smiles.

"How's your ankle."

She shakes her head. "Vicodin took care of it. It doesn't really hurt at all."

I raise my glass. "A toast."

She raises her glass.

"To the most beautiful woman here."

"I'm not," she says.

"Every man in this places wishes he was me," I tell her truthfully.

"You're not so bad looking yourself," she says, taking a delicate sip.

Taking a step closer, I bow and open a hand to her. "Will you do me the honor of dancing with me? It gives me an excuse to feel you up in a public place," I tell her with a wolfish grin.

"I'm not very good at ballroom dancing," she says, taking a small step back.

I take the glass from her hand and leave it by the ledge. "All you have to do is follow my lead, baby."

She puts her hand in mine and I pull her toward me. Wrapping my arm tightly around her to help take some weight off her ankle, I lead her toward the middle of the dance floor.

She looks up at me. "I feel as if I'm a princess in a fairytale," she whispers, and her breath is like a magic mist.

"Well, for what it's worth, you make me feel like a prince with a kingdom," I say as I twirl her about the room, lost to everything but her lovely face looking up at me. I let my fingers trail down her naked back and feel her take a sharp breath. Circling her waist, I take her through a series of spins that leaves her breathless and wide-eyed.

"We need to talk," I say into her ear. I feel her shiver beneath me and bury my nose in the top of her head. I can't let her go. I will never let her go.

"How about we talk after the dance?" she compromises. I notice her eyes start swimming with tears again. She blinks them back furiously.

What the hell is going on? "After the dance," I agree. I'd agree to almost anything for her.

She presses herself against me and allows herself to move in every direction that I move. I could stand this close to her all day and be perfectly content, but my contentment will only last until she moves. She continues looking into the skylight and at the slowly darkening sky, but I don't know why.

As the ending melody of the song plays, I look down at her. Her phone rings. "I need to go to the bathroom," she says with a sad smile. "We can talk after that, all right?"

I nod and give her a small peck on the cheek. I reach to the floor and grab her crutches for her. "And you're going to tell me the verdict on your foot," I say.

"It's sprained," Tamara whispers. "Okay, I'll be back. I'll miss you, Lars," she says before turning and walking away.

I stand in place and make small conversation with the people around me for a while. I check the clock periodically, wondering where she could have gone. She's got a bad ankle, but she shouldn't be taking this long.

I begin walking around and scanning the crowd. My nerves grow tense the longer I look, so I ask people around me if they've seen her.

FORTY-NINE
Cass

Lifting my long skirt, I hurry as quickly as I can to the ladies' room. There are only two women in there, chatting and touching up their make-up. As I walk past, one of them smiles at me and compliments me on my dress. I thank her distractedly and go quickly toward the last stall.

I try the door and find it is locked. I knock softly and Tamara opens it instantly. Glaring at me, she yanks me in and closes the door. She is dressed exactly like me and her hair is done up like mine too. The only differences are her breasts are bigger and her waist is smaller. Selena told me that she had had a rib taken out to achieve that look. The only way Lars won't notice is if she gets him really drunk. Or maybe he won't care. Maybe he will prefer her narrower body and bigger breasts.

"What took you so long?" she whispers fiercely. "I've been stuck in this smelly toilet for nearly an hour."

"Ms. Moore called me less than three minutes ago," I say.

"Whatever," she huffs. "So, where is he?"

"By the pillar on the left-hand side of the main room."

"What's he wearing?"

"A white shirt, black tux, black pants, and a black mask."

She wriggles her shoulders and pushes her chest out. "How do I look?"

"Great."

"Better than you, anyway," she says nastily and fits her mask over her face. She giggles. "This is such fun."

I don't say anything.

"Is he good in bed?"

I look at her coldly and refuse to answer.

"Never mind, I'll find out myself tonight. I might send you a little video of us doing it."

"Why would you want to do that?" I ask her.

"Because I want you to watch the man you love fuck me."

"Why would you do this to me?" I ask.

"It's hard to find entertainment in show business," she says with a shrug.

I know she is lying. "That's not why you're doing it, is it?"

Her eyes flash with temper. "Because even though you brown nose me all the time, I know you think you're somehow better than me." She jabs me in the chest. "Well, Miss Holier Than Thou, you're not. You're nothing but dirt at the bottom of my shoe. And I can take your man any time I want. I'll take him, I'll suck him dry, then I'll kick him to the curb."

I stare at her in astonishment. She is horribly jealous of me. I have no money, or fame, or celebrity status. I don't get to experience the high life the way she does. Why would she be jealous of me?

"You hurt your leg. Which one?" she asks, suddenly changing the subject.

"Right ankle."

"What did you do? Sprain it?"

For a second, I don't answer. Then my mouth opens and out it comes, the lie that I hope trips her up and gets her into trouble. "I fractured it," I say.

Her brow furrows. "Is that like a break?"

"Exactly. I've broken my leg. Make sure you hobble up to him and complain a lot about the pain."

"Hobble?"

"Uh…huh. Like this," I say, making an exaggerated hobbling movement in the confined space.

She doesn't look happy about it. I've earned this small satisfaction. This is my pathetic little revenge for all the times she has woken me up in the early morning hours for no reason at all, for when she pushed me to the ground, and for taking the man I love and rubbing it in my face. As many times as I have cursed her, let me give her a reason to curse me instead.

"Oh, and I guess I might as well give you my bandage too. Otherwise, he'll see that your leg is not swollen."

"Hurry up," she urges impatiently.

I quickly remove my bandage and give it to her.

She lifts her skirt. "Put it on me," she orders.

I crouch down next to the toilet and quickly wrap her ankle. "It's done,"

"There's the window. Now get through it."

I look at the small window, my eyes widening. "You want me to go through that window?"

"Yes."

"I don't think I'll fit."

"Of course you will. If you get stuck, I'll give you a shove from this end."

"Why can't I just walk out. Nobody will notice."

She puts her hand on her hip. "And if someone does?"

I look again at the window. Maybe I can squeeze through it. "Where do I go once I get out?"

"There a car waiting for you outside."

"A car?"

"Oh, for fuck's sake, go already."

I take a deep breath. The sooner I get out of her presence the better for me. I slip my shoes off, put my good foot on the toilet seat, and climb on to it. The window is not locked, so I push it open and put my head through. The ground is not too far away, it is grassy, and there is nobody around.

"Watch that your fat ass doesn't get stuck," Tamara chides.

I get the first half of me through easily, but the skirt of the dress is big and I struggle to free my hip. I give a good tug and hear a loud tearing sound, but my hips are through.

"Hurry up," Tamara says impatiently.

I drop to the ground and feel a sharp pain in my ankle. I stand up. The skirt of my dress has been ripped away and is still caught in the window. Only the tulle underneath is still attached to the bodice of the dress. Tamara throws the torn skirt after me.

"Pass me my shoes," I whisper, holding my hands up to the window. Instead of giving them to me, she flings them out. What a bitch! I find one but can't find the other, and my ankle has started to throb with pain. I see a long black limo waiting by the curb. Someone opens the back door from the inside. My carriage awaits.

Fifteen minutes ago, I was the princess in a fairytale. It is clear now that there is no happily ever after to my story.

Oh, what the hell, I don't need that shoe anyway. Holding my one shoe and my torn skirt clutched against my body, I limp toward the car. I duck my head and look through the open door.

Ms. Moore is in the car. I get in, and close the door.

"Well done. You just earned yourself $30,000.00," she says.

FIFTY
(One Week Later)
Cass

Nothing ever hurt as bad as leaving Lars at that Town Hall with Tamara Honeywell. Obviously, my lame attempt to get her in trouble had no bearing on anything. I guess I kept a secret hope in my heart that he would realize she is not me. It cuts me to think he never even realized that I wasn't her.

Even if he had an identical twin, I'm certain I would be able to tell the difference between him any anyone else. I'd know by his taste, his smell, his touch, his smile, the little nuances about him that make him uniquely him. My mind always goes into a tailspin thinking of him doing to her all the things he did to me, and it makes me sick to my stomach.

Even though I know now that he couldn't even tell the difference between me and that repulsive witch, my heart aches for him and my body craves his touch. I wake up at night, restless, my soul longing, hurting. It's dangerous, but I get into my sweats and go out running until all my muscles are screaming.

My heart is broken and I don't know if I'll ever be whole again, but I don't regret Lars. Yes, it hurts badly, but I wouldn't change one second of it. It was the time I felt most alive.

Also, how can I regret something that has paved the opportunity for me to have a new life? I was drowning in debt and indescribably desperate. I didn't know which way to turn. Now, I've paid Dad's hospital bills and put the rest of the money (a sizable chunk) into an account for anything else he may need. I thought hard about paying Lars back, but doing that would have revealed that I'm not Tamara.

I need to make big changes to my life, but I will wait for a while more. I intend to keep my job stocking shelves while my father is still alive.

Once he is gone, I will leave Chicago. I have decided to learn to be a horse trainer. I know now, that I belong on a ranch. I want to look up at the night sky and hear my soul sing. There has not been one night that has passed when I have not longed for the big sky of Montana. Just remembering those nights I sat alone watching the stars shine brings a new wave of sadness to my heart.

A sigh escapes me.

I look at my watch. It's nearly five. Emma Jean will be starting dinner about now. I pray that Tamara was not rude to her before she left. She doesn't deserve that. She is one of those special people.

I lift my head and look at my father, his chest rising and falling gently. He is sleeping, but sometimes he seems so still, I panic and have to hold my hand next to his nostrils to make sure he is still breathing. I lay my hand on his wasted arm and he shows no reaction. He is so near and yet so far away. In my heart, I am aware it is nearly time. My father is all but gone. His moments of lucidity are fewer and fewer, and they are always accompanied by pain and with no recognition of me or his surroundings.

Quietly, I stand and walk to the window. The evening sun is bright, and on the well-maintained grounds, patients are being pushed about slowly in wheelchairs. There is something very depressing in the sight and I turn away from it and rest my eyes on my father's pale, shrunken face. Pain has hollowed out his cheeks and eyes. His eyelids are a network of fine blue and purple veins, and his thin lips are shiny with the lip balm I applied.

My phone starts vibrating in my pocket and I take it out and look at the screen. To my surprise, it is not Jesse, but Mrs. Carter. I haven't heard from her since she wired the money into my account. I slip out of my father's room and go into the corridor.

"Hello, Mrs. Carter."

As usual, she skips the pleasantries. "You must have done a wonderful job last time because Tamara Honeywell wants to rehire you for another gig."

"What?"

"It's very late notice, I know, because you'll have to ship out tomorrow," she says, and before I can get a word in edgewise, rushes ahead, "but it's a very exciting one this time. You're being sent to New York! It's just a single day, but you can stay on for another day and get your shopping fix. You'll have to take comfortable shoes, but old, throwaway ones. The streets of New York are filthy. And here's the best part of all. You won't have to muck dirt or fall off a horse this time. You'll get a thousand dollars just for cutting a ribbon at the opening of a new wing at a center for children with cancer or something like that."

"It sounds like a wonderful job, but I'm not interested, Mrs. Carter."

"Why not?" she shoots back in a surprised voice.

"My dad is very ill. I can't leave him."

"Oh! Well, uh, it's just for one day. You don't even have to stay for the shopping if you don't want to."

"No, maybe you can offer the job to the girl who usually impersonates Tamara."

She pauses. I can imagine her frowning. "Is it the money? Because I'm sure I could get them to pay a bit more."

"No, it's not the money."

"How about if I arrange it so that you are back on the same day?"

I groan under my breath. Might as well just come out with it. "Look, I'm sorry, but I really don't ever want to impersonate Tamara again. It's just not for me."

There is a moment of silence. "You do know you won't have to meet her this time."

"Yeah, I gathered that. I just don't want to have anything to do with her, that's all. Sorry."

"Hmm…yes, that is rather a shame. Well, goodbye, Cass." She sounds very disappointed and it makes me feel bad to let her down, but even the thought of pretending to be Tamara again makes my skin crawl.

"Bye, Mrs. Carter."

I put my phone back into my pocket and return to Dad's room. He is lying in the same position I left him in. I kiss his forehead. His skin feels cold.

"I love you, Dad," I whisper before I leave him. As I walk down the corridor, my phone buzzes again. I look at the caller ID and come to a dead stop.

"Hello, Ms. Moore."

"Cass. How are you dear?"

"I'm fine, thank you."

"Mrs. Carter tells me you don't want the job."

"That's right. I don't ever want to impersonate Tamara again."

The line goes silent for a few seconds. "Would you please do it as a favor to me? Just this once. I've messed up badly and booked this engagement when I knew she wouldn't be finished with the reality TV thing she signed up for. I'd really, really appreciate it if you could do this one thing for me."

"Oh, Ms. Moore. I really don't want to pretend to be her again."

"It'll just be for an hour or so. I'll double the fee."

"It's not the money," I almost wail. I hate saying no to Ms. Moore.

"Please," she begs. "I would never ask if it wasn't important."

Ms. Moore has always been kind to me, and it makes me feel horribly ungrateful and churlish that I cannot return the kindness when it sounds like such a short and easy gig to do. What harm can it do to help her out once? "All right. I'll do it this once, but please don't ever ask me again."

"Thank you, Cass. Thank you, very much. I promise you, you won't regret it. It'll be the easiest grand you'll ever earn. You'll be picked up and flown by private plane. A chauffeur will take you to the ceremony. Once you get there, someone will be there to hold your hand and make sure that everything goes well. Afterwards, you can decide if you want to stay for a few days, or I can arrange for you to be returned back to Chicago on the same day."

"I'd like to return on the same day, please."

"Of course."

"What time will I be picked up tomorrow?" I ask.

"Nine-thirty in the morning, your time."

"Fine."

After a week of trying to heal myself, I'm being forced to stick a bandage over a gunshot wound and crawl back to pretend to be the woman who destroyed me.

FIFTY-ONE
Cass

I'm in Carrie Bradshaw's New York and dressed in something she would wear, right down to a pair of blue and white striped Manolo Blahnik shoes. As the limo crawls through the streets, I crane my neck to look at the cityscape and the crowds of people, much better dressed than in Chicago, hurry along the streets.

Despite myself, I get caught up in the ceaseless energy and excitement that is New York. It's crazy, but the graffiti, trash, and dirt contribute to the distinct character of the city. It is almost cinematic. One day, I promise myself, when my Dad is no longer here, I'll come back here to visit, shop, and take in a show on Broadway.

The building is a glass and chrome high-rise in lower Manhattan. As soon as we arrive, an Asian woman with very shiny, shoulder-length black hair comes out and opens the door.

"Hello, Miss Honeywell. I'm Simran," she says. "It's so great that you could make it. Did you have a good flight?"

"Yeah, it was great, thanks," I say, stepping onto the sidewalk. Even the air smells different.

She looks at my dress wistfully. "Love your dress. It's gorgeous."

"Oh, thank you."

"Well, my job is to take you somewhere you can freshen up. Somebody there will also give you a rundown of your itinerary."

"Sure," I say and follow her into the building.

She ushers me quickly past the security guards and into one of the gleaming elevators. I stand in the elevator alongside her as she inserts a key. I'm amazed as we continue gaining floors all the way up to the penthouse. As soon as the elevator doors open, she turns to me. "This is you. Susan will take care of you from now on."

"Thank you," I say politely. I'm not doing that rude thing to random strangers anymore. I'm done with all that. If Tamara doesn't like it, she can kiss my fat ass.

"Goodbye," she says and I enter a reception area with black marble floors. It has a nest of pristine cream leather couches and a desk, behind which, a woman is sitting. She stands and comes forward. She is immaculately coiffured and dressed in a formal gray pant suit.

"Welcome to New York, Miss. Honeywell. I'm Susan Baxter. I'll show you into Mr. Redmond's office. He wants a quick word first."

"Er…who is Mr. Redmond?"

She looks at me strangely. "The owner of Trans Corp"

I have no idea what Trans Corp is. Thanks, Ms. Moore, for dropping me into another weird situation. Well, I'll just wing it as I go along. "Thank you," I say, wiping my sweaty palms down my dress. For some weird reason, I've started to feel a bit nervous.

She leads me to a set of tall mahogany doors. With a smile, she opens one of the doors and holds it open for me. I walk through and hear her close it behind me. I am standing in a massive room with a lofty ceiling and floor-to-ceiling glass windows. From every angle, all you see is the blue sky, the tops of all the skyscrapers, and the glittering city below.

From where I am standing, the view is mesmerizing, but my attention is riveted to the big black desk across the room and the black, leather swivel chair behind it. The chair is turned away from the door and all I can see is the top of a man's head.

I bite my bottom lip and clear my throat.

"Beautiful, isn't it?" a man's voice says.

My heart stops in my chest before restarting and beating at triple the speed it had been going at before he speaks. My metaphorical gunshot wound tears wide open and my knees turn to JELL-O. I stumble forward and sink into one of the two chairs in front of the desk.

The black leather chair turns around slowly and I blink and stare at him stupidly. He's not wearing a cowboy hat. And he's dressed in a suit. One that looks incredibly expensive. And he looks amazing. "You?" I gasp.

He smiles long and slow. "Hello, beautiful."

"What's going on, Lars? What are you doing here?" I whisper.

"You left something behind, Cass," he says and pushes a box toward me.

My hands shake as I lift the lid of the box. It's the shoe I lost outside the Town Hall. Dazed and blind-sided, I look up at him without any real comprehension. My brain feels like mush. He stands from his chair and reaches my sitting figure in a few confident strides. I shake my head in disbelief. He looks so different. So polished and unreachable.

He crouches beside me. "That's not all you left behind."

I frown, too confused to make heads or tails of what is going on. "No?"

"You left a broken heart behind, Cass. Mine."

My eyes open wide. "I broke your heart?"

"Into a million fucking pieces."

My eyes fill with tears and roll down my cheeks.

"Goddammit," he exclaims and pulls me toward his chest.

"I'll ruin your beautiful suit." I bawl like a two-year-old kid.

"Fuck the suit, Cass. I don't give a damn about anything but you. From the day I laid eyes on you, I didn't know what hit me. You led me a merry dance, young lady, and made me fall so crazy in love with you, I swear I don't know whether I'm coming or going."

"I love you too," I admit with a great sob.

"Well, that's nothing to cry about."

"I'm just sorry I lied. I had no choice."

"Listen to me, baby. I don't care that you lied about who you were. I lied about who I was too. I'm not a ranch hand. I own that ranch. I own all this too."

I look at him through a haze of tears. "You mean, you're rich?"

"Yup."

"Why would you hide something like that?"

He shrugs. "It suited me to let Tamara think I was a ranch hand. I wanted to know how she would treat my other workers. Besides, when I made that decision, I hadn't met you yet, and I thought I didn't want to deal with the likes of her coming onto me just because of my family name."

It hits me like a flash. My eyes widen. Redmond. Like Tamara's family, the Redmonds are another old-money family. "Your family is *the* Redmonds?"

"Guilty as charged."

I shake my head in disbelief. "So, there is no ribbon for me to cut?"

"Nope."

"Was Ms. Moore in on this too?"

"Of course."

"But how and when did you find out that I was not Tamara?"

"I threatened to expose Tamara to her father if she didn't tell me. She sang like a canary."

I swallow hard. "Did you do…anything with her that night at the ball?"

"Anything?"

I take a deep breath. "She was planning to trick you into bed with her."

He laughs harshly. "Are you kidding me? I wouldn't touch that mean bitch with a fucking bargepole."

A big smile of sheer relief spreads over my face. It grows wider and wider. I can't stop beaming at him.

"Actually, I still can't get over the fact that you would think I could be fooled even for a minute. Hell, I'd been eating, sleeping, and breathing you for weeks. I know every inch of your body, Cass. Of course, I'd know it wasn't you."

"I thought if you were drunk enough."

"Drunk? I'd have to be blind, deaf, and dumb to think she was you. She's nothing but an empty, selfish, soulless, tired, nasty, plastic doll. And she's stupid and rude to boot. You, on the other hand, are as fresh-faced as a rain-washed apple, intelligent, kind, warm, sweet, sexy, complicated, fun, deep, caring- Hey, are you crying?" he asks, frowning.

"Yeah, tears of happiness, you dork."

"Dork, am I?"

I nod vigorously.

"Tell me more about that girl I fell in love with under the big sky?"

"Cass Harper lived in a drab little room in a horrible area of Chicago. She worked hard to earn money, but it all went to pay for her sick father's hospital bills. When that was not enough, she took a loan from some loan sharks and they kept on adding more and more interest to it. It got so that she didn't even have enough to pay her rent. That was when she took a job to impersonate Tamara Honeywell on a ranch in Montana."

"I'm so sorry, Cass. I'm here now. From now on, you'll never need to work a day in your life if you don't want to." Standing on one knee, he takes my hand between his. "I love you, Cass. For better or worse, I'm here."

"Well, I've loved you since the day I stopped hating your arrogant ass," I say with a chuckle.

He laughs and pulls something from his pocket. "Now, don't think I'm proposing just yet. I'm gonna do it, just not now." He shows me a velvet box. "I don't know you, and you don't know me, but I want to know you, and a year from now, I'll bring you back here and give you this ring and ask you to be my wife."

He opens the box. I look down at the ring and gasp. It is a beautiful pink stone set in white gold. "Oh, Lars. It's beautiful."

I look into his molten gray eyes, soft with love and tenderness. I push him back a few inches and reach for my blue contacts. I take them out and hold them in my hands. "I have green eyes."

He looks at me for a moment before smiling. "I like green even more," he says, kissing my knuckles.

A smile tugs at my face. I push the chair backward and kneel on the floor with him. "Do you know what I'm desperate for right now?"

He pulls back and slides his calloused fingers beneath my eyes, wiping away the remnants of tears. "I really hope it's a hard fuck, because my cock's fucking starving for you, Cass. He's going to rip right through my pants if I don't get inside you soon."

I giggle. "Well, what are you waiting for, big boy?"

EPILOGUE
(Three Years Later)
Cass

I wake up suddenly and with a strange knowing. Dawn in already in the sky and its pale light is creeping in through the open windows. I turn my head and look at Lars sleeping next to me. For a few moments, I simply stare at him in wonder. He is so beautiful, it's like watching a living breathing painting.

Sometimes, I still can't believe he is mine.

My finger lifts to touch his cheek, but I stop myself. I don't want to wake him up yet. Gently, I slip out of bed and pad over to the bathroom. From the cabinet, I take out my pregnancy kit. I tear it out of its wrapper and hold it in my stream of pee. I flush the toilet and clean the stick. Then I wash my hands and sit at the edge of the bath. It's only seconds, but it feels like a long time while I wait for the seconds to tick by. When enough time has passed, I look at the stick.

A bubble of joy rises up from my belly and erupts as a giggle. I lay the stick by the sink and go back into the bedroom. Lars is awake.

"You made the bed cold," he complains.

I walk over and look down at him.

He lifts the duvet and shows me his erection. "Want to come and sit on me," he invites, his eyes dark with desire.

"There isn't enough time," I say, even though my body has started clamoring for him.

"I'll be quick if you will," he says persuasively.

"Oh yeah? That's what you said the last time and look what happened then."

"You're wasting time. Come on, I'm dying for you."

I climb on the bed and looking into his eyes, slowly impale myself on his strong, thick cock.

"Jesus, that feels good," he groans softly.

I lift myself along his shaft, and drop down on it, slowly building my momentum until I get into a good rhythm. My heart is full of happiness; and my body is full of Lars and the tiny life quietly growing inside me. When I break apart it is different too. The waves are slow, languorous, and so incredibly intense they make my body shake. I open my eyes, and Lars is looking at me.

"Are you all right?"

He knows me so well. He can even tell when my orgasms are different. With my secret and him still buried deep inside me, I feel almost too blissful to speak.

"What is it, Cass?"

"Daddy," I whisper.

His eyebrows rise and his eyes flash. "Are you being kinky, or are you trying to say something to me?"

"What do you think?"

"I think…I like the idea of you being that kinky at this time of the morning, but the other idea is making my heart pound like crazy."

I smile slowly. "It's the other idea."

His eyes widen and he starts beaming. "Really?"

I beam back happily. "Really."

He laughs with joy. "A baby?"

"A baby," I confirm.

"Take your gown off," he murmurs.

I grasp the edges of my nightie, lift it over my head, and toss it to the floor. Underneath I'm naked.

His eyes rove my body greedily, hungrily, as if he has not just had me. As if he has not already seen my body a thousand times. His hands move towards my stomach. He cups it gently. "I love you, Cass. I never thought it was possible, but I love you more everyday. It's got so that I love you so much it actually hurts."

I grin. "That's because I'm such a pain in the butt."

"You said it. Not me."

A small cry comes from the baby monitor.

"My son has perfect timing," Lars says.

I get off Lars lovely cock, wipe myself, and go to pick up my gown.

"Don't," he whispers. There is something warm and alive in his eyes.

"You want me to go get our son naked?"

He nods. "Why not? Soon you won't be able to."

I shake my head and roll my eyes, but I walk naked to the next room.

My boy is already standing up and gazing at me from his cot. He takes his thumb out of his mouth and calls out, "Mommy."

"Good morning, darling, I greet as lift his small body into my arms. Then I do what I always do, I bury my nose in the crook of his neck and smell him. He still smells of milk.

"Shall we go see, Daddy?"

"Go Daddy," he replies.

So I carry him to our bedroom.

Lars.

I sit up and wait.

I want to remember this moment.

One day when I am old and there are grandchildren running around me I want to be able to recall this precious moment. I hear her footsteps in the corridor, and a lump forms in my throat.

Then she appears.

My mind clicks the image. My naked woman and my child. There is nothing more beautiful in the world. That's my whole world right there. If everything else I have burns down to the ground tomorrow and I still have what's standing in that doorway, I'm a happy man.

I swallow the lump in my throat. "Morning, Cody."

"Daddy," he cries, lifting both his hands towards me.

I watch my woman walk to me, the insides of her sweet pussy still coated with my seed, my son wriggling in her arms to get to me, and another child growing in her belly, and I know there is not a man in this world who can tell me he is happier than me.

The End

DELETED SCENES

(I wrote this scene, then realized that the story was better without it. Still it seemed a shame to waste it, so for those of you who would like to know what happened at the ball when Lars realized that Cass was not Tamara read on…)

Lars

I spot Tamara coming towards me, but her head is bent, and she is limping badly. What the fuck? I leave my drink on a table nearby and walk quickly to her side. "Are you all right?"

She looks up at me, the movement is unfamiliar and unlike her. "Not really. Can we get out of here? My broken ankle is killing me," she says in a whiny voice.

I take a rear back and stare at her in horror. I don't know what the hell is going on, but the woman standing in front of me is *not* Tamara Honeywell. My eyes quickly sweep over her body. Her breasts are much bigger and obviously fake, and the rest of her is horribly malnourished. Almost skeletal. I return my astonished eyes to her face. Even from under the mask her nose looks dangerously over-worked.

"Your ankle is broken?" I ask slowly.

300

Her eyes narrow. A look of uncertainty comes into them. "I thought you knew that."

"I was under the impression it was sprained."

Something flashes in her eyes. Fury. Not the kind of fury I'm used to seeing in Tamara's eyes. This fury is vindictive and malicious. These are not the eyes I know. I take a step forward and whip the mask off her face.

She blinks with surprise, then, tries to smile.

I scowl at her fiercely. "I don't give a damn who you are or what kind of sick joke this is. All I want to know is where is the real Tamara."

She lifts her nose. "I *am* the real Tamara," she announces grandly.

Of course, she is. This woman is everything I feared she would be: a proud, spoilt, plastic brat. Everything makes perfect sense now. The one I love is the imposter. I feel a flash of pure joy. All those horrible rumors weren't about my girl.

"And who is the other girl," I ask softly.

She makes a dismissive gesture with her hand. "No one. She needed a job so I helped her out."

I stare at her for moment, my face deliberately cold. "Does she have a name?"

"Cass something," she replies sulkily.

Cass. Yes, the name suits her. An image flashes into my mind. Cass riding Thunder, sunlight in her hair. Cass. Yes. My Cass.

"Where is she now?" I ask sternly.

She shrugs. "Who knows. Gone back to wherever she crawled out from."

What a sneaky bitch. She didn't fancy spending a month mucking out horse stalls so she hired a lookalike. "And you don't know how to get in contact with her?"

"Nope." Her voice is spiteful.

This is easier than I thought it would be. "Fine, I'll just ask your father."

The change in her is instant. She becomes red with fury. "My father? Who the hell do you think you are? You think my father has the time to get involved in your pathetic sex life? Mind your manners or I'll make sure you're thrown out on your ear."

I look at her curiously. "Who do you think I am?"

For the first time, she looks unsure of herself. "One of the ranch hands?" she asks hopefully.

"Nope."

Her forehead furrows then her eyes suddenly widen when the penny drops. "Lars…Oh, fuck. You're not. Noooo."

I nod slowly. "Afraid so."

Another change comes over her. She starts simpering like some nineteenth-century heroine. "I'm so sorry I was rude to you. I thought you were one of the ranch hands." She licks her lips nervously.

I laugh. "What's the matter? Doesn't Daddy know that you got an impersonator to take your place?"

"No. Please. Please, don't involve Dadddy. He's got enough worries on his plate already."

"Bullshit," I say harshly.

She flinches at the hard threat in my voice, but I don't soften my expression. I need to know where my girl is.

"All right," she says. "I'll tell you everything. Just don't tell my dad, okay?"

"I'm going to have to tell your dad either way, but you can make it easier for yourself by telling me where she is."

"If there's nothing to be gained by telling you, I won't bother to. I know how to work my father, let's see how you find that little tramp without my help," she says, a taunting smile playing about her lips.

I want to grab her and shake her.

"Her name is Cass Harper and she works for a lookalike agency called Cinderella.com," a voice behind us says.

I turn around and see an elegant woman dressed in a deep red suit standing a few feet behind us. She has gray hair and that kind of daring chic that you only find in Paris.

"How dare you interfere, you stupid old bitch?" Tamara screeches.

"This time you went too far," the woman says in a calm dignified voice.

"This time you're fucking fired," she hurls back furiously

"Good," the woman says softly, and turning around, walks away.

I spend one second more looking at Tamara Honeywell's flushed, frustrated face, then I go after the gray-haired woman. She and I have unfinished business.

I need to know where my Cass is.

Thank you for reading!

Made in the USA
Lexington, KY
08 June 2017